Colors of the Ocean

ENDORSEMENTS

Colors of the Ocean leaves the reader yearning for the tang of salt on their lips and the freedom of the open ocean, whether a seasoned sailor or armchair explorer. The author takes the reader on a transformative journey. The character's endless horizon symbolizes opportunities, the trials and storms represent conquering adversities, and each new landfall is a journey of self-discovery. One of the novel's greatest strengths is its realism both in nautical details and in the emotional honesty of its characters. The book's ending was my only letdown as I craved to continue the adventure and discovery. Perhaps Cheryl has a sequel in her future.

—**Diana Lee Moran**, author of *Floppy Ears and Puppy Dog Tales: How to overcome Grief from Loss and Other Life Lessons I Learned from My Pet*

Teens and adults alike will gravitate towards this multigenerational coming of age story. Cruise along with Roxi and her grandmother as they navigate relationships, new cultures, and storms—both in life and at sea. *Colors of the Ocean* does a brilliant job of helping us to see God is in

every detail of our lives, the easy sailing and the turbulent waters.
—**Jennifer Noel Wilson**, author of *The Best Trophy*

Sail to tropical ports around the world in this coming-of-age story. Drawing from her own years at sea, author Cheryl Fitzgerald introduces readers to the unique life of cruisers when a teen reluctantly boards her grandmother's boat for an extended voyage. The journey to discover who you are and where you fit in the world comes to life in *Colors of the Ocean*.
—**PeggySue Wells**, USA Today bestselling author of 45 titles including *Homeless for the Holidays* and *The Patent*

Praise for *Colors of the Ocean*, a richly layered novel filled with exotic settings, gripping action, and unforgettable characters. It is more than a book about sailing around the world. Cheryl Fitzgerald's debut smoothly navigates into choppy life issues of family and faith, taking the reader below the surface to what really matters.
—**Sue Stewart Ade.** Her debut novel, *Friends Forever,* was a Nancy Pearl finalist, and *Displaced*, her recent novel, was a finalist in the Pacific Northwest Literary Association's Contest.

While *Colors of the Ocean* makes for an entertaining travelogue in story form for a YA audience, Cheryl Fitzgerald offers us a novel of hope as a young teen learns what counts most when it comes to family.
—**Linda Sammaritan**, author of the *World Without Sound Series*.

If you enjoy sailing and the open sea, you are going to love reading this book. The colorful descriptions put the reader in the moment. I have never sailed, but it seems like

I have after this read. Hopefully, you'll learn many lessons on this journey. I loved every bit of it. This book is good for anyone but especially for people who love the outdoors. Those who have a challenging teen in their life might gain a few insights as well.

—**Phyllis Dow Bex**, Author of *Life on Turkeyneck Hill: A Memoir, More Tales on Turkeyneck Hill, Turkeyneck Hill and Beyond*

A beautiful story of second chances, faithful love, and redemption. Vividly written, this story leaves you feeling as if you lived it. Cheryl Fitzgerald takes you on a journey that lingers long after the last page is read.

—**Emerson Ford** (pseudonym), author of *What the Silent Say*, and *Every Bend in the River*

When choosing a novel, we want it to take us places exotic and unknown yet freshly familiar. *Colors of the Ocean* delivers all that and more with intricate descriptions, relatable characters, and evolving story of sailing around the world. When Roxi and her grandparents leave the dock, with her mother fading in the distance, we fight tears. When Carol and Jon struggle with danger, we bite our nails. When sailors and strangers invade the story, we're curious, When Roxi senses God's presence, we exhale. All to say, Cheryl Fitzgerald's debut novel, *Colors of the Ocean* is well worth the journey.

—**Joyce Long**, author of *Real Mothers*, and *Trinity: Walk in Love, Forgiveness, and Peace*

Colors of the Ocean

Cheryl Fitzgerald

ELK LAKE PUBLISHING INC®

PUBLISHING THE POSITIVE
Plymouth, Massachusetts

A Christian Company
ElkLakePublishingInc.com

COPYRIGHT NOTICE

Scripture Version: Scriptures marked NIV are taken from the NEW INTERNATIONAL VERSION (NIV): Scriptures taken from THE HOLY BIBLE, NEW INTERNATIONAL VERSION ®. Copyright©1973, 1978, 1984, 2011 by Biblica, Inc.™. Used by permission of Zondervan

Cover and Interior Design: Kelly Artieri, Deb Haggerty
Editor(s): Carol McClain, Cristel Phelps, Deb Haggerty

PUBLISHED BY: Elk Lake Publishing, Inc., 35 Dogwood Drive, Plymouth, MA 02360, 2025
Library Cataloging Data
Names: Fitzgerald, Cheryl, Cheryl Fitzgerald
Colors of the Ocean / Cheryl Fitzgerald

290 p. 23cm × 15cm (9in × 6 in.)
ISBN-13: 9798891344778 (paperback) | 9798891344785 (trade paperback) | 9798891344792 (e-book)
Key Words: Christian women fiction three generations sailing; Mother-daughter relationship Jesus ocean adventure; Grandma teen granddaughter God relationship novel; Godly women's fiction sailing adventure family; Family life fiction coming of age Jesus love faith; Mother daughter granddaughter fiction God love; New Zealand sailing fiction godly family discovery
Library of Congress Control Number: 2025949807 Fiction

Dedication

To my granddaughter, Ashley, who didn't go on a sailing adventure with us—but I wish you could have. And for future generations of cruising adventurers whose dreams are as vast as the ocean.

Acknowledgments

There are so many wonderful people to thank for the reality of this book, way beyond who I've listed below.

I especially want to thank my editors at Elk Lake Publishing for believing in this novel. You have treated me like family and taught me so much, sharing your expertise with kindness and encouragement. Carol McClain: The parallels in our lives and stories are uncanny. Deb Haggerty: For taking a chance on a first-time author. Cristel Phelps: You made me feel welcomed from the very beginning.

To my friends and critique group at Heartland Christian Writers: Joyce Long, Linda Samaritoni, Phyllis Bex, Jane Bowman, Seana Zoderer, Lorraine Richardson, Jennifer Wilson, Hayden Garris, Rachel Hills, Amanda Graves, Nesha Anderson, John Walker, and Mary Kay Jones. It takes a village to get a novel into shape for submission. You all are that village. A special thank you to Joyce, who has been both a writing mentor and friend these past nine years. Publication would not have come to fruition without your experienced guidance.

My husband, Jerry. If you hadn't taken me on the most thrilling sailing adventure, there would be no story. Lots of work and challenges, but what a marvelous escapade.

Many thanks to the offshore cruising community. You were more than cruising buddies—you were family with whom we shared holiday potlucks, exploration of foreign lands and cultures, ham radio check-ins, and an amazing odyssey. Through tears, laughter, frustration, and loss amid the wonder of God's glorious creation, you were people we could rely on in the midst of every storm. Also, humongous hugs to sailing mates, Susan & Steve Ticehurst. We not only crossed an ocean together, but now land cruise, exploring remarkable and unique settings within the United States. I always look forward to what's around the bend on our next adventure.

My path to publication began at Taylor University's Writers Conference. I attended Jeff Crosby's *Advanced Fast-Track Publishing workshop* and also became acquainted with Peggy Sue Wells who steered me to Elk Lake. A grateful note of thanks to you both for your incredible knowledge of the industry and motivation to take the next step.

My long-time friend, Diana Lee Moran. As I observed you work through the process of publishing your first book, *Floppy Ears & Puppy Dog Tales*, you gave me hope that this could become a reality for me also, not only an unreachable dream.

Sue Ade, a friend and fellow author who invited me to join her critique group when I moved to Indiana. Thank you for always encouraging my writing and story.

My son, Shannon. You brought an emotional depth to my story that hadn't been there until we traveled through that dark valley together.

And finally, my deepest gratitude to the Captain of My Soul, Author of Life, and true author of this book. *Colors of the Ocean* may have started as my novel but became yours as you guided me down new paths of inspiration.

Chapter One: Leaving—1998

ROXI

Roxi McKay clung to the rail of the wobbly sailboat *Dawn's Dove* as the vessel motored away from the slip. Her insides crumbled like a sand sculpture as the tide rushes in. She glared through brimming eyes at her mother, Star, who stood at the end of the dock. As the distance between them grew, Star posed like a model with one sleek hip thrust out. Her low-cut halter top left little to the imagination. A delicate swan-like neck led up to her sultry Hollywood smile. She parade-waved to Roxi, blowing goofy air kisses.

Face it, Rox, she's probably elated to be rid of a fat, ugly loser like you. Still, she couldn't help but admire her mom's thick auburn hair, flawless face, and Barbie body. Everything about Star was the complete opposite of how she looked. Roxi half waved and turned away from everything and everyone important to her—Mom, Alexis, her best friend, and her bunny, Thumper. Who knew where he would end up?

PJ stood at the helm grinning as he steered the thirty-six foot sailboat past California's Long Beach jetty. Roxi called him PJ because Papa Jon wasn't her *real* grandpa, only someone who married Mama Carol. His freckled complexion and surname Fitzpatrick left no doubt of his Irish ancestry.

He chuckled as Mama Carol leapt up, dark hair bobbing in a short ponytail, and flung her arms out. "We're free! The world is ours to explore." Dark shadows beneath her grandma's brown eyes couldn't hide their gleam of excitement. "Just keep following the sun, Jon."

"Yep, like Robin Lee Graham did. 'Course he wasn't lucky enough to have two beautiful gals with him." PJ winked.

"Whatever." Roxi had heard the story that inspired this insane voyage a gazillion times—the young solo-sailor who sailed *Dove* around the world in 1965. Blah, blah, blah. She shuffled to the bow and turned her back to grandparents who were as old as dinosaurs. Her tangled strawberry-blonde curls felt frizzy beneath her fingers as she tucked loose strands behind her ears. She licked a salty film off full lips and grimaced as she recalled that final day with her mom.

Instead of being sad, Star had acted ecstatic, prancing around the small apartment, making messy piles of both their stuff.

"I'm gonna miss you, Mom. Will you miss me?" Roxi murmured.

Star had taken a long drag on her cigarette and let the smoke out slowly. "Well of course, snuggle bunny. But what an opportunity for both of us. This new part on the soap opera is going to make me rich and famous." She flashed a fake smile. "And you're embarking on a fabulous adventure."

Roxi tried one last time, hoping to change her mom's mind. "Really? You don't even care that I could die out there?"

Star's eyes flashed with alarm for an instant, but then narrowed. "You're more of a drama queen than I am. Stop thinking only of yourself." Her voice hardened. "Do you know how much I've sacrificed for you? My career, freedom, relationships, pretty much my life!"

It always came back to this same argument. Now Roxi found herself stuck on this dumb boat with grandparents she barely knew.

After Star calmed down, she had finally promised that if Roxi still felt unhappy after a year of traveling, she could return home.

Can I survive this? Roxi stole one last glance toward the distant shore. Star was long gone. The scent of the sea conjured images of squiggly jellyfish and giant squid lurking beneath its murky surface. She shivered in the damp October wind and squinted toward the horizon. Like her future, the vast gray ocean stretched out before her, bleak and unknown.

Chapter Two: Cabo Welcoming

ROXI

On the day before Thanksgiving, a humongous gray whale breached not more than thirty feet from the bow as *Dawn's Dove* sailed near Cabo San Lucas's Arch along the Mexican Baja Coast. The thunderous slap as the leviathan landed on its side rocked the boat. Roxi grabbed the starboard's wire shroud. "Oh snap! Is that creature welcoming or warning us?"

Mama Carol was slow to respond after the overnight sail from Magdalena Bay. "Maybe both." She winced as they rounded the tall rock leading into the large anchorage crowded with all types of boats. "What a zoo. I thought we left all this behind in Southern California."

Flags flapped atop a shiny white cruise ship anchored at the mouth of the bay. Jet-skiers zipped around anchored yachts, creating artificial storms. Noisy party-boats and sport-fishers cruised in all directions. Above all the chaos floated colorful parasails.

Sweet. This looks like much more fun. Roxi spun around the deck. All those empty anchorages and days at sea along the coast of Baja had stunk of total boredom. Well, except the night of November 17th. Her thirteenth birthday.

They'd lounged on cushions in the cockpit as meteors from the Leonids zigzagged across the midnight sky, leaving long glowing trails. Others exploded in brilliant flashes. More magical than Disneyland's fireworks. Mama Carol had proclaimed the heavens lit their candles just for Roxi.

"I'm sooo ready for some excitement!" Roxi grinned. "Let's get this party started."

PJ shrugged, but Mama Carol frowned. "You sound like Shalimar when you talk like that."

"Mom's new name is Star, remember?" Her mom was a chameleon, changing hair color weekly and nails daily to match her mood. Sometimes she even took on new names as her acting career grew.

"Hah! Exploding Star is more like it." Mama Carol's lips tightened into a thin white line.

Roxi rolled her eyes and huffed. "Well, I'm nothing like Star." *Unfortunately.*

Deep grooves formed between her grandma's eyebrows. "Thank goodness." Her voice turned bitter. "But I see a bit of her wild, rebellious streak in you."

PJ diverted the gathering squall. "Kinda sounds like her grandma." He yawned while pointing to a small open space between yachts. The conversation halted as her grandparents concentrated on anchoring procedures.

They gathered information from the yachties next to them and set out early the following morning to begin the tedious mandatory task of checking in with the three offices—*Capitan del Puerto, Immigracion,* and *Aduana*—Customs. Of course, all three were in different parts of town.

Mama Carol's Spanish had baffled the officials. The slow pronunciation she used with her Hispanic special-ed students back home proved unintelligible to them.

They didn't complete all the paperwork until halfway through Thanksgiving. By then Roxi's mood had soured and her feet sizzled like tortillas in a hot skillet. The only good thing to come from the whole boring process had been meeting Brittany, a girl close to her age, whose family was also checking in. The two girls made a plan for that evening, something to add a bit of fun to this tiresome journey.

In late afternoon, Roxi and the dinosaurs joined about thirty sailors on a deserted stretch of beach to celebrate their first holiday in a foreign land. The diversified group ranged in age from five to seventy-five. Most reclined on beach chairs or towels encircling an overturned inflatable dinghy, its flat bottom ladened with food.

Mama Carol chuckled. "Well, I'm thankful for this feast we're sharing, but this definitely doesn't resemble a Norman Rockwell Thanksgiving."

"That's a fact," Roxi snarled. She'd studied the American artist in her home school art history curriculum and was also learning to paint whenever conditions were calm. Not that she'd admit to Mama Carol her love of the magic of swirling dabs of paint onto paper until colors evolved into a picture—almost as enjoyable as dancing. Both made her forget how homesick she felt.

Roxi's mouth watered as she focused on the juicy turkey, savory stuffing, mounds of mashed potatoes, exotic salads, curried and candied vegetables, and decadent desserts.

Golden flecks sparkled in PJ's green eyes. "Mmm, mmm—where do we start?"

"With a prayer, of course." Mama Carol closed her eyes and spoke softly. PJ bowed his head, but Roxi ignored her and dug in.

When bellies were full, adults gathered around a bonfire and began sharing embellished sailing tales. A few kids worked on a huge sand fortress. As the sun sank into the reflective orange-red ocean, voices blended in a mix of folk songs, hymns, and sea shanties.

It's definitely time. Roxi's mouth curved into a mischievous smile. She glanced over where her coconspirator, Brittany, sat with her dad and brother and gave a slight nod. Being the only two teenagers among the cruisers, the two girls had gravitated toward one another. Roxi's stomach quivered. She ignored the nagging inner voice whispering in her head that she shouldn't be doing this.

Both grabbed backpacks and slipped away into the night, past groups of boisterous tourists and obscure couples sighing in the shadows. Giggling, they raced up the beach. At one of several resorts, the girls peeled off shorts and T-shirts, revealing tanned, bathing suit-clad bodies. Brittany, tall for fourteen, had slender boyish hips. Self-conscious, Roxi faced away. She hated her short body that showed a hint of curves padded with a gross layer of baby fat.

They showered on a tiled platform built on the sand and then tiptoed onto the patio landscaped with potted flowers and palms. A glimmering pool beckoned. The place looked empty except for an oblivious couple whispering and making out in a dark corner.

The girls watched for a minute. Brittany whispered, "I'm thinking they're way too busy to notice us."

Roxi snickered. "That's for sure." She perched on the edge of the pool.

After diving in, they splashed each other playfully. The air felt balmy, the water cool velvet against Roxi's skin. She floated onto her back and gazed at the twinkling, rhinestone-sprinkled blanket above, identifying both Big and Little Dippers.

Ahh ... once in a great while, life can be good. She sighed with contentment.

Voices sounded behind them. Hotel security? Double quick the girls ducked underwater and swam behind a small waterfall. When they surfaced, peals of laughter rang out. Two scrawny Mexican boys, about their age, stood above them at the edge of the pool.

They tried to lure the girls closer with hand gestures and warm smiles. Shaggy black hair framed their burnt umber faces and unreadable dark eyes.

Roxi couldn't put her finger on what was bugging her. Were they sincere or mocking?

"*Buenas noches, senoritas. Cómo están?*"

Brittany replied in timid Spanish. "*Bien. Y ustedes?*"

"*Bueno. Somos Carlos y Jaime, primos.*"

"Does that mean brothers or cousins?" Roxi caught a few words of their next sentence as she and Brit climbed out of the pool.

"*... una fiesta de la familia.*"

"Totally cool." Roxi grinned and nodded.

Brittany shook her head and mouthed, "No way."

"Come on." Roxi bounced up and down on her toes. "Don't be such a fraidy cat. Wouldn't you like to meet their family? This party could be fun."

Brittany twirled a strand of long blond hair. "Well, I am intrigued by new cultures." Her foot tapped nervously. "But I don't feel comfortable going with strangers."

Exasperated, Roxi gritted her teeth. "Oh, come on—just for a bit."

Brittany sighed. "I guess." Both girls dried off and pulled their clothes back on.

The two boys led them through a maze of streets. Roxi caught a glimpse of the quarter moon peeking between low-lying buildings. Conversations were awkward, with each of the four speaking a mixture of English and Spanish along with lots of pantomime. Roxi didn't notice when they left the tourist section.

Without warning, Carlos grabbed his cousin and growled something unintelligible. Jaime gave his head a forceful shake. They bickered back and forth.

Jaime punched his cousin's arm. "*Callate!*"

He must have said shut up because Carlos grew quiet. He turned toward the girls, eyes calculating, but with a dazzling smile. His finger made little circles next to his temple, then pointed to Carlos.

"What was that all about?" Brittany's soft voice shook.

Roxi's eyes widened, then blinked with trepidation. "I haven't got a clue."

The dim, squalid neighborhood was eerily silent. Roxi's heartbeat pounded in her ears. Something smelled rotten. Dead. Howling echoed in the distance. *Where were they?*

Chapter Three: The Dark Monster

ROXI

Carlos and Jaime pushed the girls into a gloomy, deserted alley.

Roxi broke into a cold sweat. *Should we run?*

Brittany edged closer to Roxi, whimpering.

Like a raging bull, Carlos snorted and shoved Roxi to the packed dirt, then kicked her in the stomach.

Brittany screamed as Jamie attacked her.

Breath whooshed out of Roxi. She clenched her fists. *Jump up, Rox. Smash his face.* While she strived to suck in air, Carlos ripped off her backpack. Searing pain radiated from both shoulders. Roxi fought the urge to throw up and struggled to her hands and knees. Where was Brit?

Her friend leaned against a crumbled adobe wall, sobbing. Brit's bleeding lip had already begun to swell and her right ankle lay twisted beneath her.

Carlos flung the pack to the dirt and spit. "You got nuthin'." He almost looked like he might cry. As the two hooligans slipped into the darkness, Jaime shouted, "Go home you *gringas estúpidas*."

Brittany's moan turned into a wail. "Oh, Roxi, what are we going to do? How will we ever find our way back to our families?"

Roxi grimaced as she stood and rubbed throbbing shoulders. She tucked her disheveled hair behind both ears. "We'll be okay," she croaked, then coughed. "PJ made me learn how to find my way by using the moon and stars. That seemed unnecessary with a GPS on board, but I guess that knowledge could be useful at a time like this."

Roxi grabbed her friend's hand and pulled. Brit wobbled to her feet and winced as she held onto Roxi's shoulder for support.

"Are you going to be okay?" Roxi craned her neck up at the night sky that no longer sparkled, but now held a forbidding gleam. "Can you see the moon? I remember the glow in the east after we left the hotel."

Standing a head taller than Roxi, Brittany hobbled in a tight circle, then pointed. "There."

The girls clung to each other as they slowly backtracked. Brittany sniffled and occasionally let out a squeak if she stepped wrong.

The brutal attack flashed through Roxi's mind in strobe-like pictures. She wanted to crawl in a hole. *What a gullible idiot I am. Why didn't I listen to Mama Carol? She and PJ were probably sick and tired of her crummy moods and behavior by now. Maybe they'd send her home. Yeah, in your dreams, Rox.*

Music pulsated from a main road ahead. Drunken teens shrieked and hollered, dancing in the street. Skeletal dogs dug through rotting garbage and lapped up spilt beer. Roxi breathed through her mouth as the girls crept along the shadows. Even the dogs ignored them.

Her grandma's words haunted Roxi. She'd warned her before they came ashore that Cabo San Lucas could be dangerous. A dark monster lurked beneath its festive atmosphere, bright serapes, and glittering silver jewelry. Poverty. Vulnerable locals thrust into a world of survival-of-the-fittest at a young age. Clashing with this, a mass of wealthy tourists threw their money and arrogance around while fishing out their ocean.

Roxi bellowed. "We didn't deserve to be attacked. Brit and I were only being friendly." She stamped her feet.

Brittany stumbled. "Whoa. What did you say?"

Roxi caught her and frowned. "I'm thinking how much I despise this place—and this trip. What a Thanksgiving."

"Yeah, worst ever. Hopefully, Christmas will be better." A teensy smile hovered.

Roxi bit her lip. "Don't even go there." She dreaded the thought of another holiday away from home.

They walked in silence until the hotel and its beach came into view. "We made it," Roxi whispered with relief. She raised her head. *God, if you exist and are listening, which I doubt, thank you for protecting us. But why do you allow bad things to happen?*

A wonderful, English-speaking voice called out. "Over here, I've found them." A mob of faces closed in around them.

Brittany started to cry again, but Roxi felt numb, her eyes dry as the desert wind. Embraced by the community of cruising friends and family, the girls attempted to answer questions. Where had they been? Why did they go off with strangers? What did the boys do to them? The air buzzed with too many voices. Grim faces. But Roxi could see and feel the group's gratefulness for the girl's safe return in their hugs and tears.

Brittany's dad, Jeff, who everyone called Red, and older brother, Toby, whisked her away.

The scene around Roxi dimmed as a roaring grew in her ears. Her heart fluttered with an irregular rhythm, and she gasped for air. She felt herself lifted and then settled into their dinghy. Like a deflated raft, she slumped against Mama Carol.

PJ rowed the dinghy with forceful strokes toward *Dawn's Dove*. He spoke through clenched teeth. "I'm gonna find those boys and when I do—" He grumbled under his breath when Mama C put a finger to her lips.

"Doggone it, what were them gals thinkin', runnin' off like that?"

"Jon, shh. We'll talk about everything in the morning. Let her rest." She rubbed Roxi's back with a shaky hand.

Paddles dipped and sloshed. Silence hung in the air, thick as a winter fog. Her grandma whispered in her ear, "I'm so sorry for forcing you on this voyage. I never wanted to put you in harm's way. I only meant to ..."

Only meant to what? Was my grandma or my mom to blame for me being held captive on this floating prison? Roxi shifted away. Her whole body ached, but not as much as her heart. Would Star let her come home now that she'd almost been killed? Did that count for anything?

Life wasn't fair. After years of moving all over LA and Orange County, Roxi had finally made a real friend, Alexis, who preferred to go by Alex. Both of them shared a love of dancing. She hung out at Alex's house as often as possible and missed her. Lots! Brittany seemed okay, but they didn't have much in common—except being stuck on this stupid *adventure*.

Half an hour later, Roxi lay in her bunk scrunched into a tight ball. She clutched her stuffed rabbit, Snuggles, to her chest and finally allowed the scalding tears she'd been holding in to pour out. She muffled a groan into her pillow.

Nightmarish images assaulted her as the boat's gentle rocking lulled her into a restless sleep. Roxi dreamed she and her mom were standing waist-deep in a stormy ocean. Star's grin morphed into a sneer. Her arms became tentacles that weaved around Roxi, sucking her down into a deep, black nothingness.

Chapter Four: A Different Kind of Christmas

CAROL

Carol blinked and slowly opened her eyes. Above, Jon's footsteps shuffled in the cockpit at the back of the boat as the ship's clock chimed seven bells. She yawned and began back stretches on the aft bunk located beneath him as she planned the day—Christmas day! A wave of childhood holiday memories washed over her.

Carol could picture Mom sipping her cup of coffee, a cigarette smoldering in an ashtray. But what she remembered most had been her mom's heartwarming smile that lit up her face. Beneath the tinseled fresh pine tree loaded with homemade ornaments were lots of presents. Her mom loved giving, way beyond her budget, and always cherished her and Jimmy's homespun items. Dad always had a drink in his hand and a scowl on his face while trying to maintain order. Jovial grandparents usually gave clothing gifts that were hideously out of style. Carol smiled as she thought of Jimmy, her rambunctious brother, who would wrestle with her for each present. She frowned as she recalled his passing almost three years ago. Alcohol and drug abuse had taken their toll. He'd left a son, Justin. Her nephew must be close to twenty-five now. A good kid in spite of everything he'd been through. She hoped he might join them later in their voyage.

On December 26, 1967, when Carol was only twenty, her recently divorced mom announced that she had breast cancer. Mom hadn't wanted to spoil the holiday for her family. By the following Christmas she was gone, and Carol's life had become a mess.

Tears spilled over. There were so many more memories, but she'd reminisce tonight and read about the birth of Jesus in her Bible. That's what this day was all about. Now Carol needed to get moving. Whip up her famous pineapple coffee cake and pop it in the oven. She climbed up two steps and poked her head out the companionway, taking a deep breath of salty air. "Morning, Jon. *Feliz Navidad.*"

Jon looked up from the stainless-steel rail he'd been polishing and grinned. "'Bout time ya got up. Sun came up an hour ago. Whatcha thinkin', today is a holiday or somethun'?"

Carol stuck out her tongue and wrinkled her nose. She gazed across the sun-dappled anchorage at La Paz, a sleepy Mexican town tucked along the eastern coast of Baja in the Sea of Cortez. Tall saguaro cacti dotted dusty, rose-colored hills. Painted adobe buildings splashed bright colors amid the landscape.

Carol stepped below into the galley, strode eight steps down the narrow aisle of the main salon, past the closed door of the head on her left, and into the forecabin.

Roxi still lay asleep in the bow's four by six-foot V-berth amid rumpled clothing, books, and candy wrappers. Long golden lashes hid those beautiful, but troubled, sapphire eyes. A sprinkle of freckles danced across her lightly tanned cheeks and nose.

Lord, please heal my granddaughter's heart. Fill her with your joy and peace today. May your will be done, Father, not mine, for I know your plans are greater.

Ever since the Cabo fiasco, Roxi had withdrawn more from Carol, but thankfully, she had found cruising friends, Brittany and Dustin, to talk with. *Be patient, give her time,* she told herself for the umpteenth time. Carol hoped this trip would bring her and Roxi closer, something she'd never been able to accomplish with her daughter. Even as a child, Shalimar had been shy and secretive.

Roxi's sketches and watercolors, taped above teak shelves that ran along both sides of the hull, caught Carol's attention. That girl really had a God-given talent. If only she'd believe in herself. She sniffed. A lingering scent of dried seaweed and mildew wafted from the chain locker hidden behind the V-berth's forward bulkhead and waterproof curtain. As Carol headed back to the galley to bake the cake, she added interior cleaning to tomorrow's chore list.

Elvis crooned *Blue Christmas* on the cassette player when Roxi finally shambled into the main salon and grumbled, "I know how he feels."

"Merry Christmas," Jon boomed as Carol shouted, "Feliz Navidad."

Roxi plopped down at the dinette table. "Whoa, take a chill pill." Silence filled the boat. Her thin smile was more of a grimace. "Doesn't feel like Christmas."

"Maybe this will help." Carol fought off a wave of despair as she dished up spicy omelets for her and Roxi, plain cheese for her tender-mouth husband, and warm slices of coffee cake. Jon poured freshly squeezed orange juice into cups.

There wasn't a crumb left on Jon's plate when he leaned back and patted the green T-shirt stretched across his belly. "That was a mighty fine meal, darlin'. And ya know what else was fine? The boaters gettin' together last evenin', stuffin' all them bags with candy, oranges, and toys for the local kiddos. Bet you enjoyed that, Roxi."

She rolled her eyes. "I guess. Way different from Christmas at home. Alex always had a tree up to the ceiling, a kazillion presents, and her mom baked all kinds of cookies. Even Star put up our fake tree so I could decorate it with loads of tinsel and glittery balls."

Carol cringed. The Baja breeze twirled the scanty display of ornaments hanging beneath each open porthole. Her heart ached for her homesick granddaughter. "I'm sorry everything is so unfamiliar here. Today must be especially difficult without your mom or friend."

Roxi's eyes narrowed. "You don't know how I feel. And I don't want to talk about them." Her voice quivered. "We should at least have a tree."

"Guess we could cut us a cactus to decorate," Jon teased. He eyed a pile of gifts on the small table and reached across the aisle.

Carol playfully slapped his hand. "Well, next year we should be in New Zealand. Plenty of pine trees there to choose from."

"Whatever. I hope next Christmas, I'll be home with my mom."

Carol clenched her teeth and counted to ten. *Don't react.* "Didn't you enjoy singing carols last night accompanied by Grandpa's guitar and my keyboard?"

A sour look puckered Roxi's face. "Yeah, great fun, if you're ninety."

"Hey, we're not that ancient." Jon winked as he reached again towards a rectangular box. "'Bout time to open these, I suppose."

Roxi took the gift from him. "That one's mine?" She tore open the package and held up a silver and turquoise necklace she had admired at the plaza's night market. A teensy smile tickled her rosy lips. "Wow, I didn't expect this."

Carol sighed with relief. *Thank you, Lord.*

Roxi's fingers stroked her next present, a soft, white cotton blouse embroidered with bright parrots. "Thank you, guys. Now, open yours, but they're nothing spectacular."

"You're welcome, sweetie bird." Jon opened her two paintings of Baja's western coast. One was a vibrant sunset over the ocean while anchored at windy Los Frailes—the other of the pristine bay of Santa Maria with its sparkling white sand covered in seashells and sand dollars, copper-hued hills in the background. He whistled. "Can't believe you made these. You're gonna be famous one day, known all over the world."

Roxi's face reddened. "You're only saying that because ..."

Say the words, Carol thought—*because you're my grandpa.*

"These are beautiful. I love your blending techniques and eye for detail. You really have a gift." Carol held the artwork up against a teak bulkhead. "We'll get these framed and find perfect spots for them."

"Enough already." Roxi groaned.

Jon ignored her rudeness. He cleared his throat as he handed Carol a brown paper bag. "Sorry 'bout the wrapping. Couldn't remember where you kept the good stuff."

"Well, after ten Christmases together, guess I know what to expect. You can't teach an old mule new dance steps. Besides, it's what's inside that counts." She peered in the bag, pulled out a miniature brass lantern with a scented candle inside, then gave him an exuberant hug. "This is perfect—unique, practical, and doesn't take up much space."

Delight colored Jon's voice as he opened his final gift—a large tin of chocolate chip cookies. He took a huge bite of one. "Mmm, my favorite." He licked crumbs and chocolate off his fingers and reached for another one.

"But don't eat too many at once." Carol smiled to herself. He didn't seem to notice the artificial sweetener she had substituted for half the sugar.

After Roxi wolfed down three cookies, she disappeared into her room.

Carol cleared the clutter. Then Brittany's voice came over the VHF radio.

"*Dawn's Dove* and *Harmony*, this is *Sea Eagle*. Do you copy?"

"Roxi?" Carol looked toward her granddaughter's cabin. "Brittany's calling."

Roxi rushed from her room. Before she picked up the microphone, Dustin responded. "Hey, this is *Harmony*. Merry Christmas, Brit and Rox. Let's try channel 67 or 68."

Brittany and Dustin chatted non-stop for a couple of minutes. Her granddaughter's foot tapped a rapid staccato, and Carol braced for the inevitable eruption.

Roxi cut in. "Hey, hope you geeks don't mind if I join the conversation."

Carol shook her head as she finished washing dishes in the galley. *It's a miracle that girl has any friends. She's so impatient and sarcastic. Guess we do have something in common after all.*

Rob's gravelly voice broke the tension. "Good morning, young folks. I've been sharing this blessed day with those silly Austrians, Claudette and Jurgen on *Kashmira*. They had me in stiches until I popped a button on my Bermuda shorts!"

Lord, thank you for saving us through another awkward moment. Still smiling, Carol prayed Rob wasn't missing his late wife, Jeannie, or grown boys too much. Holidays could be tough.

Static crackled before Rob came back over the airway. "I'll pick you three swabbies up around fourteen-thirty for celebrations at the *Magoti*, if that is okay with all your folks."

Roxi glanced at Carol who nodded yes. "Sweet. See you later." She signed off, "This is *Dawn's Dove* and we're clear."

Carol took a deep breath. Things were looking up. Maybe this different kind of Christmas would produce a miracle for everyone.

Chapter Five: New Friends

ROXI

Roxi ignored Mama Carol's probing stare as she stomped up the steps after the talk with her friends on the VHF radio. PJ spoke in a low voice. "Let her be, Carol. She'll come around." His southern Tennessee twang began harmonizing along with a Johnny Cash cassette.

Frustrated, Roxi curled on top of a sail bag near the bow and heaved a sigh. What was wrong with her? Why this jumble of feelings? Being crammed into this fiberglass fishbowl didn't help. Although she should be excited for the party later today, all she could think about was her mom. Why hadn't Star insisted she be sent home after the Cabo Thanksgiving fiasco? Being apart at Christmas didn't seem right. Not that their holidays together were perfect.

Her stomach cramped when she thought about last year's holiday. Star and another loser boyfriend had partied most of the night. Finally, at noon, she got to open gifts while her mom complained about the noise and a raging headache. Roxi smiled. At least she had fun that evening watching *A Christmas Story* with Alex and her family. That movie cracked her up.

A persistent fly buzzed around her. She swatted the obnoxious insect flat on the deck. Brittany could never replace her bestest friend in California, who shared her daydreams, secrets, and passion for dancing. Roxi added excitement to Alex's predictable life while her friend brought stability to her chaotic one.

She gazed across the windswept bay dotted with anchored sailboats. Brit didn't talk about herself very much. Still, she was sweet and only a year older—much more fun to spend time with than moldy oldies. And three weeks ago they had made another friend, Dustin.

Roxi had shared a wet dinghy ride with Brit across the choppy bay to Club Cruceros. "Guess we get a salt bath before our real showers. She jiggled two quarters in her pocket needed to pay for that luxury as they tied up at the dock.

After washing off, Roxi crooked a finger for Brittany to follow her next door.

"Let's check for mail and then stop by the sanctuary." That's what they called the trading library packed with hundreds of books. She could live inside that musty little room. Hopefully, she'd score a Lois Duncan mystery or supernatural tale by Betty Wright. Harry Potter ranked first on her list, but she'd already read the first two books twice, and the third book wouldn't be out for a few months.

As they walked through the doorway, both girls froze. A teenage boy knelt in front of the nonfiction section. And wasn't wearing a shirt. *Wow, nice bod.* Roxi tried not to stare. He angled his chiseled, handsome face their way. Brittany gasped.

His mocha eyes shifted back and forth between them. The oversized World War II volume he'd been perusing slipped from his hands as he jumped up and yanked on his wadded T-shirt. "Hi. I'm Dustin Campbell off *Harmony*. What's up?" He flashed the cutest lopsided grin.

Brittany's mouth hung open slightly, not uttering a sound.

Roxi hesitated, her mind blank for a couple of seconds, before unbidden words tumbled out. "Buenos dias. I'm off of *Dawn's Dove*. My first name is Roxette, named after a goofy Swedish pop band. Last name is McKay." She bit her lip, trying to hold back the geyser erupting from her mouth. "Roxette is almost as lame as my mom's given name, Shalimar, who only answers to Star. Because she is one—well, sort of."

She narrowed her eyes, daring him to say something snarky. "Anyway, only call me Roxi or I'll use you for trolling bait! Comprende?" She squeezed her eyes shut for a second and winced. *Why did I say all that? He must think I'm a freak.*

"Ah ... sure, no problema, little one. Roxi it is. I wouldn't want to get gobbled up by a hungry fish." Dustin's mouth twitched.

Was he going to laugh? Her nostrils flared. "No short remarks either." She always hated being the dwarf in the crowd.

Brittany shot her a quizzical look and scrunched her eyebrows. Then she shook back her silky sun-bleached hair and turned toward Dustin. "By the way, I'm Brittany Ann Redfern from *Sea Eagle*. Call me Brit for short." Her voice purred.

Roxi swore she batted her eyelashes, and then Miss Sunshine gave him a dazzling smile that lit up her whole face. Why was she acting so weird? Roxi shook her head and turned to the shelves of fiction, skimming the titles and authors.

Brittany hovered near and whispered, "Want to ask him to hang out with us?" Roxi shrugged, then nodded. "Dustin, would you like to walk around town with us after we grab a couple of paperbacks?"

"Sure, if you both don't mind me tagging along." He peeked over at Roxi. She ventured a timid, apologetic smile for her earlier behavior.

After they stuffed books in their backpacks, the three ambled outside, avoiding deep cracks in the uneven sidewalks. Brittany turned her head to Dustin. "So, what are your favorite things to do?"

He didn't think long. "I'm looking forward to scuba diving the South Pacific reefs, but at home in Oregon, I'm all about bouldering and mountain climbing." His eyes brightened. "However, there's nothing to compare with the totally rad high from bungee jumping or snow kiting."

Brittany paled. "Wow, that's a bit extreme for me. I'm more comfortable in the water, swimming or dinghy racing." She cleared her throat. "How about you, Roxi?"

She only had one word. "Dance!" The two gaped as though she'd told them she was from another planet.

Dustin guided them across the potholed road, his hand held up like a traffic cop. Dented cars weaved and zoomed around them, not bothering to slow down. He seemed to have a lot of confidence for only fifteen years old. Hanging with him made her feel important. As she stepped onto the sidewalk, Roxi glanced around to see if anyone noticed them. Nope. Still invisible.

They entered the bustling open-air central market and wandered an aisle of colorful striped serapes and sombreros. Brittany chatted about her grandparents, cousins, brother, and dad. "And everyone has dark hair except me. Makes me look like I'm adopted when we get together for powwows." She got a faraway expression and was quiet for a minute before focusing on Roxi. "What about your family?"

Roxi cringed, then picked up three straw hats, one for each of them to try on. Anything to avoid that question— but the distraction didn't last long. She placed the hat back on a peg and started twirling a curl around her finger. She realized Brit wasn't going to stop staring at her until she answered. "There's only me and my mom, okay? And my grandma."

"What about your ..." Brittany stopped when Roxi turned her back, hoping to show her the subject was closed. She seemed to get the hint. "What about yours, Dustin?"

"Only child of hippie farmers from outside Corvalis, Oregon." He snickered. "Between you and me, I think Ray grew a little pot among the fruit trees and berry bushes. My mom, Juanita, raised medicinal herbs she used for healing. Something she'd learned from my *abuela* who lives in northern Mexico."

Brittany grinned. "Grandmother Redfern also is a healer. During our walks in the forest, she taught me all about edible plants and their uses."

On the produce aisles, she pointed out a purplish-red fruit. "That's a prickly pear. They grow on a cactus and are a good source of vitamin C and antioxidants." When Dustin held up a large tan oval fruit, she smiled. "The mamey's taste is a cross between a cantaloupe, sweet potato, and pumpkin pie. They're yummy and good for your heart and digestion."

Caged chickens squawked as they turned into the butcher section. Flies swarmed everywhere. When the odor of raw, bloody animal carcasses hanging from hooks hit them, their steps slowed. Brit made a gagging sound and clamped both hands over her mouth and nose.

Roxi averted her gaze from the staring, glassy eyes of cow and pig heads displayed atop a grimy countertop. Goosebumps sprang up on her arms as they scurried by. "This area gives me the creeps."

At the end of the row, Roxi studied a stall with no customers around. *Something's off.* They crept closer and she sniffed. "What's that smell?"

Dustin edged toward the table and glanced around. "Hola, señor. Where are flies?" He flapped his arms. "Bzzz ... bzzz."

The old man behind the counter flashed a toothless grin, reached beneath the table, and held up a can of Raid. "See, I spray. No flies." He dispersed a fine mist over his toxic meat.

"Gross." Roxi fake-barfed.

Brittany backed away looking like she might really throw up. "Just another reason why I'm a pescatarian."

"Well, I've had enough of this buggy mercado." Roxi rushed the door and led the way out. When they strolled past the panaderia, she drew in the mouthwatering scents of baking bread, cookies, and cakes.

Dustin halted at the corner of Degollado and Franciscan Madera. "Want to get some tacos for lunch? I'm starved." He trotted to the taco stand. The girls followed and everyone piled their fresh grilled fish tacos with lettuce, tomatoes, and tonsil-blistering salsa. He devoured his within minutes.

"Dustin, I can't believe you ate five tacos!" Roxi puffed out her cheeks.

"Told you I was hungry." He wiped his mouth using his shirt sleeve.

"Changing the subject, do you mind if we stop by Martin's produce truck?" Brittany held up a half-empty canvas bag.

"My pack is full, but tonight's dinner still needs a few more veggies."

At the dusty marina lot, the three sauntered to the antique pickup with a striped awning that shaded the full bed of fruits and vegetables. Martin shared a jovial smile plus gifts of juicy orange slices.

Brit picked out a jicama and scrutinized the tomatoes.

Roxi followed Dustin over to an old white guy. "Hi, Rob. How're you doing?" Dustin introduced her as she studied the deep furrows etched on Rob's weather-beaten face and wondered how these two had connected.

As if he could read her mind, Rob explained how he and Dustin knew each other. "This lad and his parents rescued me at the dinghy dock awhile back. My outboard wouldn't start, so they offered me a tow back to my boat. I made tea, and we ended up chatting away the afternoon."

Dustin grinned. "Yeah, and I got to hear his totally cool stories about serving under MacArthur in Papua New Guinea, Australia, and the Philippines."

"Yes, well, we don't want to bore this young lady with all that right now." He chuckled. "Meeting you was such a pleasure. I hope our paths cross again soon."

"Me too." Roxi watched Rob's gray-blue eyes crinkle at the corners and the kindness that shone out of them warmed her all the way to her toes. As he shuffled away, she yearned to know him, although she couldn't understand why. He had to be way more ancient than Mama Carol.

What could they possibly have in common?

Chapter Six: Working Things Out

CAROL

Carol felt as if ants were marching across her scalp as she fidgeted in the galley. She scratched her head with both hands. Stress. Roxi's emotional roller coaster had her reeling. Like those years after Shalimar's dad, Joe, died from too many days battling depression and booze. The loss of her father when Shalimar was eleven had been devastating and the catalyst for her daughter's downward spiral.

Before she could continue down that vortex of despair, she heard the squeak of an inflatable rub the hull. One of their fellow cruisers had arrived, probably Rob.

Jon shouted from the deck, "Welcome, Rob. Appreciate you pickin' up Roxi and her buddies."

Roxi bounded into the main salon, glowing in lemon-yellow drawstring shorts and a lime-green T-shirt. She wasn't wearing her new blouse, but the turquoise necklace around her neck pleased Carol. "Wow, you're bright. Have fun with your friends. We'll be over to the Magoti in a bit when I finish the fruit salad." She forced her words to sound upbeat.

Roxi gave a wide smile, no indication of her earlier moodiness evident. "Okay." She leapt up the companionway steps.

Carol gritted her teeth as she noticed the laughing wizard on the back of Roxi's shirt that read, *I mean, it's sort of exciting, isn't it, breaking the rules?* "Hey, be safe and stay with your friends."

No response of course.

Carol climbed out into the cockpit and plopped heavily onto a cushion, staring after Rob's departing dinghy as the group headed toward the cruiser's Christmas party. A lively rendition of *Joy to the World* from Dustin's harmonica rippled across the water. Roxi sat beside Brittany who strummed a glossy guitar. Dustin's and Brittany's families' dinghies fell in behind Rob, everyone singing.

Jon took a seat opposite Carol. "Almost ready to head over, hon?"

Carol inhaled a ragged breath. "Not really. I'm so frustrated. Roxi is not adjusting well. I can only imagine what will happen when we head across the Pacific. We'll be captives on this boat with a ticking time bomb."

"Come on, darlin'. Give her time. Roxi will figure things out. After all, we've only been out sailin' a little over two months, and she's havin' to learn a whole new way a livin'." Jon crossed his arms. "Although, that gal's gotta learn to be more respectful."

"I don't know my granddaughter anymore. She used to be so sweet when she was small." Carol blinked back tears. "If I hadn't spent the last five years living with you in Washington, maybe things would be different."

Jon's eyes narrowed. His normally soft voice grew gruff. "Well, if that don't beat all. You sayin' you regret our meetin' and marryin'?"

She groaned. She hadn't meant to upset her husband, but he had no clue. "That's not what I intended. I love you, but you've never raised children. You don't understand teenagers or what can happen when they've been traumatized."

Jon's face tightened into a scowl. "Do we need to be talkin' 'bout this stuff right now?" He jumped up. "This is Christmas. Let's go join our friends and have fun." He stomped to the mast and lowered their dinghy.

Carol shuffled below, stomach burning, and dug her fingernails into her palms. "That's the other problem," she snapped. "You never want to talk about difficult things."

Without a word, Jon focused on rowing to where thirty or more dinghies lined the shore. He landed theirs on the sloping, windswept beach of the Magoti.

Carol's stomachache diminished when Jon jumped out and pulled the dinghy onto dry sand so her sandaled feet wouldn't get wet. He held out his hand.

"Thank you." She gave a tentative smile. "And I'm sorry."

He squeezed her hand. "Me too."

Carol didn't wriggle out of his firm grasp as they trudged up the soft sand to a walkway leading to a large, tiled patio. Yesterday the abandoned resort had been swept clean, debris tossed into the pool already half-filled with sand, broken furniture, and other refuse. She tugged Jon's arm. "Let's go enjoy ourselves. Maybe grab a drink first?"

He kissed the top of her head. "There's the gal I married." He drew her into a warm embrace before they headed toward the coolers of *cerveza,* sodas, and water.

Tables with festive red and green cloths held bottles of wine, rum, and tequila.

Cruisers know how to party, Carol thought as the two found shade and sat beneath one of several palm trees circling the patio. She sipped her rum and coke. "Wow. There must be forty or fifty adults and teens here, and I count at least twenty kiddos. They're going to love the piñatas we stuffed and strung between the trees yesterday."

Jon didn't answer. Carol looked over to see what he was staring at.

Beneath a thatched roof, cracked blue-tiled counters formed a rectangle. She inhaled mouth-watering smells that drifted from an array of food covering them. The loud rumble of Jon's stomach made her chuckle. He took a swig from his can of *Tecate*.

"Sounds like someone's ready to eat." Carol stretched as she stood up. "And I see our granddaughter and her gang. Let's check on her and then grab some food."

After they exchanged a few pleasantries, Carol and Jon moved into the food line. "Roxi seems to be enjoying herself. What a relief." Her elbow nudged Jon as he heaped his plate with juicy slices of ham, a huge scoop of scalloped potatoes, and a teensy serving of mixed vegetables. "And you do too. Don't forget to save room for a small piece of your favorite chocolate cake."

Jon chuckled. "When have I ever not had room for dessert?" After they finished eating, Jon and Carol ambled over to Red who was in an animated conversation with Drew Stuart. They had met Abbie and Drew Stuart in Long Beach at Alamitos Bay Marina a few months before *Illusion*, the couple's Deerfoot 50, had departed for Mexico, a year ahead of *Dawn's Dove*.

She found Abbie bent over in a beach chair rubbing her feet. Carol felt so grateful to have reconnected with this woman of faith. "Feliz Navidad! Having a rough day?"

Abbie's face wore a pinched expression, but her pale blue eyes lit up when she saw her friend. "Oh, Merry Christmas to you also." She slipped her sandals back on. "My feet are killing me. Probably arthritis." Her eyes filled with unshed tears, and she took a shaky breath.

"And you're missing your family," Carol ventured softly. Not that she could completely relate.

Abbie nodded. "We always spent the day visiting our son, Andy, his wife, and the twins who recently turned three. I can just picture the excitement on their precious little faces."

Carol handed her a napkin, and Abbie wiped her eyes. "And our daughter's sweet son, Benjy, two-and-a-half, has probably been a pint-sized ninja turtle. We'd be millionaires if we could bottle his energy." Abbie chuckled. "He wears out our daughter Hannah. She and her husband had planned to take Mom to California so they could celebrate the holidays with Andy and his family." She paused a moment. "But her obstetrician advised against travel since she's suffering with gestational diabetes. So, they're making the most of an Indiana white Christmas."

"Brr ... I can't even fathom snow." Carol got goosebumps thinking about frigid temperatures. She felt thankful for the sunshine that warmed her skin. She turned and eyed the drink table. "Want something to sip? I'm thinking one more rum and coke, since this is a holiday."

As Abbie rose, she tilted to one side. Carol caught her arm and steadied her. "Careful, girlfriend. Why don't you wait here, and I'll get yours?"

"An ice-cold coke sounds heavenly. Minus the rum, please. I'm having enough trouble with my balance."

Carol returned, carrying two drinks, handed Abbie hers, and leaned back in the beach chair. She closed her eyes for a moment and blew out her breath. "Jon and I had an argument this morning."

"Everything okay now?" Abbie's brow creased.

She nodded. "Yes, but now I'm thinking about Roxi. One moment she's laughing, the next she's either screaming or stomping off." Her throat closed up. When she could finally speak her voice trembled. "What if she's bipolar like her mom?"

Abbie rubbed Carol's arm. "Oh hon, from what you've told me, she's nothing like Shalimar. Roxi has been through so much, and you have to admit, this trip is probably not the way she wanted to spend eighth grade and maybe high school. Plus, she's a teenager. That's never easy."

Carol shook her head. "I know, but she's so headstrong, and I can't seem to break through that rock fortress."

Abbie's smile was tender. "Just keep chipping away. That wall will eventually crumble and then you can rebuild your relationship."

"I only pray she doesn't implode or explode and destroy us all." She took two large gulps of her drink, then gasped. "I hope I'm not turning into my dad. He always got wasted on holidays. Maybe I'm the one who needs help."

Abbie searched Carol's face. "I'm quite sure you're not an alcoholic. I've never seen you even tipsy, Miss Control Freak."

"Guess you're right. This is only my second drink." She poured the remainder into the sand and studied her friend.

Abbie's eyelids drooped over reddened eyes, and new worry lines furrowed her brow.

"Everything else okay, Ab?"

Abbie lowered her gaze. "Yeah, guess so. Well, not really. Drew and I also had a small spat earlier. I love my husband, but sometimes, he irritates me."

Carol felt shocked by Abbie's confession. Guess even perfect couples had disagreements. She gave a grim smile. "I can totally relate."

"Before we set sail from California over a year ago, Drew promised we'd fly home at least twice a year. And that hasn't happened yet." Her eyes narrowed. He's always got an excuse. I know how much he's enjoying the fulfillment of his dream, but this isn't how I envisioned our retirement." A soft hiccup interrupted her. "I always hoped we'd live close to our kids in California half the year and Indiana during the warmer months."

Carol wanted to comfort Abbie, but she wasn't sure what to say. "So, what are you going to do?"

Abbie smiled weakly. "I have no idea. I want to be with Drew, but I also need to be part of my grandchildren's lives. And Mom won't be around forever. She's almost eighty and has health issues."

A stab of guilt pierced Carol. She felt selfish for hoping her friend wouldn't go home, but also for the years she'd abandoned her granddaughter. She almost wished she hadn't poured out that drink. Her neck muscles were taut as a bowstring. "There sure are lots of things to work out when you go cruising."

"Probably a good topic for our women's prayer group." Abbie took Carol's hand and gave it a squeeze.

"Definitely. Hope we're meeting soon."

Chapter Seven: The Gift

ROXI

The line of cruisers moved forward, and Roxi jabbed a hunk of pineapple, flinging the fruit onto her overloaded plate.

"Hey, don't forget to save room for these awesome desserts." Dustin licked his lips several times making Roxi laugh.

"You look like you're ready to devour all those cakes, pies, and cookies, but make sure you save me a gooey fudge brownie. My fav."

Brittany scrunched her whole face. "Ugh, even more food than at Thanksgiving. I'm going to gain ten pounds just looking at all of those calories."

Roxi flinched at the memory of that horrific holiday. She glanced at her skinny friend's plate of salad and veggies. "Yeah right, like you have anything to worry about."

In between bites, Roxi chatted with Rob and her grandparents. While Brit picked at her food, she and Dustin inhaled theirs. Roxi patted her bulging stomach. *Whew, thank goodness for elastic waistbands.* The trio waved to the elders when they finished eating and headed to one of the resort's buildings to exchange gifts in private.

Brit's long slender legs seemed even longer in skimpy jean shorts as she ascended the rickety wooden ladder onto the flat roof. Roxi felt a twinge of envy when she glanced at Dustin who steadied the ladder. His eyes were glued to those flawless legs. She scowled. *Shouldn't have had that second brownie.*

Up on the roof, all guilt for overeating vanished as Roxi drank in the panorama of vast desert and wide bay leading out to islands in the sea. "Wow. What a totally cool view." She spun several pirouettes on short, muscular legs. Leaping and bounding in widening circles, her arms fluttered gracefully like an albatross soaring high above the ocean. A wave of deep joy swept over her. Passion for dancing always freed her from worries and negative thoughts—for a while. Roxi bestowed an elaborate curtsy toward her friends and tried to catch her breath.

Brittany's eyes popped wide open. "That was magnificent, Rox. But please, stay away from the edge. You're making me a nervous wreck."

Dustin gawked like a puppy waiting for another treat.

Only Alex, her far-away friend, truly understood what dancing meant to her. They alone shared these feelings. Was Alex missing her too?

Roxi hunkered down beside her sailing friends and pulled rumpled gifts from each pocket of her shorts. "They aren't much, but I made these bracelets in your favorite colors." She thrust the presents toward them. "Merry Christmas, Muggles. I'd go bonkers without you guys."

"Awesome. Love the blues, like the ocean and your eyes." Dustin's lips curved into a crooked grin.

"Oh, I love friendship bracelets. I'll never take this off." Brittany crossed her heart.

Roxi tied them around her friends' wrists.

Brit gave her a gentle hug. "I know what you mean. I'd be a mental case if all of us hadn't met. It is sooo difficult being away from the rest of my family, especially Grandmother Redfern. She's like a second mother to me." She sniffled and wiped her eyes before handing Roxi a package bound by multi-colored curled ribbons. Then Brit reached over and gave Dustin an awkward half-hug and presented him a shimmery silver box with a bright blue bow.

Dustin fidgeted and stammered, "Umm uh ... thanks guys." He fumbled through his over-stuffed pockets, retrieved two small drawstring pouches, peered inside, and handed one to each girl.

Roxi opened her gift from Brit and slid the beaded band on her arm. "Sweet. Like a rainbow on my wrist." A gasp made her look up.

Brittany held a multi-strand woven bead necklace to her slender neck. "Oh, Dustin, I adore this necklace," she squealed. "And the colors match the golds and greens of the bracelet Roxi made me. Now open yours." A smile whispered at the corners of her mouth.

Dustin squirmed and ran fingers through his dark wavy hair as Brittany focused adoring eyes on him. He looked as though he'd swallowed a large gulp of hot sauce when he glimpsed the scrolled silver wristband inside the box.

"Uh ... um, *Muchas gracias, mi amiga.*" He licked dry lips, not meeting Brit's seeking gaze, and turned toward Roxi. "You haven't opened your gift yet," he said in a low voice.

She gave up trying to comprehend the strange vibes between Brit and Dustin and shrugged as she unwrapped the final gift. Her mouth opened but no words came out. She slowly lifted a delicate dove carved from abalone that hung from a thin leather cord.

Roxi's throat dried up like desert sand. "Oh, to-ta-ly su-u-weet." She'd never received a gift like this from a boy.

Brit's mouth and eyes drooped.

Did I do something wrong? Well, whatever it is, it is. Roxi jumped up. "Let's bounce." In silence, the three friends clambered down the ladder, holiday cheer lost amid a dust devil of conflicting emotions.

As Roxi's feet hit the ground, a hand grabbed her elbow and spun her around. *Uh-oh.*

Mama C scowled, inches from Roxi's face. Her voice shook. "What on earth were you thinking? Dancing on the roof?"

Before Roxi could reply, her grandma continued her tirade. She tried to tune most of the words out but winced at *irresponsible* and *self-centered*. Thank goodness PJ came to her rescue and led his wife off for "somethun important."

Dustin and Roxi headed to the patio where a group crowded around one of the piñatas. She soon forgot all the previous drama. A boisterous, blindfolded two-year-old was spun a few times, and allowed five whacks at the colorful paper-mache donkey dangling above.

Dustin hollered with laughter when one little boy swung so ferociously that he sprawled on his back, still swinging. Kids shrieked with laughter when a supervising teenager got smacked on his butt—twice.

Roxi snorted, which caused Dustin to howl. She took a wild swing, and he caught her wrist. Over his shoulder, she spied Brittany standing alone, watching them.

"What's Miss Gloomy-Face's problem?" Roxi asked.

Dustin turned. "I dunno." He quickly dropped her hand.

All five piñatas eventually showered their sugary treasures, and kids scrambled to gather candy. In the end, the older ones shared their larger stash of goodies between the younger kids so everyone got an equal share. Roxi imagined this was what being part of a large family was like—working and playing together, helping one another. She'd often longed for a brother or sister. Someone to share the many lonely nights when Star was out.

The holiday ended around a crackling bonfire. Several strumming guitars, five humming harmonicas, two warbling flutes, one rumbling saxophone, and Rob's lively accordion accompanied over seventy joyful voices. The sublime harmony of "Silent Night" resounded in the starry night. Roxi, her grandma, and PJ sauntered toward their dinghy, now high on the beach, abandoned by a low tide.

"You know, this wasn't such a horrible Christmas after all." Roxi's confession surprised herself.

"The day had its moments." Carol gave Roxi's arm a playful punch. "But overall, the holiday was unique and memorable with two of my favorite people and many new friends.

PJ patted his belly. "Don't forget all that amazin' food."

Roxi chuckled. "My holidays at home are usually like the movie, *A Christmas Story,* but without the dad. A couple years ago my scatter-brained mom raced around our kitchen, actually cooking as she chugged wine like soda pop, mashed lumpy potatoes, and scraped Jello from a mold. Christmas music blared and timers rang as she pulled the turkey from the oven." Roxi covered her mouth and nose as her giggle ended in a snort. "Unfortunately, Star tripped while carrying it toward the counter. That bird took flight toward *Uncle* Scott, her boyfriend at the time.

He caught the thing like a hot potato and flung the searing projectile towards me."

Mama C laughed, "Oh no, what did you do?"

"That thing was steamin' hot, so I ducked. The dripping fowl whizzed by me and smacked poor JoJo, our neighbor, on his bare chest. He'd stopped by to see if I wanted to go to the beach for an hour while he surfed. He squawked like a turkey being chased with an ax, plucked it off, and launched the greasy bird. The turkey splashed down in a sink full of bubbles."

A belly laugh erupted from PJ as he doubled over.

Mama C's grin changed to a tight line. "I bet your mom wasn't too happy about that whole fiasco."

Roxi's smile crumpled like Star's face had that day. She recalled her mom's wail that pierced the sudden silence. She shook her head. "Mom stormed into the bedroom and slammed the door. The holiday was quiet after that."

Roxi helped push the heavy fiberglass dinghy toward the shushing bay. She never knew what to do with her mom's tantrums. Whether she ignored Star or sympathized, Mom would give an academy award performance, swearing to leap off the nearest bridge or an equally disgusting death. *Was Star serious or only wanting attention?*

Roxi felt helpless and scared that she wasn't there to soothe her mom's lows. She fought off clawing fingers of apprehension. Why couldn't she be five again? Life was so much simpler then—cuddled in Mama's arms amid comforting murmurs of "I love my snuggle bunny so much" and singing "It Must Have Been Love" over and over in her sultry voice.

PJ dipped the oars into and out of the placid water as the three headed back to *Dawn's Dove* and Mama C hummed "Silent Night." Contentment mingled with an aching emptiness. Roxi tilted her head skyward and scanned the twinkling Christmas heavens. Yearning for something. Or someone.

Could she handle the upcoming crossing? Would Rob be okay sailing alone for twenty-plus days? What was going on between Dustin and Brit? And where would she be in ten months? So many unanswered questions.

God, are you real? If you're there, I could really use some answers.

Chapter Eight: Provisioning

CAROL

"I'm sick of stupid boat chores. Sick of this boring town that has no malls, arcades, or dance studios. And sick of this trip!" Roxi paced from stern to bow, back and forth, like a caged lion cub.

Carol cringed at Roxi's withering scowl. *Just say it—and sick of my grandparents.* This outburst likely stemmed from yesterday's mail packet containing four letters from her friend, Alex, and not even a post card from her mom. That had to hurt. "I understand ..."

"Nothing," Roxi roared and glared. "You can't understand how much I miss home—singing at the top of our lungs while Star and I rollerblade along the beach trail, spying on the world from Alex's huge avocado tree, and dancing in her bedroom until we collapse." Tears glistened as she turned away.

Carol ached for Roxi. Maybe sharing her own distress would help. "You aren't the only one to miss people."

Roxi shrugged. "Whatever."

"My friend, Anne, and I grew up in Washington and have known each other since we were your age. We double-dated through high school and college, were in each other's weddings, and have battled many storms together." Talking about Anne made Carol a little homesick too, but she had Roxi's attention. "And my California friend, Micki, and I not only taught at the same school, but being two single hotties, took country-western dance lessons and power-walked beaches, sharing dashed hopes, dreams, and even a few of our deepest secrets."

Roxi chuckled when Carol called herself a hottie. Maybe opening up would comfort Roxi and let her know that missing people you love was normal. Besides, this eruption couldn't compare to the night of Jon's and her worst altercation ever. Remembering still caused disquieting pain.

Last month Brittany's dad, Jeff, who liked to be called Red and shared Jon's passion for woodworking, read about an incident on the internet that involved a Catalina 36—a boat like *Dawn's Dove*. Their rudder had sheared off halfway to Hawaii, making the sailboat impossible to steer. Carol shuddered. *How frightening that must have been.* Thankfully, the crew had been rescued the following day. Jon stayed up half the night chugging Dr. Pepper while he wrote a long list of extra safety items needed for their voyage.

"Why do we need more junk for the boat?" The thought of more delays and expenses had driven Carol a little berserk. She tore up the list and threw the darn thing overboard. *Guess I overreacted a bit, huh, Lord? I could use extra help with patience.*

Jon usually stayed out of her way when she got agitated. But not that night. He jumped into the ring fighting mad, his stubborn Irish temper flaring. Towering over her, he bellowed, "I'm going to the marine stores in San Diego and will buy every item on that list and install a new rudder or this here boat won't be leavin' Mexico."

Carol could see Roxi curled in the center of her berth hugging her bedraggled Snuggles, but she didn't back down. Even as alarm bells clanged in her head, she ignored their warning. Her pent-up frustration unleashed. "Another decade wouldn't fulfill your wish list for this boat."

"Yeah well, there ain't many marine stores in the middle of nowhere. And these spare parts might keep our boat afloat and us livin'."

She threw her arms up. "You're going to mess up our monthly budget that I've planned for the next three years. Besides, every locker is jammed full. There's barely room left for food that we *do* need to stay alive."

Jon crossed his arms, his face crimson. "Well, maybe we should head home and work another ten years so we can buy a bigger boat for all them supplies and food."

"Great idea," Roxi yelled from her room at the bow.

Carol glared through the doorway at her, then at Jon. She blinked back tears as her voice wavered. "Fine. Do whatever you think you need to do. I give up." Her stomach in knots, she stomped up the companionway and stayed on deck long after sunset.

Jon and Red left on a bus heading north the following day. During her husband's absence, Carol teetered between anxiety and hope. In the quiet of night, she prayed her favorite verse from Philippians. "Do not be anxious about anything, but in every situation, by prayer and petition, with thanksgiving, present your requests to God. And the peace of God, which transcends all understanding, will guard your hearts and minds in Christ Jesus."

Roxi drove Carol crazy between complaints of not being allowed to accompany Jon to California, then fretted over his not returning. Carol was thankful her granddaughter was safe here and would not be tempted to flee home. The poor kid needed stability and consistency, something Shalimar had never provided.

But what if Jon doesn't come back? Will we have to fly to California alongside Abbie on Thursday? And then what? Another wave of misery crashed over Carol's fragile state as she thought about her friend's imminent departure. Abbie wasn't feeling up to the strenuous crossing but she would join Drew in Tahiti where they could all cruise French Polynesia together.

Everyone exhaled great sighs of relief when Jon and Red stepped off the bus from hell, as they referred to their ride, shaken and worn out. Red's son, Toby helped the two men unload the new gear.

Carol frowned at the huge pile, and her exuberance dampened further at Red's mention of enduring several checkpoints guarded by armed soldiers.

Jon jumped into the conversation. "But them soldiers were a downwind sail compared to the bus screechin' round them curves and nearly runnin' over goats and cows standin' on that skinny dark highway."

Carol's blood pressure swerved upward, and she gripped her husband's hand tighter.

Red nodded. "That Indy 500 bus driver would curse and press the accelerator to the floor, brushing a hair-width past the poor creatures. We're lucky to be here."

"Luck had nothing to do with it. I prayed for both of you the whole time." Carol looked to heaven. "God protected you and brought you back safely."

Back aboard the boat, she and Jon reconciled their chilly goodbye with a passionate kiss and hearty hug. Roxi pretended to ignore them, but Carol noticed her grin. Things were back on track. *Praise the Lord.*

Sounds of an approaching motor and then Rob's gravelly voice carried through an open hatch. "Come along, polliwog." He coughed, then cleared his throat. "Are you and your grandma ready to venture ashore for some serious shopping?"

The thumps of Roxi pacing the deck above her head finally ceased. Roxi poked her head in the doorway. "Mama C, Rob is here. Time to bounce."

Carol snapped out of her reverie and grumbled as she struggled to fold up yards of canvas covering the main salon table and floor. She had been stitching a sail awning to hook onto the dodger that protected the companionway and cockpit from salty spray. The dodger's pliable plastic windows had really challenged her minimal sewing skills.

"Be right there. I'm definitely ready for a break. By the way, did you finish today's schoolwork?"

Roxi muttered, "Take a chill pill."

Carol locked the companionway hatch.

"Everything except math. I'll do that page later."

Carol took a deep breath and stared at her granddaughter.

Roxi scurried down the stainless ladder hinged to the side rail and plopped onto the plump tube of Dustin's inflatable, sitting between Rob and Brit. "Grrr ... I hate being told what to do all the time like I'm five."

Carol tensed when Roxi's lip curled as she scrutinized her friend's flowered sundress and silky hair bound in a high ponytail with matching scrunchie.

Her granddaughter glanced down at her own baggy shorts and rumpled chartreuse T-shirt. "Kinda fancy for a trip to the grocery store, doncha think?"

Brittany blushed and gave Roxi the evil eye before turning her back on Roxi.

Carol settled in the dinghy beside Dustin, who drove, and shook her head at Rob, mouthing, "Kids." She'd deal with Roxi's rudeness later.

The ancient mariner nodded and gave her a sympathetic smile. "Good afternoon, Carol." He turned to Roxi and Brittany. "You know, everyone gets a little out of sorts as departure day draws near. There is so much to do and worry about. Life can get a bit overwhelming." He cleared his throat. "That's why it's so important to be extra patient, kind, and forgiving, especially now."

The girls gawked at each other for a few seconds. "Sorry," they both murmured, their eyes downcast.

"That's the spirit." He winked at Carol. "Things will calm down once you settle into your routines at sea."

"I doubt that." Roxi rolled her eyes.

As they headed toward shore, the soft breeze caressed Carol's tense muscles. She did a few shoulder rolls, breathing in the fresh briny air, and tried to relax.

As the dinghy weaved through a maze of anchored yachts, Roxi swiveled her body to face the back of the inflatable. "Hey, Dustin, what's up?"

"Wondered when you were gonna acknowledge my presence." He gave her a mocking grin and bowed his head. "Of course, I'm only your humble chauffeur."

Roxi stuck out her tongue. "That's right, and don't you forget it, slave."

"Yeah well, only a couple more days until you'll have to find someone new to boss around. Dad informed us at breakfast we're almost ready to bust outta here. I'm so ready for something new."

Brittany squeezed her eyes shut and chewed morosely on her fingernails.

"I guess *Harmony* can blaze the trail and let us know what lies ahead." Roxi shrugged, and the outboard motor's high-pitched whine filled the silence until they arrived at the dock.

Jon and Brittany's dad, Red, waited outside Club Cruceros, chatting with an acquaintance who had been cruising the Sea of Cortez for the past fifteen years. Red waved them over. "Hi, guys. I ran into Gary, and he's offered us a lift to the CeCeCe in his vintage van."

Jon patted the round VW insignia on the front of the van. "I always liked these sixties buses. Great on gas and run forever."

Skeptical, Carol studied the grimy van's swirling fluorescent flowers and rainbows. Would this old clunker get them to the store? "Uh, thanks, Gary. Sure this won't be out of your way?"

"No problemo. Had a few errands to run anyhow." Everyone piled inside, and Gary slammed the sliding door shut. The vehicle coughed and sputtered a few times, but they reached the super mercado on the outskirts of La Paz in one piece.

Gathering provisions over the next two hours proved exhausting. Especially for Rob, whose gait grew slower and whose body leaned heavily over his cart. Carol was happy to see the kids assist him. Roxi kept asking for help to decipher Mexican labels, while Brittany simply translated and pointed to items. Carol figured that with Brit's experience as primary shopper and cook for her dad and brother, Toby, she could calculate what and how much Rob would need and then triple amounts for her own family's cart.

Brittany stayed glued to Dustin like his shadow. Her adoring gaze never drifted off him as he lifted heavy cases into Rob's squeaky cart. Jon, like Dustin and Red, was in charge of loading while Carol made selections—except for the economy-sized bags of candy and cookies he tried to sneak in. She allowed a few.

Outside the store, they hailed a taxi van. She prayed without ceasing as the battered cab screeched out of the lot, careened around corners, and zoomed through intersections.

Dustin laughed gleefully. "Feels like we're in a video game."

Brittany moaned, her face pale. She clutched Dustin's arm as they barreled into the marina's dusty lot.

Carol wasn't sure which squealed louder, the brakes or Brittany.

"Awesome! We got to the finish line without being destroyed." Dustin gently disengaged from Brit's grasp and stepped from the taxi. "I'm gonna find a couple of dock carts to load all this stuff in."

The others took a minute to get their bearings before staggering out. Rob paid the kamikaze driver before Carol led them to Martin's pitted produce truck with its faded green and white striped awning.

Roxi chuckled. "He always reminds me of Humpty Dumpty with a mustache."

Brittany poked her ribs. "Shh, he might hear you."

"Ah, *Buenos días señora, señoritas, and señores.* How you, today?" Martin's brown cheeks puffed out with his smile.

"*Muy bien, y tú?*" Carol glanced over his fruits and vegetables for the least ripe and longest lasting produce.

Rob limped around the small pickup, looking every bit of his seventy-five years. "Too much activity today. My nemesis, Arthur, is visiting my hips and knees again."

Carol rubbed her low back. "My arthritis is acting up too. That taxi ride didn't help either." She grew concerned. *Will he have the stamina for sailing over three thousand miles alone?*

Rob paid for his purchases as Martin threw a couple of handfuls of red and green chilis into his canvas bag. "Good for *el corazon*." The produce man pointed to his heart.

"*Sí, sí. Muchas gracias, mi amigo.*" Rob shook his hand.

"Better eat lots of those," Roxi advised, a quaver in her voice.

Dustin arrived, pushing a wobbly, overflowing dock cart. He gestured over to Red and Jon. "They've got another full one. Hope we don't sink the dinghies."

Everyone bid farewell to Martin. Carol felt a little sad. "I'm going to miss your generosity and warm smile."

"*Vaya con Dios, mis amigos,*" the jolly produce man sang out as the group headed to the gangway leading to the dock.

The group crammed into their three dinghies tied next to each other and stuffed bags around themselves and onto laps. Wind-swept swells struck their bows as they headed across the bay. Saltwater rained over everyone and their canvas grocery bags.

The group of dinghies arrived at Rob's sailboat, *Romance,* and everyone passed his damp bags up onto the deck.

"Darn, another northerly must be on the way." Dustin's lower lip curled into a frown.

"Maybe you should wait a few more days before heading off." Brittany's eyes held a hopeful gleam.

Dustin scowled. "Are you nuts?"

Brit's face flushed, and she gasped.

Dustin apologized. "Sorry. I'm just anxious for a change of scenery. You know—diving, rock-climbing, those kinda things." He directed his wonky grin at Brit. "Anyhow, this weather probably won't last."

Rob shook his head. His Tilly hat blew off, saved only by the strap looped under his chin. "Get used to harsh conditions, scallywags. This breeze is nothing compared to Pacific gales and squalls."

"Too bad we can't beam across to the Marquesas like they do in *Star Trek*." Roxi's smile was stiff.

Carol winced and wished Rob hadn't brought up stormy weather. That would stress the girls out even more. She felt a tiny bit nervous, too, but mostly excited. There was a huge ocean to sail across, but with their own resourcefulness and God's protection—that would be enough.

Chapter Nine: Adios Mexico

ROXI

Roxi leaned against the stern rail of *Dawn's Dove's* and waved. The thirty-five-foot sloop, *Harmony*, glided past under perfect sailing conditions—clear skies and a warm fifteen-knot breeze. But it *was* April 1st.

"Only a fool would leave today," Roxi shouted to the passing sailboat, not that she was superstitious.

Dustin grinned and pumped his arms in the air. "That's us, a ship of fools. Hey, Rox, don't forget the radio sched."

"Don't worry." She planned to keep close tabs on her friends, so she'd know what to expect. Anxiety mixed with a teeny dab of excitement. The *real* adventure lay ahead. Problem was, she wasn't that adventurous.

Dustin's family would explore a few islands in the Sea of Cortez before the lengthy passage southwest to the Marquesas. He intended to paddle his inflatable kayak, free-dive, and rock climb before camping on secluded beaches each night. His dad, Ray, planned to sketch and dabble with paints while Juanita, his mom, dried herbs, grew jars of sprouts, and canned meals in the pressure cooker.

Harmony shrank to a speck as Brittany rowed over from *Sea Eagle*.

Roxi ignored Brit's blotchy face and swollen eyes. Instead, she pointed to her friend's bandaged toe. "Now what happened?"

Brittany blushed. "I ran into an inner shroud watching Dustin leave instead of where I was going."

Roxi snickered. "Yeah, those wire cables will jump out and trip you when you least expect it."

Brittany's face crumpled, and she began to cry. "Oh, Roxi, I already miss him."

Grrr. "Whatever. It's only a few weeks before you and Dustin catch up—not forever."

Brittany sniffled and wiped her nose. "You don't understand."

Nope, I don't. We might only be eighteen months apart in age, but sometimes I feel like we came from different planets.

"Dustin will probably fall in love with a Polynesian beauty before I get there."

Roxi twirled a curl around her finger. She wanted to tell Brit not to be such a crybaby. Her fists clenched. "At least you guys are almost ready to leave. I'm stuck here another three weeks thanks to PJ's bottomless list of projects. He's driving Mama C and me batty."

Eyes downcast, Brit hiccupped. "Sorry for only thinking of myself. That's even worse. By the way, when's *Romance* leaving?"

Roxi drew a deep breath. "Rob thinks by the end of the week if his mail arrives. He's expecting more books from Swami. Can you believe his son lives in a Himalayan monastery? Crazy, huh?"

Brit hesitated, and a frown etched a line between her eyebrows. "Do you think he's going to be okay sailing alone?"

Roxi ran fingers through her messy strawberry curls. Her lips stretched thin. "Rob will be fine. He's tough as Mama C's pot roast."

A few mornings later, Roxi wasn't so optimistic. As she boarded *Romance*, she found Rob seated below. Thick bandages covered his right eyebrow and one elbow. She gasped. "Hey, what happened to you?"

No response.

She squatted in front of Rob. "Are you okay?"

His forehead wrinkled. "Hmm? Oh, quite all right. Yesterday, I was studying a chart and must have had a spell of vertigo when I stood to fix a cuppa tea. This dizziness doesn't occur often. I only banged up my head and arm a bit."

Roxi's eyes narrowed. "You never told me that happens."

"Now, dear, don't be fretting over me." Rob patted a purplish bruise on his cheek. "My boys have done enough of that. They're very much against this excursion." Rob moved to the galley with a stiff shuffle, popped several vitamins into his mouth, and washed them down with a swig of papaya juice. He offered her a glass.

She pursed her lips and shook her head. "Maybe you should find someone to help you sail across the Pacific."

Rob rubbed his temples in slow circles. "No, this is my quest—alone. Besides, Jeannie will be right beside me through every storm and lonely night watch."

"Oh great, a helpful ghost." Roxi locked away her worries as she and Rob stored the remainder of his provisions and miscellaneous gear. She wasn't an organized neat freak like Mama C, but she did try to number each locker and write a list of the contents as her grandma had suggested.

Rob interrupted her thoughts. "Have I mentioned that I grew up in Franklin Lakes, New Jersey? The town was a boy's paradise with air shows at the small airport and plenty of fishing, swimming, and sailing dinghies on the lake."

She straightened from her bent-over position at a galley locker. "Sounds like a cool place. So what did you do after high school? Go sailing?"

"I wish. No, I served in the army during WWII. Then attended MIT, majoring in electrical engineering with a minor in metaphysical philosophy."

"That's a strange combination."

Rob's eyes twinkled. "Engineering satisfied my mind while philosophy quenched my soul's desire to understand our existence—who we are and why we're here."

Roxi's eyebrows rose. "So, did you find all the answers?"

He chuckled. "Not in books, although they got me thinking. My professors did too. No, I actually gained the most insight when I met Jeannie."

"You mean about love?"

"In a roundabout way." His smile crinkled his whole face. "She introduced me to her country church where I fell in love with God, who is love."

"If you say so." Roxi twisted up one corner of her mouth, and she gave him a sideways glance. "Sounds like another fairy tale adults feed you."

Rob massaged his scalp for a minute. His gaze pierced her. "Why do you suppose we met? Out of all the billions of people and places on this planet, why did our paths cross?"

Roxi fidgeted. "I dunno. Things happen. Does there have to be a reason?"

"God always has a reason, a purpose for everything, good and bad."

"Ha. I find that hard to swallow." She squirmed. "Let's not go there."

"Sure, polliwog. We're pretty much done, anyway." Rob sank onto the settee, breathing heavily. "Come and rest a moment before we say our goodbyes."

Roxi slid in across the table from him, glad chores were over. Leaving her friend was going to be difficult.

"Jeannie was the best wife a man could have. Our life together had everything we'd ever hoped for, except a daughter." His voice held a hint of regret, but then he chuckled. "Not that raising two rambunctious boys wasn't a full-time endeavor. But if God had blessed us with a girl, we'd have wanted her to be just like you."

Whoa, how do I respond to that? Her feet tap danced on the teak floorboards.

Rob reached across and patted her hand. She glanced up. "The most precious gift you can give or receive is love. Without love, life doesn't mean much."

She could only nod as her throat constricted. Did she agree? *I've done fine so far not having much love. Haven't I?* Her foot tapping increased to the level of a dancer in *Riverdance.*

Rob cleared his throat. "Don't be afraid to open your heart."

"I'm not scared." She blinked away tears.

"Relationships can sometimes be painful. Believe me, I understand regret and sorrow, being so broken you can barely breathe." His gentle smile flattened for a moment. "But I've also experienced extreme joy when mutual love is shared between two people." A beatific glow lit up Rob's face.

Roxi nibbled her bottom lip. "But what if you love someone and they don't love you back?"

Rob gingerly touched his bandaged forehead and grimaced. "Many people are afraid of, or not good at, expressing how they feel. But God places every person in our life for a day, a season, or sometimes eternity—like Jeannie and me." His voice broke, and he paused. "Each person challenges, encourages, or teaches us to love as God loves—unconditionally."

Roxi hopped up. "Not sure I understand all that." But her heart lightened with a slight glimmer of hope. *Maybe there is a purpose to why I'm here and why we met.*

Rob groaned, rubbing his hip as he stood, then wrapped her in a hug. His blue-gray eyes glistened. "Thank you so much for your help and friendship, but most of all, for the love you've shown me. You are the daughter of my heart."

She couldn't speak for a minute. "Well, make sure you take good care of yourself on that humongous ocean." Her voice quavered as she fought the urge to cry. "Don't forget, we're meeting Brit and Dustin in Tahiti for Fête." Her eyes narrowed to slits. "You'd better be there!" She spun toward the companionway and raced up the steps. "Love you," she whispered.

By the time Rob reached the top step, Roxi had slipped the dinghy line and pushed off. He waved at her, wiping his time-worn face. "I love you too, polliwog," he cried. The only reply came from a shrieking seagull circling above.

The following day, Rob departed amid a flotilla of cruisers bound for the South Pacific. His final advice had been, "Don't forget to keep your sails adjusted." He loved Arthur Ward's quote: "The pessimist complains about the wind; the optimist expects it to change; the realist adjusts the sails." Roxi thought he meant she needed to stay flexible, not fight life's currents and winds, or they would drag her down.

Easier said than done. Roxi puckered her lips. *I want what I want when I want it and don't need any help getting it.* However, that attitude didn't seem to be working with Mama C and sure hadn't with Star.

Before Brittany left Mexico, the girls ate lunch at an outdoor café. They shared stuffed papas—potatoes filled with chicken, peppers, and onions, all smothered in a creamy cheese sauce. Her friend scraped off most of the sauce. What a waste, but more for Roxi.

As they strolled back to the marina, Roxi couldn't stop complaining about the upcoming three weeks at sea. "Sleeping, eating, and walking circles around the deck. Boring," She felt like throwing up that yummy lunch.

Brittany pulled her long ponytail tighter. "There should be lots of time to read and journal. I know how much writing your thoughts and feelings helps."

Roxi kicked a pebble, stirring up a puff of dust. "Guess I can learn French from Rob's cassettes." Sidestepping the dust cloud, Brittany followed Roxi down to the dinghy dock. She undid the line and pushed them off. The dinghy puttered across the bay to the anchorage.

When they passed a new arrival at anchor, Roxi's eyebrows shot up at the wooden boat half the size of *Dawn's Dove*. The name *Songwriter* had been carved into a board mounted on the stern. She snickered. "Looks as if a waterspout twirled that junk heap around, then spit the sailboat out. Must not have tasted good."

Songwriter's tattered mainsail hung limp. Salt-encrusted gear and clothing were strewn everywhere. Brit's face scrunched. "The boat probably belongs to a pot-smokin' hippie who got lost at sea." Roxi burst into hysterical laughter, and Brit joined in.

Roxi wasn't laughing a few days later when *Sea Eagle* disappeared over the horizon. She already missed Brit. Hanging her head, she turned to go below. A movement caught the corner of her eye. She spun around, astonished at a restored *Songwriter*—steering a course straight toward them! A lean young man stood at the mast, winching up the mainsail, oblivious to the forthcoming disaster.

"Watch out!" Roxi screamed like a banshee.

He glanced up, secured the halyard, hopped into his cockpit, and looking nonchalant, swung the tiller to port. His boat changed course less than forty-feet off *Dawn's Dove's* starboard beam.

The most stunning creature gazed across at her. Tall, with chiseled features that made her forget to breathe.

"Sorry, my fault. Doing too many things at once as usual." He pushed curly, dark-blond hair from his eyes.

Roxi's heart ping-ponged as she struggled for a rational thought. "Oh, uh, no problemo. Where you headed?" The wind caught his sail, sweeping him past. She ran to the bow.

His smooth baritone wafted across the water. "The Marquesas."

She cupped her hands and shouted, "Maybe I'll see you there." For a moment she felt disappointed, afraid he hadn't heard.

He waved. "It's a date."

Suddenly, the day and her spirits brightened. She didn't know his name, but anticipation of catching up with this intriguing stranger made the crossing feel a teensy less dreadful. Roxi hummed softly as *Songwriter* grew smaller and her dreams grew larger.

Chapter Ten: Life At Sea

ROXI

The first days out from Mexico were pure misery. Thirty-knot winds propelled them westward as vast Pacific swells tossed Roxi about like laundry in a washing machine. She awoke screaming in the early hours of their third day at sea. The room rocked like a giant cradle as wave after wave of nausea swept over her. She moaned.

PJ rushed in. "You okay, sweetie bird? Havin' that bad ol' dream again?"

His soft drawl wound its way through Roxi's foggy brain. Her gaze darted about in the gloom as she recalled the nightmare—climbing a tall swaying pine, an explosive snap as the limb gave way, her shrieks carried off by buffeting winds before she plunged into a churning canyon river.

Roxi struggled to sit up. "I'm gonna be sick again," and quickly covered her mouth.

PJ guided her to the doorway of the head, only large enough for one person, and waited outside. Roxi grabbed the small countertop with her right hand and sank onto her knees. She dry-heaved into the pump-style toilet before curling beside the bowl. *Would anyone even care if she died?*

But she didn't. Within a week, the seasickness disappeared, and Roxi stopped stumbling as she got her sea legs. The three-man crew developed a routine for mealtimes, sleep, watches, and of course, never-ending chores. And for her—schoolwork.

Tonight, she stood the 6:00 to 9:00 p.m. watch. The sea gurgled while rushing past the hull. Rigging creaked. Sails rustled. Amid billions of sparkling gems in the night sky, Roxi located the Big and Little Dippers whose outer bowls pointed toward the North Star and on to Cassiopeia. She breathed in the salty air and relished a rare moment of contentment and connection. With what or who, she wasn't sure, but she felt like a small yet vital part of everything. Maybe she did matter. And there might be a reason for existing. Even for being on this boat?

Not likely.

PJ had been teaching her how to use the GPS to plot the position of their boat on the chart, figure out how many nautical miles they'd traveled in twenty-four hours, the number of miles until landfall, and what their arrival time would be. Working out all of the equations was kinda fun, and her grandma included navigation as part of school assignments. At noon today, they were at Latitude 05 18' North/ Longitude 127 05' West. Only 318 miles until celebrating their first equator crossing. That would officially make them Shellbacks, according to ancient sea lore. Sounded dumb, but she guessed that would be something to look forward to. Mama C planned to cook a special dinner of canned ham with glazed pineapple, crispy fried potatoes, and a surprise dessert. Hopefully PJ would be feeling better. Since leaving Mexico, he either felt ravenous or nauseous. According to the *Medicine at Sea* book, her grandma suspected a gastrointestinal disorder. *Nothing serious, right?*

By the next afternoon, now 240 miles to the equator, the cerulean sky had turned an ominous slate gray. Towering clouds loomed ahead. Chilling rain pattered against the deck. At dusk, they ate a simple supper of canned chili and jicama coleslaw. Then all three shrugged into waterproof jackets and pants. Huddled in the cockpit, Roxi was grateful not to be alone on watch as lightning crackled and thunder boomed.

At 8:00 p.m., PJ rose to head below and turn on the ham radio. "I'll check us in on the Seafarer's Net. Maybe Bob can give us an idea of when we'll be outta this foul weather."

Mama C nodded, mouth drawn tight. "Soon, I hope."

"Don't ya'll worry. We built *Dawn's Dove* strong enough to handle much rougher weather than this." He squinted into the murky night. "Keep an extra-close eye out for lights from other vessels. Visibility is mighty poor in this storm."

The boat lurched sideways as PJ turned to step below and he fell into Roxi's lap.

She squealed. "Ouch! Get off me."

He jumped up and almost toppled the opposite way, but Mama C steadied him.

"Sorry 'bout that." A sheepish grin spread across his face. "Guess we all need to keep ahold of somethun' when we get up. Hope I didn't squash ya too bad, sweetie."

"I'll survive," Roxi mumbled as she gingerly rubbed both legs.

A long thirty minutes later, PJ poked his head out the companionway hatch.

Roxi glanced up. "Well, what did he say?"

He held up his hand. "Hang on. Before it slips my mind, *Harmony* and *Sea Eagle* say howdy. Both are still in the

Marquesas enjoyin' life on Oa Pou but preparin' to head for the Tuamotus in a couple days. Dustin says the divin' is supposed to be excellent there."

"Darn. We're never going to catch up to Brit and Dustin. How about *Romance*?"

His eyes clouded for a moment.

Roxi squirmed. "Well?"

PJ licked his lips. "Still no word. But keepin' a radio schedule when sailin' alone is mighty hard. That's always when a sail needs adjustin' or other—"

Mama C broke in, her words sharp as the filleting knife she used for slicing the fish they caught. "What about the weather report?"

"I was gettin' to that. Bob said we must be close to the ITCZ."

"Whatever the heck that is." Roxi stuffed stray curls whipping her face back inside her hood.

"Stands for Intertropical Convergence Zone." He hunkered down beside her and patted her still sore thigh. "No serious weather. Just lots of little squalls and fluky winds."

Roxi glared and brushed his hand away. "Oh, that explains things sooo much better."

Her grandma cleared her throat loudly. "He means winds that often change direction and their force—which leads to lots of sail adjustments. For how long, Jon?"

He shrugged his broad shoulders. "Can't say for sure, maybe a day or two. 'Course then we'll hit the doldrums where there's likely to be no wind."

The deck tilted as the boat slid over a large swell. Roxi squeezed into the cockpit's corner and braced herself, trying to escape the rain and saltwater spray.

"Wonderful," Roxi sighed and wiped her face. "This trip sucks."

PJ scowled at her before shuffling to the mast. He yanked more mainsail down and put in a third reef so the sail resembled a small triangle. Next, he lowered the staysail, headed to the bow, and sank onto knobby knees. Spray showered him each time the ship dipped into a trough. He bundled, then lashed the sail to the railing. Gripping the handrail, he sidestepped back along the side deck and ducked beneath the awning, shaking water off like a dog.

Roxi covered her face with both hands and peeped between her fingers. "Hey, stop that. I don't need another saltwater bath."

He gave another jiggle and stomped his boots. "Could get to thirty-five knots tonight, so I slowed us down. That should make us more comfortable."

"Thanks, hon. That looked scary at the bow."

He beamed when Mama C planted a kiss on his cheek.

"Yum, salty."

PJ turned to Roxi. "See. Yer grandma likes salty."

Mama C glanced across the cockpit as Roxi yawned. "Sweetie, you don't have to stay out here. Why don't you grab a few hours of rest in your dry bunk?"

"No thanks. Down below is like trying to sleep on a Tilt-A-Whirl." She shuddered and her stomach convulsed as she thought about becoming seasick again. "At least we're kinda sheltered from the storm by the awning and dodger."

"I'll put up the side panels if things get too nasty. Here you go." Mama Carol handed over an extra cushion and smiled. "You're quite the trooper. Let's pray for a calmer ocean tomorrow."

"You pray. I'll sleep." Roxi tucked the cushion against the bulkhead and rested her head. *Quite the trooper. What does that even mean?* Drowsiness overcame her as she stared into the impenetrable night lit only by infrequent flashes through the clouds.

Do you even care how dangerous this crazy voyage is, Star? Well, six more months until New Zealand—then she was outta here. A girl could only take so much. Mom had given her word she could come home if things weren't working out. No way would she let her worm her way out of this promise like she had so many others.

Roxi shivered as she slowly awoke. She felt clammy and wrinkled beneath her foul weather gear. At first, she thought this had to be another nightmare. Six-foot swells bashed the hull from every direction.

PJ's erratic snores rose and fell, sometimes ceasing when he stopped breathing for a few seconds.

That freaked her out, but she had sort of gotten used to the noise and then the silence that followed. Roxi leaned forward and peered at Mama C.

"Don't worry. I'm awake. Keeping watch. Besides, who can sleep during all this racket from the storm and ..." She gestured toward her husband.

"Is it almost morning?"

Mama C gave a weary smile. "A few more hours." She carefully stood and stretched. "How about some hot chocolate and cookies?"

"Sounds yummy. My stomach hurts, but maybe that will help." Roxi stretched her neck in each direction to get the kinks out. She opened the door for her grandma and gazed inside. The cozy cabin beckoned, but her stomach declined.

Halfway down the steps, Mama C reached up to slide the hatch shut. A powerful wave slammed into them and the boat tilted with a violent thrust to port. Her hand flailed about for the other handhold. Legs swung off the steps as her torso twisted like a pretzel.

Roxi recoiled at the thwack of her grandma's back smashing against the heavy wooden steps.

Mama C yelped like a wounded animal before crumpling into a heap beside the stove.

Chapter Eleven: Overcoming

CAROL

Stunned, Carol lay on the floor, afraid to move.

Roxi screamed for help.

Footsteps pounded. A dim light clicked on. Jon crouched beside Carol in the narrow galley and gently cradled her head. "Tell me you're all right." His hand shook as he brushed tangled hair off her face.

Carol twisted to face him. She clenched her teeth at the pain exploding in her back. For a moment a red haze shadowed everything. "Oh no ... my ... back."

Roxi braced herself in the doorway, sobbing. "Is she okay?"

Jon looked up. His face struggled between a frown and hopeful look. "Wrenched her back pretty bad, but nuthin' is bleedin' or appears broken." He searched Carol's eyes. "Bet yer gonna have quite a few purty bruises, though. Think you can get up if I help you?"

As she stood and leaned against Jon, the blood drained from Carol's head. She forced herself not to faint as he half-carried her to the aft bunk. When he pulled off her wet gear, she whimpered but stifled a groan. "Jon, can you get me two extra-strength acetaminophen and a water bottle?"

He fetched a bottle from the fridge, shook out two capsules, and handed them to Carol. After he tucked a quilt around her, he stood and assisted Roxi down the companionway.

Roxi perched on the bottom step and unzipped her jacket with shaky fingers.

Jon pulled off her heavy rubber boots.

She wriggled out of waterproof pants and crawled beneath the covers beside her grandma.

Jon snugged pillows around them. "Both of you, get some rest. I'll stand watch until daybreak."

"This is all my fault." Roxi's voice shook. "If I hadn't wanted that snack, none of this would've happened."

"Honey, you didn't cause my fall. We're not at the helm and can't control the weather, the ocean, or accidents."

Roxi sniffled. "I'm such a loser. You'd be better off without me."

Carol laid her hand over Roxi's. "Not true. You're one of the best gifts God has ever blessed me with. And remember, God works everything for our good—even falling down ... the ... steps." Her voice faded. She blinked several times before drifting into a sleep as restless as the surrounding sea.

Noon-time sun blazed through the portholes. Jon poked his head through the companionway to check on Carol who lay in the bed at the back of the boat. He uttered the same discouraging report as he had earlier. "Not a breath of wind or ripple on that glassy sea. Hard to believe last night's storm ever happened."

Carol could only summon a grunt in reply as she wrestled to a standing position. Two fans swirled the sweltering air below deck. Sweat beaded her forehead as she hobbled to the head. Angry purple welts mottled her legs and arms, but thankfully, she'd only strained a couple of her back muscles.

Long swells continued to lift and rock the vessel throughout the day. At the apex of each, Roxi would shout, "Any sight of land yet?"

By late afternoon, Carol could hear the frustration in Jon's voice. "No, Roxi Dawn, I've told you a hundred times, we have at least ten more days."

"That's like forever."

Carol shook her head when Roxi whined. She hoped her back would heal quickly so she could lighten Jon's burden a bit.

The next evening Jon's guttural snoring crescendoed and ebbed from the settee behind the table in the main salon.

Roxi climbed below after first watch and knelt beside the aft bunk. Carol shifted around and tried to find a comfortable position. Roxi's forehead creased. "PJ's okay, right? I mean like, he's been kinda cranky. I'm almost afraid to wake him up for his watch."

Carol's concern had also been mounting. Jon complained his fingers felt tingly. He dragged around, even nodding off during meals, and his thirst seemed unquenchable. Her musings led to his horrible diet.

"Probably all those Dr P.s and candy bars he stuffs himself with." Roxi crinkled her nose as she stuck out her tongue.

Her granddaughter must have read her mind. Carol nodded. "Yep, I've been warning him about all those sweets.

He says the caffeine and sugar keep him awake since he's got extra duties now. I can't deny that." But twinges of guilt gnawed at her. She sighed in frustration as Roxi shook Jon awake and then climbed into her V-berth at the bow. *God, please don't let anything else go wrong.*

Three days becalmed in the doldrums pushed Carol and everyone else close to their breaking points. They growled and grunted in place of words. Finally, a five-knot breeze blew in from the southeast.

Jon plodded to the bow to fasten on the light-wind drifter. Pillows were propped around Carol who reclined in the cockpit.

At the mast, Roxi found the sail's halyard stuck, dangling off the self-tailing winch.

Jon grabbed binoculars from an open cubbyhole near Carol and raised them up. "The line for raising the forward sail has somehow wrapped around the forestay."

Not more bad news. Jon rubbed his brow and described their dilemma, "Of course the problem is at the top where the wire stay attaches to the mast."

"Oh no." Carol's eyebrows arched high. "What are we going to do? This will slow our trip even more if we can only use one sail."

Jon ran shaky fingers through his reddish silver hair. "Only see two choices since you and me ain't doin' so hot. Sail by the main alone which will add days to arrival, or—"

"Or what?" Tendrils of fear crept up Carol's spine.

He hesitated, his haggard face grim. "Send Roxi up the mast."

"I knew you wanted to get rid of me!" Roxi dashed below, into her cabin, and slammed the door.

Twenty minutes later, Carol knocked softly. "Time to come out, honey." What a lousy grandma, to be making her granddaughter do something so dangerous. "I know you don't want to go up the mast, but there aren't many alternatives."

Roxi shuffled from her room shaking her head. "This is *not* going to happen. You know I hate heights."

Carol exhaled. "I understand and wish I were going up that mast instead of you. But I can't, and your grandpa said we'll have to sail an extra four to five days to get to the Marquesas if we only use the mainsail." That should clinch their plan. Roxi was beyond anxious to get off this boat. They all were.

Roxi's eyes swam with tears. "Well, this better not end like my treetop nightmare."

Jon called from the cockpit, "You ready yet, shortcakes?"

Roxi's breathing increased until she couldn't catch her breath.

"Give us a minute," Carol shouted up to Jon. "Honey, take a seat, and let's try to relax. Breathe in through your nose, out slowly through your mouth."

Roxi held her stomach. "I think I'm going to throw up."

Carol squeezed Roxi's hand. "This is scary, but you're going to be fine. If being raised in the bosun's chair wasn't safe, I wouldn't allow you to go up. And I've been praying."

"Like that's going to save me." Roxi stomped up on deck.

Carol eased herself up and sat on the raised coaming of the cockpit. Pain exploded across her back. Everything went dark for a moment. *Get a grip, Carol. Stay alert. Jon and Roxi need you.*

Jon grasped the bosun's chair attached to the mainsail's halyard, his face whiter than the sail.

Oh, Lord, please give my husband strength. Her gaze followed Roxi as she shuffled to the mast. *And my granddaughter courage.*

Roxi threaded her legs through the two openings of the flimsy canvas seat. Jon buckled three straps around her. His fingers trembled. He then used a separate line to hook a safety harness around her for added protection.

"Are you sure you want to do this?" His voice shook.

"No, but the other option is worse," she grumbled. "Let's just get this stupid job over."

Jon's eyebrows creased together accompanied by a frown. "Sorry 'bout this. Should be me goin' up." He held out his hands. "But these doggone fingers ain't workin' right. Feels like they're sleepin'."

Roxi didn't say anything. Her lips drew into a thin line.

"Remember, as I hoist the seat up, keep a light hold on the mast. Wrap yer arms and legs 'round the post if you need to. But whatever you do, don't let go."

"Don't worry. Nothing will be able to pry me loose."

Jon patted her shoulder. He hobbled forward to the anchor windlass, then fumbled with the electric cable before nodding, and pushed the toggle switch.

Roxi's eyes squeezed shut as the slack line of the bosun's chair tightened and she felt her bottom supported by the stiff canvas seat. Her feet left the deck. "Oh snap." She grabbed the mast. "This can't really be happening."

"Okie dokie, here we go, sweetie. Holler and wave if you need to stop or come down."

"Right now would be awesome," Roxi yelped.

The chair rose slowly.

Carol sucked in a deep breath. *Lord, I'm trusting you. Help us through this ordeal.*

Roxi's wide-open eyes held a terrified gleam.

Jon wiped sweat from his brow. "By the way, when you get to where the line is stuck, you'll have to stretch out to reach the forestay. Might even have to let go of the mast, but only for an instant."

Carol's stomach nose-dived. She couldn't breathe.

Roxi screeched, "Yeah, like that's going to happen. Stop, right this minute!" She hugged the mast as if she were about to leave her best friend. Silence pulsated like the beating of wings. Two minutes passed. "What do I do now?" she moaned, her voice barely audible.

"When you get to the top, untangle the halyard. I'll be waitin' to crank in and secure the line. Afterward, I promise to bring ya down, pronto."

"You better." Roxi scowled and turned her face toward Jon.

Twenty-five feet off the swaying deck, the chair halted. Roxi's head bent down. Her eyes locked on Carol before her sturdy arms and legs again clung to the mast like a barnacle on a piling.

Her granddaughter's fear left a sour taste in Carol's mouth. "Honey, don't look at me. Stare at the horizon and take a few deep breaths."

"Too late, Mama C." Seconds ticked by until Roxi called down, "Okay, guess I'm ready." She loosened her hold at the precise moment an immense swell broadsided *Dawn's Dove*. They listed forty-five degrees, and Roxi spun into space—away from the mast.

"No!" Carol screamed and struggled to rise.

Roxi thrashed around. Her arms flailed as though searching for anything to grasp onto.

Carol braced for Roxi's impact against the aluminum mast. Somehow, her granddaughter stretched muscular legs out in front of her and cushioned the blow by using her feet. As her knees rushed up to meet her chin, Roxi grasped that lovely post and kissed it.

Carol wanted to do the same.

"Good recovery, sweetie." Jon hit the switch, and Roxi continued the risky ride to the top.

She kept both ankles secured against the mast, stretched both arms out, and managed to grasp the forestay. Minutes ticked by as she untwisted the tangled halyard using one hand. At last, she raised her arm and gave a thumbs-up.

Forty feet beneath her, Jon shouted, "You got 'er done. Great work!"

"Amen," Carol whispered.

All about them, glittering light danced upon the ocean's ripples as Jon lowered Roxi to safety.

She unbuckled several straps, unhooked the harness, and kicked off the canvas contraption.

Jon engulfed her in a hug. "Tweetie bird, I'm so proud of you."

"Thanks, but hopefully, I'll never ever have to do that again."

Carol stood and gripped the boom gallows post to brace herself. Roxi slithered by her into the cockpit. Her body quivered. "I'm exhausted."

"I can only imagine." Carol moved with caution and followed Roxi below. As she backed down the steps, she felt her granddaughter's hand press against her back. "Thanks for watching out for me, hon, although I should be the one protecting you. Now, how about a few brownies and a hard-earned rest?" Roxi's smile crinkled her eyes. Carol sensed a new warmth emanating from their deep blue depth. "Something's different about you."

Roxi blushed and studied the ceiling for a moment. "I just remembered something Rob once told me. *The sea will wage its wars against you. At times, the sea will be your only friend, but most of all, the sea will change you.*" She took a deep breath. "I'm still not ready to sail around the world. And I'd rather have a popcorn party with Alex than climb masts. But I feel this weird kind of shift, like I'm ..." She ran fingers through her messy strawberry curls and shrugged.

Carol smiled. "You're growing up, Roxi, learning to overcome your fears and to work as a team." She hugged her, and Roxi didn't squirm away as she normally would.

"That was a very brave thing you did." Carol's eyes glistened as her heart swelled with pride. "You're my hero."

Chapter Twelve: Land Ho

ROXI

Roxi sprawled in the only patch of shade beneath the cockpit awning. She'd reluctantly completed schoolwork and straightened her cabin, sort of, if you didn't count the closet where she'd dumped everything. She wiped beads of sweat off her brow and opened her book. This miserable heat had zapped all motivation except for reading. At La Paz's trading library she'd scored a duffle bag full of books including a few Judy Blume and Nancy Drew, but no Harry Potter. She was dying to read Rowling's newest, *The Prisoner of Azkaban.*

She could listen to those boring French cassettes Rob had loaned her. Nah, there'd be time for that *if* they ever reached land. But when they did, she first planned to dance, dance, dance. Roxi picked up a spray bottle and misted herself from head to toes, which cooled her body, but not her rising impatience. Mama Carol had that zombie look again, staring right through her, but with thoughts a trillion miles away. Roxi pressed her lips together to keep from spouting something nasty like *Isn't this exactly like you dreamed this trip would be*? The middle of nowhere definitely wasn't anyone's dream.

Bubbles hovered around Mama C as she knelt beside two heavy plastic buckets in the cockpit, lifting one lathered piece of laundry at a time. She rinsed each item and then handed them to PJ, who hand-cranked them through a wringer.

Beside Roxi, the pile of wrung items grew. She turned the page of *Here's to You, Rachel Robinson*, and buried her head back in the book.

PJ cleared his throat, and Roxi glanced up. He pointed at the pile beside her.

"What? On a schedule or something?" She slammed her book shut and jumped up. Now she had the thrilling job of securing clothes over the rails with wooden clothes pins. Like in the Dark Ages. Star would laugh her head off if she could see them. Her mom certainly would never be caught dipping her long manicured nails into soapy buckets. She seldom did laundry, even though there was a machine down the hall. Dirty clothes were normally piled in corners or stuffed in cupboards and closets. If Roxi needed something clean, she'd gather an armful and wash a load herself. Star fantasized about disposable clothing, or better yet, none. She loved walking around naked. *Who does that*?

PJ handed Roxi the last item to hang. "Woo-hoo! Wind's up to fifteen knots. Bet we'll make 120 miles today."

Looking heavenward, Mama C shouted. "Praise the Lord. I'm done barely moving in those doldrums. All those sail adjustments wear a soul out." She rose stiffly and emptied both buckets over the side.

"So, how much longer?" Roxi scowled. "I need off this flotsam."

Her grandma's smile wilted like parched flowers in July. "This morning the logbook showed only 348 miles to Hiva Oa."

"Might as well be 3,048 miles. I'm never going to catch up with Brit and Dustin." Her bad mood nosedived. Which is what she felt like doing. Diving deep into the sea and never coming up.

"Not true, sweetie. Remember last night on the Seafarer's Net? Yer friends reported they're at Rangiroa in the Tuamotus." Jon winked. "Shoot, that's practically tobacco-spittin' distance."

Roxi pouted, and her lower lip quivered. "Yeah, right. Bet they're having all kinds of fun—without me."

"Anyhow, ain't you thankful Rob is safe in Fakarava and preparin' to head west? From that side of the Tuamotus it will be a quick jog to Tahiti."

"Sure, if you can walk on water." She doused herself again using the spray bottle.

"Enough!" Mama C slammed her hand against the coaming. "You'll see your friends soon."

Roxi stomped toward the bow, counting from one to ten in English, Spanish, and French. Then backwards. No one understood her, or they would realize how desperately she needed privacy. And lots of space to leap, to twirl, to dance.

"Land Ho!" Roxi pranced around the deck. Everyone had been awake since before dawn, anticipating their first landfall since Mexico at Hiva Oa. Roxi nibbled a stale oatmeal muffin and savored the miraculous image through a pinkish haze. At first, the island appeared as nothing more than a dark bump on the horizon.

PJ stretched. "Mmm, I smell flowers."

Mama C sniffed. "There's an earthy scent mixed with a whiff of campfire."

Roxi's nose twitched. "You're both nuts. Something definitely smells fishy." She leaned over the side of the boat. Splash. Something squealed. "What the ...?" A sleek gray shape hovered inches below the surface. The creature rotated, looked up, and showed a silly grin. "Wow, a dolphin!"

From the bow, PJ shouted, "Look, we're surrounded by them." He raced below and came back up holding his camera.

She and her grandma circled the deck, giddy as two kids at the fair. Over a hundred round-nosed dolphins leaped, somersaulted, and glided alongside their sloop. Roxi giggled, not sure who was more delighted, the humans or sea creatures.

"They must be the official greeters here to escort us in." Mama C whistled, trying to mimic their sounds.

Roxi dangled her legs over the side of the boat and attempted to imitate the dolphins—squeak ... click click click ... chirp chirp. They probably thought she was one very sick dolphin.

The pod slowly dispersed as they drew closer to the island. PJ chuckled. "Guess they're off to guide another boat, or it's feedin' time." He adjusted the autopilot attached to the tiller.

"You set our destination in the GPS for Traitor Bay, right Jon?"

"Yep. Gonna run parallel, about two miles off the coast to be safe.

Mama C grinned as she handed Roxi the binoculars. "Twenty-three days at sea has been more than worth all the misery to experience this."

Mountainous peaks rose from the ocean's depths into a cerulean sky. The tallest were cloaked in frothy clouds. Rocky ridges jutted. Emerald valleys wound inland from small bays. There must have been twenty shades of green. Roxi's fingers itched for a paintbrush.

Most things that her grandparents found interesting were a complete bore, but this moment was an exception. Her deprived senses zinged, overloaded by colors and smells. She yearned to be on land, to touch each glorious living thing.

Mama C's eyes sparkled like the sun on the sea. "Jon, pinch me. I can't believe we're really in the Marquesas. Feels like a dream."

"My pleasure." He gave an impish grin, reached over, and pinched her bottom.

"Ouch. I was only kidding." She playfully slapped his arm.

Roxi ignored them. She felt like an over-inflated ball, ready to pop. Part of her wanted to bounce up and down, yelling at the top of her lungs, *We're here*! At the same time, she sensed a hushed reverence emanating from this South Pacific Island. "This place is like a beautiful cathedral," she whispered.

"You're so right." Mama C nodded. "You've captured its spiritual essence perfectly."

"What does that even mean?" Roxi's harsh tone matched her surly stare.

PJ diverted the potential argument. "Better check our position, Carol. Should be gettin' close to the bay."

Mama C turned to head below, but not before Roxi caught the hurt look and trembling of her lips.

Darn. She didn't mean to hurt people. If she could only keep her big mouth shut, there wouldn't always be a foot sticking out of it.

"Roxi." Jon gave her a stern look, then an understanding smile. "I'm going to drop the lapper, that large sail in front. You bundle it up and secure the sail to the side rail using sail ties. Then, I'll trust you to man the bow and keep a lookout ahead for any dark patches in the water. Could be uncharted rocks or coral heads."

"No problemo." Helping felt much better than hurting.

A few minutes later, her grandma peeked her head out the companionway. "Only 2.3 miles to the entrance. About thirty minutes at our current speed."

"Good work, hon. Take fixes of our position on the chart every five minutes." He glanced at the compass and then bent over and made a slight adjustment on the autopilot. "Let me know if we drift off course. Could be tides this close in. Also, tell me when we're a quarter-mile from the entrance into the bay. Might be easy to miss with so many inlets. Don't want to turn in the wrong one."

"Aye, aye, Captain." Carol saluted sharply. A playful grin crept over her face as she turned and gave Roxi a thumbs up.

Thank goodness. Mama Carol was smiling again.

Roxi smiled too.

Chapter Thirteen: The Garden

ROXI

Roxi fidgeted with her curls, tangling them into hopeless knots as PJ deployed and set the anchor deep within Atuana's protected harbor.

He began clearing the foredeck as Mama C dashed about below doing who-knows-what.

"Really? Does all that need to be done right now?" Roxi growled. "What's with you two? Aren't you guys dying to step foot on land? Twenty-three days at sea must have fried your brains."

Finally, PJ lowered the dinghy, and the three climbed aboard. Yachties waved and called out greetings as they navigated the crowded anchorage.

Roxi hunkered down when the dinosaurs roared back replies. Embarrassing.

A jumbled mass of dazzling green, red, and yellow foliage and flowers speckled the shoreline and beyond. As they drew closer, an avalanche of fragrances, colors, birdsong, and chatter from a dozen or more people bombarded Roxi. For a moment, she felt overwhelmed. She focused on the clearing ahead and jumped up. The dinghy rocked violently, and she fell back onto the wooden bench seat.

Mama C glared at Roxi, clearly irritated. "What are you thinking? You almost overturned the boat." She motioned to a rough cement slab set into a muddy bank. "Looks like that's where we tie up, Jon."

"Sorry, Mama C, but could that stone structure be an outdoor shower? That would be sweet. Although kind of a bizarre spot to bathe."

Her grandma only gave a small shrug as they drew close.

PJ's forehead bunched. Several inflatable dinghies were tethered to short metal stakes and bounced vigorously against the dock. "We're gonna have to tie our dinghy on the outside so the fiberglass don't get all banged up."

Roxi was the first to clamber out, sliding and crawling over three inflatables. Stepping ashore, she teetered for a minute as the ground tipped. She wove a crooked line a few feet up the path, then turned around, grimacing. "Oh, great. I feel like I'm still on the boat."

PJ spread his legs wide, his torso swaying slightly. "Don't worry. You'll quickly get your land legs."

"I kind of look like my mom when she's drunk too much wine." Roxi shook her head, which made her dizzy, and she almost fell. "Why would anyone want to feel like this?"

Mama C gave her a funny look, her mouth half-open like she wanted to say something. Suddenly, she dropped to her knees.

PJ rushed over. "Is your back botherin' you again, hon?"

Mama C shook her head and pressed her palms together. "Thank you, Lord, for a safe journey." She bent over and kissed the red earth. "I've waited weeks to do that." She wiped dust off chapped lips and applied a fresh coat of lip balm.

PJ wagged his head. "Been at sea too long," he muttered to a nearby couple.

"Oh, I understand completely. I felt like doing that myself a few hours ago." A woman held out her hand. "I'm Susie, and this is my husband, Steven. We're off *Camelot*."

PJ shook their hands. "I've heard you check in on the Seafarer's net. Nice to meet you both and put faces to those voices. Actually, I feel like we've met before. Maybe Mexico or California?"

After chatting a few minutes, they moved on toward a cluster of cruisers gathered near a primitive stone sink that had wide counters. Several people were in various stages of laundry duty.

Roxi's eyes pierced her grandma. "Don't even go there. I've got more important things to do, like getting lots of exercise and checking out this wacky place, even if this is only a dinky island in the middle of the Pacific." She high-kicked and almost toppled even though her foot barely swung to shoulder height. Frustrating. Would she ever dance again?

They encountered a Dr. Patterson among the crowd, and Mama C bombarded him with questions regarding PJ's health.

"Well, orthopedics is my specialty, but there's probably not a decent English-speaking MD until Tahiti." The lean, silver-haired doctor swatted a mosquito feasting on his forearm. "He could have an intestinal parasite, in which case a round of antibiotics should be started."

Mama C shook her head, frowning. "I already tried that. Didn't change a thing."

Dr. Patterson nodded. "Might also be a precursor to diabetes. Symptoms are similar. Any family history?"

"I think so, and also heart issues."

Roxi's eyes widened. "What? That's not very reassuring."

"Well, I'd advise drinking at least sixty-four ounces of non-sugary fluids per day." He stroked his chin. "And eat a well-balanced diet with plenty of fresh vegetables and fruits, cutting back off of fatty foods and sweets."

"Yeah, PJ. You've gotta give up all that junk food that Mama C warned you about." Roxi gave him a stern look. *Because if something happens to you, then what happens to me?*

PJ had been hanging back but now stepped forward, almost nose to nose with the doctor. "Excuse me. I'm Jon." His voice held an edge of exasperation. "I can handle all you said except I'm never givin' up my chocolate."

The doctor backed up, holding his hands out in front of him as if to protect himself. "Understood. I'm only saying to decrease sugar as much as you're able. You don't want to end up somewhere in the boondocks with serious complications such as—" He looked over his shoulder as someone called his name.

"Thank you so much, Dr. Patterson. I'm Carol by the way. We'll be sure to take your advice."

He shook her hand. "Call me Larry." Scrutinizing PJ, he added, "Start with small modifications in your diet. And ease into activities. Changing lifelong habits is a slow process."

Mama C pulled her ponytail tight. "By the way, what did you mean by complications?" But Dr. Larry was already out of earshot. Looking smug, she stared at her husband. "See, I was right about your diet."

Roxi noticed the stubborn set of PJ's mouth. She cut in before he could argue more. "Enough socializing already. I'm totally bored. Not a single kid close to my age around here." She stomped toward a steep, twisty dirt road she'd spotted. "Let's go check out Gilligan's Island."

Her grandma's brow furrowed, but PJ nodded. "I'll be okay. We'll go slow." He reached for her hand.

The last few yards up the hill made Roxi's atrophied legs shake with fatigue. On the rise, she paused as sweat trickled down her back.

"Whew, this weather's oppressive." Mama C exhaled in rapid huffs as she caught up. She used a tissue to wipe her face, but within a minute, she glistened again. She glanced back. "You okay, Jon?"

His face appeared pale. "Yep ... nuthin ... a few ... cookies ... can't fix."

Mama C's eyes narrowed, and her mouth bunched when PJ mentioned sweets that the doctor had told him to avoid.

"Just jokin'." PJ gave a small chuckle, then a cough. He hunched over, hands on knees, panting.

Mama C glanced around. "Let's rest in the shade for a bit." Taking his arm, she led him to a row of tall palms lining the road.

He leaned heavily against a smooth trunk, sagged to the ground, and tilted his head back. "Sure hope none of them coconuts drop off."

Her eyes twinkled. "Couldn't dent that hard head of yours."

"Good one, Mama C." Roxi snickered as she skipped with an awkward rhythm over to a bush that sprouted gigantic yellow hibiscus flowers containing deep scarlet centers. She plucked one and twirled its stem, creating a kaleidoscope of color before offering the flower to her grandma like she used to do as a preschooler.

Mama C smiled at her, a delighted gleam in her thoughtful gaze as if she were remembering too.

"Thank you, sweetie." Mama C tucked the gift gently behind one ear. "Doesn't this land look like we're walking through the Garden of Eden?"

A flowery rainbow enveloped them. "Reminds me more of Oz. Think there are any munchkins around?" *And maybe a yellow brick road and wizard to whisk me home?*

"Only munchkin I see is the one standin' in front of me." PJ chuckled.

Roxi scowled, not amused. "And you're the scarecrow without a—"

"Hey, let's be nice." Mama C uncrossed her arms and pointed to the ground. "Check out all these coconuts." A mixture of shaggy brown and sleek green ones lay strewn about. She handed one to PJ.

He smacked the coconut against a large rock and the thing bounced out of his hands without a mark on it. "Hmm, that's tougher than a two-dollar steak."

An amused hoot burst from Roxi. "Better ask the locals before trying that again."

Insects buzzed, birds chirped, and palms rustled as they continued their snail's pace stroll. Mama C played amateur botanist, rattling off names of various plants. "Look at those enormous red and yellow-veined crotons. Must be eight-feet tall." She stopped in front of a small tree with white and yellow star-shaped flowers and leaned in. "Frangipani, also known as plumeria. Isn't the smell scrumptious? An exotic, spicy blend of citrus, jasmine, gardenia, and more."

The strong, perfumy scents made Roxi's nose itch, and she rubbed it. A couple of wooden houses peeked from amid the foliage. "Where's all the people? This is Dullsville."

"Must be siesta time. Remember the middle of the day in Mexico?" Mama C tucked one of the tiny smelly stars behind the other ear.

PJ yawned, then took a swig from his water bottle. "Sounds like a purrrfect idea."

"Well, I want to meet kids my age and learn the local dances. Can we go a little further?" Roxi pleaded. She wasn't ready for the suffocating confinement of the sailboat yet. She spun in a slow circle and beheld steep hillsides and verdant valleys. Besides a ka-zillion coconut palms, trees brimmed with mangoes, bananas, and several weird-looking fruits. *Nobody starves around here.* Her empty stomach growled.

They rounded a curve and came upon a roadside stand. Among papaya, guava, and huge bunches of bananas were several grapefruit-sized fruits. The Marquesan shopkeeper's dark eyes lit up with a smile. "*Kaoha.* Hello." He lifted one of the large greenish balls Mama C was poking and offered the fruit to her. "Pamplemousse. You like?"

She shrugged, then handed him two American dollars for two of those thingies plus a cluster of bananas. The man's smile almost reached his ears.

"I have no idea what these taste like, but I always enjoy experiencing new foods." Mama C winked. "Right, Roxi?"

PJ inspected the fruit and gave a slight frown.

"Hmm? Oh, whatever." Roxi yawned and stretched her arms wide.

"Think it's time to turn around and get some rest?" No one protested. Mama C scratched at a bite on her neck, already pink and swelling. "We'll have plenty of time for exploration in the days ahead. And tomorrow will be busy with all those fun, first-day-in-a-new-country routines."

Roxi groaned inwardly. Her grandma was always planning, making lists. Couldn't she just live in the moment? Not dwell on what *had* to be done tomorrow.

On the walk back, an old pickup passed, stirring up the dust, and rumbled to a stop a few yards ahead. A dark-complexioned man leaned out the window and motioned to the truck bed. Grateful, the trio climbed aboard. "*Koutau.* Thank you," Roxi and her grandma shouted.

Three young girls peeked through the cab's back window, smiling shyly. Wide black eyes focused on Roxi, probably intrigued by her freaky, frizzy strawberry-blonde hair. Ugh—she hated to be stared at. She crossed her eyes and stuck out her tongue. The girls giggled and made similar faces. For the remainder of the ride, they all took turns making grotesque faces. Looks like she'd found one way to communicate.

On the hill above the anchorage, PJ attempted to pay the driver. The man shook his head. "No, no."

Mama C handed each of the girls a dollar bill. "Okay?"

The father nodded his approval. "*Koutau.*"

Roxi waved as the truck pulled away. "*Apae.* Goodbye."

Looking up from her pocket dictionary, Mama C added, "*Koutau roa.* Thank you very much." She turned to Roxi. I'd say our first day on a South Pacific Island went very well."

"Hmm, definitely different." At least they were not still bobbing like a cork in the middle of the ocean. Roxi traipsed down the road, a mixture of anticipation and anxiety upsetting her stomach. Each day was an unknown in a cruiser's life. She didn't welcome all this *adventure* like Mama C and PJ did. They came from completely different worlds—their desires and needs at opposite ends of the universe from hers.

What lay ahead in the upcoming days, weeks, and months?

Did she even want to know?

Chapter Fourteen: The Meae

CAROL

In the galley, Carol peeled, then sliced a large, green-skinned pamplemousse and set the platter on the table. Roxi's face scrunched, and Carol braced for the anticipated sarcasm.

"If that tastes like a yucky grapefruit, then forget it." Roxi made a sour face.

Carol started to reply, but Jon stepped down into the boat right then with two freshly baked baguettes tucked under his arm. "How did everything go at the *boulangerie*?" Carol's mouth watered. "That bread smells delish."

"Busy. Had to fight for the last two loaves." Jon chuckled when Carol frowned. "I'm kidding. Let's eat. Worked up an appetite climbin' the hill."

Roxi took a tentative nibble of the unfamiliar fruit and cocked her head. Her bunched mouth softened into a slight smile. "Hmm ... not too gross."

Carol chewed a juicy chunk. The slight melon sweetness blended with a hint of lime. "Yum, this is delicious. Give the fruit a try, Jon."

He grunted and forked a piece onto his plate, then returned to slathering canned butter and globs of strawberry jam on his bread.

Her eyebrows knit together. "Isn't that your fifth or sixth slice? Remember what the doctor said, not so much fat and sugar." Trying to retrain a stubborn man was frustrating, if not impossible.

As Carol cleared the breakfast table, she eyeballed her granddaughter. "So, what would you like to do later today?"

Roxi's eyes lit up. "Really? I get to choose? Well, I'd love to find a beach, go for a swim, and maybe work on a few dance moves."

"That all sounds wonderful." Carol shook her head. "But first we have to clean up the boat, finish a few chores, and run several errands. Then we can have some fun, okay?"

Roxi glared. "You're just like my mom. You never listen or do want I want." Her voice rose. "If you already had a list longer than my Christmas one, why'd you even ask?" She stomped into her cabin and began cramming everything scattered on her bunk onto side shelves and into her messy locker.

Carol rolled her shoulders—up, back, down, relax. Up, back, down, relax.

Roxi's grumbling continued. "Besides, what's the point of coming all this way to your dreamy islands if all we do is work? Cruising life sucks."

Carol clambered into the cockpit before she added fuel to the explosive atmosphere. Deep breathing helped. Her emotions calmed as she focused on the deep greens of mountains and Windsor blue sky. She found a young teen on board more challenging than she'd anticipated.

Concentrate on the blessings, not the difficulties. That's what Abbie had taught her. Carol desperately missed conversations with her friend whom she hadn't seen since Mexico and counted the days until their reunion in Tahiti.

Finally, boat chores were completed. Carol tried to stay positive through Roxi's silent treatment for the remainder of the exhausting morning. At the *gendarme*'s office there were plenty of *excusez-moi, s'il vous plaît,* and *merci*—excuse me, please, and thank you, as they checked in. Jon stayed quiet as her bungled French puckered the official's face as though he'd swallowed a lemon, but the man eventually stamped their passports.

Their second stop at *Banque Socredo* baffled all three of them. A dozen locals reclined around the room's perimeter, chatting in their native tongue— definitely on island time. But everyone seemed to know when their turn with the bank teller was. The exchange rate made Carol choke, but their colorful French Pacific francs that depicted island landscapes, and then gorgeous stamps purchased at the closet-sized *bureau de postes* soothed a little of her tension from the tedious wait times.

Later, at a small *marché*, Jon and Roxi let Carol make all the selections. She grimaced. "These store prices are outrageous! We're only going to buy chicken and a few of these excellent *fromages*. Thank goodness the cheese and meat are subsidized by the government and somewhat reasonable." Her lips pulled into a puckish grin. "And we can probably afford one bottle of French wine. I only wish Abbie were here to share and pair the bubbly with some cheese and fruit."

Jon shook his head. "The wine and cheese are all yours, hon. You know my tastes run more towards Boone's Farm, and the only cheese I eat is cheddar."

After a brief lunch break onboard and the passing of an early afternoon squall, the weary trio headed back ashore to tackle the large pile of salt-encrusted laundry. Jon and Roxi looked a bit frazzled, wearing droopy faces.

At the wide stone sink, Carol promised her weary ship mates, "This is our last chore. I've planned many great activities, beginning tomorrow."

"I feel like a captive on a slave ship," Roxi whined. She hunched over a sudsy bucket and pushed the plunger up and down. "And I want off."

Nothing, not even Roxi's grumbling, could diminish Carol's ear to ear grin. "I know this is hard work, but this limitless fresh water for rinsing is such a luxury." She couldn't stop marveling.

"Can you imagine what them ancient mariners aboard Captain Cook's fleet musta gone through?" Jon cranked the wringer, feeding each item through the rollers. "No washin' clothes or bodies unless they chanced upon a rainstorm. And no healthy meals like your gramma cooks. They were nuthin' but smelly skeletons by the time they got to these here islands—if they survived."

Today will be full of new and exciting adventures. Carol smiled. Yesterday's bone-weary workload had not been much fun for any of them. She gasped as the SUV that their guide, Roger, drove rounded a sharp corner. The spectacular scenery held her spellbound. "Look at that waterfall plunging from that cliff up ahead." She nudged Roxi who sat beside her in the backseat. "Having more fun today?"

Roxi remained silent, staring out the window.

Carol's gaze fell on Roger in the front seat. He and his wife were their tour guides today. The burly Marquesan had arms and legs the size of a wooly mammoth. Perched next to him, his young wife, Sabina, glanced back often with an unpretentious smile that spilt warmth into her cocoa eyes. Carol couldn't help herself from being a little envious of that thick, lustrous black hair cascading over smooth brown shoulders almost to Sabina's waist. Carol touched the clip that held her own frizzy mess off her neck. Definitely cooler, but not so glamorous.

The vehicle wound over jungle-clad volcanic mountains on a deeply rutted road. With each jarring bounce, the sound of Sabina's tinkling laughter filled the interior. Carol smiled as she tapped Roxi. "Well?"

"What? Am I having fun?" She poked back, only much harder. "Beats chores, that's for sure. Aaah!" She squealed as the vehicle swerved dangerously close to a steep drop-off.

Time hung suspended for a long moment. Carol prayed, thinking this might be her final glimpse of earth. Far below a silvery ribbon wound through tall grassland and across the river a blur of vines and blossoms intertwined among tall trees. She sputtered, "Uh, um, that might be a shortcut, um, Roger, but um, I'd prefer taking the road."

Roger guffawed. However, his foot stayed glued to the accelerator.

Only by a miracle did they arrive intact at the tiny village of *Pau Mau.* "Praise God," she murmured as Jon awoke bright-eyed from his nap and stretched his neck.

"Here already?"

Carol and Roxi exchanged a look, their eyebrows raised. She shook her head. "I can't believe you slept through that crazy ride."

Jon gave a shrug and grinned.

Their gentle giant guide introduced them to a jumble of cousins, aunties, and uncles who all crowded around jabbering at once in broken English intermixed with their indigenous language. "Sounds as if half of the village is related to Roger." Carol chuckled.

"Come, come," several women beckoned, attempting to lead them toward their unadorned plywood houses covered by thatched roofs.

"So sorry, no time, but thank you." Carol slowly shook her head, longing to stroll through every luxurious natural garden that embraced each home.

After a short visit, the SUV followed the road down along the ocean where drying nets hung over fishing skiffs that lined the rugged shoreline. Naked children scampered on a narrow beach, hopping over small volcanic boulders, and splashed in the surf. Their giggles mingled with the swish of waves and cries of gulls.

Roxi kept repeating in a shocked voice, "They're not wearing any clothes."

"Is that all you can see?" Carol shook her head. "This is such a different world than what we're used to. Simpler. Slower."

Turning inland, they headed toward an opening in the jungle. Roxi's eyes bugged. "We're going in there? Looks spooky." Branches scraped the vehicle, and mud squished beneath the tires as the track narrowed within the dim forest.

"End of road. Now walk." Roger led them along a twisty path, their footsteps cushioned by moss and damp leaves. An occasional screech or hoo-hoo-hoo broke the eerie silence.

Carol kept a close watch on low limbs and dangling vines for all things creepy or crawly.

Roxi chanted in a jittery murmur, "Spiders and monkeys and snakes, oh my."

"That's not helping," Carol hissed.

Jon boomed, "Mighty big limes you grow here." He gestured toward several broad-leaf trees.

Carol placed a hand over her thumping heart at his loud remark and gave him a frosty look.

Sabina picked one up off the ground and handed the giant fruit to her. "They *uru*—breadfruit."

Running her fingers over the pitted green ball, Carol bounced the fruit in her hands. "Hmm, feels heavy, like a melon. Good to eat?" she pantomimed.

Sabina nodded yes. "Cook in *umu*."

Carol gave Roger a puzzled look. He explained, "Umu is below ground oven or large pit. Everything be cooked there."

Roxi made a face and pinched her nostrils together, sounding like Daffy Duck. "Whew, what's that stinky smell?"

Roger sniffed the thick air. "Ah, that be rotting breadfruit." He pointed to the ground around them where dozens lay in various stages of decay.

"I guess fermentation causes that yeasty, mushroom smell." Carol took shallow breaths and agreed with Roxi. The decomposing fruit did stink.

Ferns, flowering tiare, shrubs, pink and green variegated nono plants, and other bushy vegetation eventually opened up into a clearing the size of a school gymnasium. Roxi turned in a slow circle. "What is this place?"

"This is an ancient *meae*, a sacred area used only for special occasions." Carol grabbed Jon's hand and practically dragged him over to Roger, who lounged beneath one of several rough stone tikis. The fierce-looking warrior, coated in green and gray lichen, stood at least a head taller than their guide.

Roger's eyes danced with sparkles as he shared ancestral legends that had been passed down through the centuries. His deep voice and strange tales held them spellbound. Jon especially loved all things historical and sat as still as a rabbit caught in the vegetable garden.

"This powerful meae used for court, religious and political meetings, and important ceremonies." Roger pointed at a shoulder-high platform of flat boulders illuminated by shafts of sunlight. His voice grew ominous. "Only king allowed up there. Always keep distance from subjects. Anyone come too close—they be killed."

Roxi pulled up her knees and clasped her arms around them, shivering.

Carol's skin prickled. She could almost envision shadowy forms lurking in the impenetrable foliage that encompassed them like a prison cell and imagine their moans and cries.

Roxi jumped up and circled two six-foot rocks, running her fingers along horizontal scars.

Roger gave an amused, slightly wicked smile. "You know what those used for?" He paused. "Unlucky strangers and enemies from warring villages captured and tied to rocks." His belly jiggled with suppressed laughter. "After few days, they be cooked alive on hot bed of stones." He bellowed, "And then eaten!"

Roxi's hand jerked off the boulder like she'd been burned. She made a gagging sound. "Yuk. That's disgusting."

"You probably enjoy freaking tourists out telling that outlandish story." Carol's stomach churned.

Roger gave her a wink.

"Not very hospitable folks." Jon clucked his tongue. "In Tennessee, where I'm originally from, we invite strangers to share a meal, not *be* the meal."

Carol shuddered. "I'm really thankful they stopped practicing cannibalism—sometime in the early 1800s, I think, when Christian missionaries arrived."

"Yeah, or we might be someone's lunch." The half-smile on Roxi's pale green face faded.

Jon shook his head. "Only blood-thirsty savages left 'round here are them pesky mosquitos and no-see-ums."

On the trail back, Carol gave more thought to those early missionaries. Crossing oceans back then to uncivilized countries had taken immense perseverance and trust.

Would she have had the courage to risk her life and follow God's plan into the unknown?

And was today's modern, fast-paced world any more civilized?

Chapter Fifteen: Reunion

ROXI

Roxi sulked as she knelt over another sudsy bucket. Besides disgusting laundry, scrubbing the yucky boat inside, topside, and bottom, she'd spent hours on brain-numbing schoolwork. On top of that, Mama C had made her learn more French words. *Parlez-vous anglais? Parlez lentement—Do you speak English? Speak slowly.* The only thing she'd like to say is *au voir* to Hiva Oa and move on to Tahiti where Brittany and Dustin were hopefully anxious to see her and were quite despondent without her vivacious presence. *Yeah, keep dreaming, Rox.* Pushing a sopping ringlet off her forehead, she jumped like a kangaroo as a vaguely familiar voice spoke behind her.

"I see you're having a marvelous time in paradise."

Roxi pivoted around on her knees. A sassy reply stuck in her throat. She nibbled her lip as her gaze traveled up muscular legs, past flowered swim trunks and tanned torso, then lingered on blue-green eyes the color of the outer bay.

"Oh snap! What are you doing here?" Her face warmed at her outburst and grew hotter as she became aware of her gross appearance and the close proximity of *Songwriter*'s captain.

His eyes penetrated beyond her rudeness and creased in apparent amusement. "It's good to see you too." He extended one lean arm. "Remember our close encounter in La Paz? I didn't have time to properly introduce myself. I'm Kyle."

For a moment, Roxi couldn't move, then she sprang up and reached for his hand. Her pudgy fingers were engulfed by long tapered ones inside his firm grasp. Bubbles squeezed out between their hands. Both mouths opened in surprise and the air reverberated with their laughter. A comfortable sensation settled over her as they chatted. The unexpected encounter felt as though two life-long friends had reunited after months apart. Like the way she'd connected with Rob, even though he was over half a century older. She wondered about Kyle's age. *Older than thirteen, that's for sure.*

Her grandparents approached with questioning grins.

Roxi sighed before giving a grudging introduction.

PJ studied Kyle for an awkward moment. "So, where'd you two meet?"

Kyle glanced at Roxi and winked. "Uh, we met briefly as I was heading out of La Paz, sir."

"Please, call me Jon. Where I come from in Tennessee, we never met a stranger." He grinned, scratching his head. "You sailin' alone? And where are you from?"

Roxi managed a quick wink back before tucking her head between her shoulders at his interrogation.

"Yep, solo. Been my dream for years. As far back as I can remember I've repaired and helped build all types of watercraft alongside my dad and grandpa at our family boatyard in Vancouver, Washington." Kyle chuckled. "Got saltwater running through my veins."

Great. The two guys will probably rattle on for hours about boats. Roxi turned her glare from PJ and gave Mama C a pleading look. She exhaled with relief when her grandma finally interrupted.

"Excuse me. Why don't we let Roxi take a break and have some time with Kyle?" Mama C's eyes locked on her husband's. "We can finish up here. Right, Jon?"

"I'm certainly not going to pass up the opportunity to get out of laundry duty. Thanks, Mama C." Roxi attempted a grateful smile as she undid her messy ponytail. She combed fingers through her hair, then pulled and secured it higher with a scrunchie. Glancing down, she tried to smooth out the wrinkles in her T-shirt. "Let's bounce, Kyle."

They ambled along the bush trail leading to Rocky Point, the promontory at the bay's entrance. She kept sneaking sidelong looks at him. "This is so amazing we ran across each other. How come you're here now when you left a month ahead of us?"

Kyle licked his full lips, chapped by sun and wind, and frowned briefly. "Well, after spending a week here, I sailed over to Ua Pou and two small, uninhabited islands. I dove on a couple of cool coral reefs and did a few radical rock climbs." His smile wavered. "Unfortunately, I caught a flu bug I couldn't shake. The low-grade fever and skull-cracking headache made me so miserable I barely ate anything for almost a week."

Roxi shook her head. "That's a bummer."

"Yep. So I came back here to reprovision a little, rest, and gain strength before the five-day sail to the Tuamotu archipelago. Scuba diving is supposed to be awesome there."

For the first time, she noticed dark circles beneath those hypnotic eyes and the outline of ribs beneath his golden tan. "Should you be traveling alone? PJ says there're hundreds of uncharted atolls and underwater reefs in that area. Seems dangerous."

Kyle shrugged. "Hey, this is what I gotta do, why I came—and I'm gonna do this voyage by myself!"

Roxi caught the determined gleam in his eyes. Stubborn, like her. "But why?"

He shortened his stride to a turtle's pace and ran his fingers through sun-bleached curls. "It's a long story. Sure you want to hear my sad tale?"

She nodded.

"Four years ago, when I was thirteen, I felt indestructible. My two buddies and I free-climbed every chance we got. One day, I got careless and slipped."

Roxi gasped as her heart skipped a beat.

"Did a barn door, swinging out sideways. I tried to catch a jug, but my hand crashed into the ledge.

Roxi interrupted. "Wait. What does 'catch a jug' mean?"

"To find an easy hold to grab onto. Anyway, I crunched a few bones." Kyle held up his left hand and flexed his fingers several times. "Good as new now."

Roxi scrutinized the three narrow white scars. "What a miracle you didn't get hurt worse. Or die."

Kyle gazed across the water for a moment. His smile drooped. "That's not the astonishing part of this story. I needed minor surgery to pin the broken bones. When my pre-op bloodwork came back seriously out of whack, the doc called to inform us I was in renal failure—my kidneys weren't functioning properly." Kyle shook his head. "I told my mom that quack was nuts and must have me confused with another patient."

The two continued their stroll in silent contemplation until spotting a narrow strip of sand about twenty feet below the trail. Kyle gracefully boulder-hopped down, obviously part mountain goat.

Roxi scooted down the embankment and skidded to an inelegant stop. "You're gonna have to teach me how to rock jump like that. Being a dancer, I have pretty good balance. Or at least I used to." She plopped near him and crossed legs yoga style. "So, then what happened?"

Kyle leaned back on both elbows and stretched out his long legs. "Had a cough I couldn't shake and felt a bit off my usual hundred and ten percent. I finally relented to more testing. Doc speculated that a virus from strep or bronchitis must have ambushed my kidneys."

He paused for a couple of minutes as his face contorted, then took a deep breath and continued. "The doctor told us there had been permanent damage." His voice cracked. "Worse moment of my life."

Roxi could relate to that hopeless feeling. She'd been there a few times, although her life had never been in jeopardy. "That must have been awful."

"And things went downhill from there." His voice dropped. "Even following a strict diet and modified exercise program, the damage progressed until I was forced to go on dialysis three times a week. That really wiped me out and altered my activities."

Kyle's stormy eyes cleared. "Lucky for me, my optimistic mom tested as a close match and donated one of her kidneys. I'll always be grateful to her for the gift of life—a second time." An exuberant grin spread across his face. "Now I have the chance to fulfill my goal of sailing solo around the world."

Roxi gave a hesitant smile. "So, you're okay now?"

"Absolutely." He flexed his biceps to prove his point. "I have to be on antirejection meds the rest of my life that lower my immune system." He shrugged. "But hey, I'm alive and doing what most people only dream about."

Both stood, and she brushed off sand as Kyle picked up a few smooth stones and began skimming them across the water.

They skip, skip, skipped along the surface as Roxi struggled to grasp the enormity of Kyle's revelation. The closest she'd ever come to her fears of death had been when she was seven and Mom OD'd on pills and had to get her stomach pumped at the hospital. That had been terrifying.

Then, the funeral of Star's Uncle Jimmy three years ago came to mind. He'd been to a few of Mama C's family gatherings, intoxicated and funny, but Roxi hadn't known him very well. She hadn't meant to look in his coffin. The zombie inside still haunted her. Cemeteries freaked her out even more, and only a couple days ago, her grandparents had forced her to visit the gravesite of French Impressionist Paul Gauguin. She shuddered, again imagining spirits bobbing among the ancient stones.

She needed to stop being morbid. Roxi forced a smile. "Well, you look fairly good for one who almost croaked and has a secondhand kidney." She grabbed a dried-up crab and threw the carcass, hitting Kyle's bare chest.

"Hey, that hurt." He lunged and tackled her to the soft sand.

She wriggled loose and raced into the water but stopped mid-thigh. "Wow, this feels like bathwater." Before she had time to dive all the way in, Kyle dunked her. Sputtering, she came up ready for battle and balled up her fists.

With hearty laughter, Kyle fought off her wild swings. He backed away at her frenetic splashing and raised both arms high. "Okay, okay, I surrender. You California girls are awfully feisty—but cute." He raised his eyebrows up, then down, several times.

Cute? Roxi's face grew hot. "Whatever," she mumbled and swam away.

Kyle followed, and they played in the bay for a while until, without warning, he picked her up with the ease of a male dancer lifting a ballerina and heaved her high in the air. Roxi didn't fly and land as a graceful swan, but splashed onto her belly, arms and legs askew, like a hippo dropped from a plane. She surfaced, gagging from a huge gulp of saltwater.

He patted her back until her coughing diminished. "Sorry, I wasn't trying to drown you. Sometimes, I get carried away."

Kyle's wide, sincere smile helped soothe her embarrassment. Roxi sucked in a few lungfuls of air until the awkward moment passed. "No problemo." She snickered. "But that's about all the excitement I can handle for one day."

"Right. Besides, we better head back before your grandparents send out a search party."

Roxi recalled Mexico with Brit. "Yeah, been there, done that."

Her new friend's steps slowed as they drew close to the anchorage crowd, then halted. "So, would you like to do something tomorrow?"

Elation quickly deflated to regret. Roxi frowned. "Wish I could. Really. But we sail for Tahiti in the morning."

He cast his eyes toward his feet and scuffled them in the dirt. "Oh well, no worries. We found each other once. We will again. I promise." He crossed his heart.

How sweet. Just like she and her best friend, Alex, always did.

As Kyle took her hand, her breath caught. She looked up and their eyes met. She could get lost in the depths of those aquamarine pools.

He cleared his throat. "I won't see you in Papeete because I avoid noisy, polluted cities. But how about an exotic, less-traveled island we can explore together? There's a bunch in the Society group. Deal?"

Her cheeks dimpled as she shook his hand. "Sounds rad. Let's keep in touch on the Pacific Seafarer's Net."

"Sorry, I don't have a ham radio but will try to find a way to get word to you when I can." A warm look emanated from his eyes. He massaged her shoulder for a moment before his long strides carried him away.

"Au revoir," Roxi shouted. "Take care of yourself."

Kyle spun around, chest puffed out. "Don't worry. Nothing will happen to me."

Yeah, right, Superman. How about your kidney and that rock-climbing accident?

For the next 775 miles unsettling thoughts tormented her, especially during lonely midnight watches.

Chapter Sixteen: Paradise Lost

ROXI

Dawn's Dove swept into Tahiti on July 3rd at the start of Fête, a month-long Polynesian celebration. Roxi rushed below to slip on her favorite electric-blue shorts and a tie-dyed shirt. Excitement tickled her stomach at thoughts of Brit, Dustin, and Rob waiting for her on the wharf. She bounded up the steps only to be met by her pokey grandparents.

PJ finished setting the bow anchor, but as he backed the boat toward the quay, a powerful gust hit them, causing them to veer.

"Watch out, Jon. You're headed toward another boat. Move the stern to the left." Mama C paced the port and starboard decks.

"I'm doin' the best I can with this squirrely wind knockin' us around," PJ grumbled. "Grab the boat hook in case you got to push us off."

He reversed the engine as they slowly glided between two tethered yachts. Mama C handed Roxi one of the stern lines and pointed. "Throw this to Brittany's dad." She threw out the other to Ray, and both lines were hitched to huge metal cleats.

"Where are they?" Roxi scanned the long cement sea wall for her friends. She finally spotted Brit and Dustin and waved wildly. Either they didn't see her or were ignoring her. Something didn't feel right. Tendrils of fear clawed at her insides as she squinted at the crowd. *Where was Rob?*

Instead of the usual festive atmosphere, sailors spoke in hushed voices like at the hospital where her mom had been a couple of years ago. Red laid a narrow six-foot plank from the quay to their boat. Roxi sprinted ashore after PJ. Mama C followed in her wake. Roxi glanced back when she heard a shriek. Two-thirds across the wooden walkway, her grandma faltered and swayed. PJ leapt forward, grabbing her outstretched hand, and yanked her into his arms.

Mama C blushed. "Whew, that was close. Almost took a salty bath."

He patted her shoulder. "Walking will get easier, sweetheart. Nine days at sea has made everyone a bit wobbly."

"Nice save, PJ." Roxi smirked but instantly grew tense again. Their mates from *Harmony* and *Sea Eagle* were huddled together watching them, but silent.

"Red, Ray," PJ hollered. "Great to catch up with ya'll." He shook their hands as if he were pumping water. Mama C stood beside Ray's wife. A look of apprehension played across Juanita's face.

Brittany scuffed over and flung slender arms around her friend. "Oh, Roxi."

Embarrassed, Roxi faked a laugh as she squirmed from the tight embrace. "Gee, I'm glad you've missed me, but this is a bit much."

Brittany stiffened and backed away. Her mouth formed a mute O.

Dustin stepped closer, his red-rimmed eyes not quite meeting hers. Roxi's bottom lip quivered. "What's going on? Why is everyone acting so weird?"

"I'm so sorry, Rox." His voice cracked. "We've got terrible news."

Icy fingers slithered down her spine. "Is it about Rob?"

Brittany clutched her hand as Dustin barely nodded. "Three days ago, Pepper and Sugar, new cruising friends off the yacht *Escapade,* came across *Romance* drifting a hundred miles from Tahiti." He cleared his throat. The sailboat appeared abandoned. Unable to raise anyone by VHF, they managed to tie alongside, and Pepper climbed aboard."

Roxi's throat closed like someone was strangling her. "Tell me."

A tear rolled down Brittany's cheek, and she sniffled. Roxi clasped her friend's hand tighter, clinging to it as a lifeline.

Dustin's voice lowered. "There were no signs of piracy or storm damage, and his dinghy and life raft were still onboard. A half-empty mug of tea sat propped in the sink." He drew a couple of deep breaths. "The couple searched the sea for hours and put out an alert on the local net to passing vessels in the area before notifying the French Navy. They've scouted the entire grid."

He paused, then stammered, "Everyone ... including the authorities ... determined that ... that ... Rob must have fallen overboard."

Roxi aimed her lethal gaze at a mouth that spewed the unfathomable. "Liar!" she roared.

Dustin jolted back as if struck.

"I talked with Rob four nights ago on the Seafarer's Net. He was fine." Her heart raced, and she grew lightheaded.

"There must be another explanation." She sucked in a ragged breath, then another. "Maybe a boat picked him up due to a medical emergency, and he's been unconscious this whole time." *Wouldn't she feel the agony of his loss if he'd died? Had she blocked out the unthinkable?*

Two sets of arms encircled Roxi, supporting her. Her head pounded in sync with her heartbeat. Maybe she would explode. Maybe she would die. At that moment, she wanted to.

She pushed away from her friends and whirled around, facing the adults. Mama C and Dustin's mom had their heads bowed in prayer. The men huddled together. Roxi flung her arms out. "Is everyone going to give up? He could still be alive—waiting for us to find him." She could taste her salty tears as she stumbled toward her grandparents. Her shrill voice shattered the stillness. "I hate you both for forcing me to come on this horrible trip. I want to go home. *Now!*"

Before anyone had time to react, Roxi fled in an outgoing tide of grief, running past boats and a blur of people. She reached a row of cottages and gave a convulsive gulp before slowing. With no idea where she was and not caring, she trudged along a brick walkway. Her broken heart unraveled a little more with each step like a ball of yarn batted around by a kitten.

Unbearable anguish pummeled her. She grasped for something ... anything ... to keep herself from falling into the dark abyss. She pictured being back home in the familiar haven of her bedroom. Snuggled in her lime-green beanbag chair stroking Thumper's silky fur. Star's muffled voice rehearsing in the next room. Even the mingled stink of cigarettes, nail polish remover, and stale coffee felt comforting.

Roxi stopped sobbing. Her breathing slowed. Numb, she crumpled in slow motion onto a grassy slope.

Chapter Seventeen: Girlfriends

ROXI

Roxi's eyes flickered open. *How long have I been sitting here? And where is here?* Her foggy brain cleared, and a familiar figure came into focus. "Brit?"

Her friend unfolded long legs, struggled to her feet, then shuffled over and plopped down. "I didn't want to be a bother, but thought you could use a friend, so I followed you." A hesitant smile whispered across her lips. "And that wasn't easy. You were running like the devil himself chased you."

"I don't even remember how I got to this place." Roxi glanced around the unfamiliar park that overlooked a bay. Brittany's soothing presence helped her tight neck muscles relax. She drew a deep breath and stared at the still water for several minutes trying to absorb its calmness. "Now what?" Roxi wailed.

Brittany wrapped her arms around Roxi's shoulders.

"I have no idea." She patted Roxi's back.

Roxi's turbulent thoughts finally tumbled out. "I have so many questions for Rob," she whimpered. "Why did this happen? Where do you go after you die? How can I ever get over losing my friend?" Her stifled sob came out as a soft moan.

"Are you going to be okay?" Brittany asked in a soft voice.

"Sure. No. Probably not." Shivering, Roxi rubbed her arms. "This doesn't feel real. I want to wake up from this nightmare." Her feet tingled from sitting cross-legged too long, so she stretched out both legs and wiggled her toes. For some random reason, that movement made her drift back to the memory of lounging on a beach in Hiva Oa with Kyle. The day had been almost perfect. She'd been so happy. "Oh, I just remembered what I was so anxious to tell you before I heard about—you know what." The teeny smile that had begun to turn up the corners of her mouth drooped. She bit the inside of her lip.

Brittany's pale blue eyes widened. "Ooh, something secret?"

"Maybe." Her long pause made Brit squirm. "Well?"

"I had a surprise encounter in the Marquesas."

"Really? With who?" She leaned forward, her forehead almost touching Roxi's.

"Remember *Songwriter,* that crazy boat in La Paz? The one that looked like a ghost ship?" She peeked up at Brit.

"You met the old hippie? Yuk." Her excited look deflated as her face puckered.

Roxi barked out a small chuckle. "He isn't a hippie and definitely not a dinosaur. Only four years older." Her heart fluttered as she pictured him. "And he's gorgeous."

Brittany's face brightened. "Awesome. So, what'd you guys do?"

The memory of their day together warmed her as drawing near a campfire on a chilly night would. "We hiked along the bay and found a secluded beach where we went swimming. Kyle told me lots about himself. He is so rad and fun to be around. I think I have a crush on him."

"Sweet. When will you see him again?"

The pleasant images evaporated, leaving Roxi icy cold again. "No idea. He only said, 'Somewhere in the Society Islands.'" Her chin dropped as she wrapped her arms around herself. "I don't know what to do—about Kyle, Rob, or my grandparents. I really, really miss home and my mom." Her arms fell to her sides, and she scrunched the hem of her shorts into tight fists.

Brittany's eyebrows drew together. She rubbed Roxi's back in slow circles. "Believe me, I totally understand." Her gaze held a mournful, faraway look, and she remained silent for a couple of minutes. When she finally spoke, her voice choked with emotion. "Uh, um, my mom died. In a boating accident. When I was five." Her hiccup ended with a sob. She stared at an ant crawling along her calf, then gently plucked the insect off and set it on a blade of grass. "She had been sailing her tiny Sunfish sailboat when a squall hit. The torrential rain must have made visibility impossible for her to see the ferry crossing her path."

Shock jolted Roxi. She squirmed, not knowing how to respond. *The ocean claimed another victim.* She shook her head and finally said, "That's horrible."

Brittany sniffled. "I don't remember much about her except through Grandma Redfern's stories. But the aroma of freshly baked chocolate chip cookies always brings back a memory of standing on a stool beside my mom, sneaking nibbles of sweet cookie dough as we scooped spoonfuls onto cookie sheets." She gave a deep sigh.

Roxi nodded, recalling times she'd done the same with Alex and her friend's mom.

"In my favorite photo, Mom is standing in a lemon-yellow kitchen. Rays of sunlight stream through a garden window setting her long blonde hair aglow. She's smiling, holding a baby against her cheek, her blue eyes radiant." Brittany paused. "That baby was me." Her voice quavered. "There's so much we never got to share. And never will."

The dam broke and a torrent of tears flooded Roxi's face. She rarely cried, and now she couldn't stop. Because of Brit's story? Fear of losing her own mom? Or anguish over Rob?

"Sometimes my dad accidentally calls me Katie—Mommy's name. I don't mind though. Makes me feel special, although I'm nothing like her." She grimaced. "Dad says my mom was gorgeous and moved with the grace of a gazelle."

Roxi wiped her face using her shirt sleeve. Her mouth opened wide. "Are you kidding? You're perfect." Her cheeks burned, and she hung her head. Giving a compliment made her feel self-conscious.

"Ha-ha. Thanks, but I'm more like a scrawny newborn fawn."

She snorted. "Well, you are a bit clumsy at times."

Brit gave a small giggle, then furrowed her brow. "I've been missing my mom a bunch too, especially when I have questions about, you know, girl stuff. I don't ever want to forget her, but this trip is supposed to help Dad move on. This is the first time he's set foot on a sailboat since the accident."

"Wow, your life hasn't been the Disney fantasy I imagined." Roxi rubbed her itchy, swollen eyes.

"Not even close. Being on that boat 24/7 with Dad and Toby is almost as much fun as breaking a leg the day before summer camp—which I did two years ago." She peered up into the cloudless sky as if searching for answers, then grunted. "All they talk about is guy things like fishing lures, boats, and mechanical stuff I don't understand."

"Ugh, boring. Sounds like my grandparents. Everything is about the weather, routes, history and cultures of each country."

Brittany's cheeks flamed. "And while *Sea Eagle's* exterior may be spotless, down below looks like a cyclone blew through. They're complete slobs, used to Gram picking up after them. I refuse to be their maid, so all their stuff just lies scattered everywhere."

"Guess we both have troubles, but you hide yours better." Roxi twisted and untwisted a curl around a finger. "I'm really sorry about your mom. I had no idea. You always seem so cheerful. I assumed you loved being out here with your family."

"Things aren't always what they appear to be." She gave a conflicted smile. "Don't get me wrong. I do love my dad and brother. And I always try to look on the bright side." She beamed. "Like if I wasn't on this voyage, I'd never have met Dustin."

A dull ache thudded in Roxi's chest. "And I never would have met Kyle. But I still have no idea what to do. My mom's kinda messed up. And Mama C and PJ think I'm just like her. A nutcase." She made a goofy face and leaped up like a startled cat. "Let's bounce."

"Wait up." Brittany wobbled to her feet and lurched after her.

Roxi slowed. "I don't even know who my dad is. Star gets totally freaked if I ask." She kicked a small stone and sent it sailing. "She probably doesn't even know." Disgust and shame tasted nasty on her tongue. She wanted to spit the vile taste out. "I once overheard Mama C tell PJ that her daughter goes through boyfriends like her endless packs of cigarettes—she craves them, enjoys them, and then throws their butts out."

Britany burst out laughing, then snapped her jaw shut. "Sorry. That must be awful for you. But your grandma is pretty funny."

Roxi shrugged and looked away, pretending like her admission was no big deal. Inside, she cringed. *Stupid! Why did I tell Brit all that?* Only Alex knew about her looney life. She hated people feeling sorry for her or thinking she was a freak.

"Maybe you should ask your grandma about your dad."

"I doubt she or PJ will ever speak to me again."

Brittany patted Roxi's shoulder. "I'm sure they'll forgive you for screaming at them after that shocking news about Rob. Besides, I think they'd do anything for you."

Flabbergasted, Roxi swiftly turned her head to see if Brit had been joking and gulped. "Really? Most of the time, I feel like I'm in their way."

"I feel like that with my family, too, sometimes." Brittany gave her a tremulous smile. "I hope you're not serious about going home. You're my best friend out here— the only one I can really talk to. About everything. Please, you have to stay."

Roxi didn't answer. As they drew near the cement wharf she paused and glanced at Brit from the corner of her eye. "Um, thanks for listening. And um, for sharing your stuff too."

"Hey, that's what girlfriends are for." Brittany's tender smile reflected in her warm eyes. "Call me later on the radio, okay? I'd like to know how things go with your grandparents. I'll be praying."

Chapter Eighteen: Memorial

CAROL

"Hi, Abbie." Carol waved as her friend wobbled across the plank toward the quay, holding the hand of her husband, Drew.

Carol flashed back on her own near dunking when they arrived in Tahiti and waited to say more.

When Abbie landed on solid ground, the two women flung their arms around each other, rocking back and forth.

Carol squeezed her friend. "I've missed you."

"Missed you too. Sorry we weren't here when you arrived. Drew and I rented a car and have been sight-seeing the past few days. Tahiti is a huge island." Abbie grabbed Carol's hand. "I hope we can explore this delightful paradise together."

Carol swiped her eyes. "We will definitely be spending lots of time with you both. I feel like we've been apart three years, not three months."

Abbie beamed. "I agree. Life back home has been a whirlwind. I divided my time between the grand-twins in California and my Indiana family. Mom's hanging in there.

Hannah's baby girl is already three months old, and Benjy is still a little wild man but dotes on his new sister."

"Sounds like family time was what you needed. Want to walk to Papeete's Municipal Market? I need quite a bit of fresh produce and more noni. The fruit may not smell or look appetizing but seems to be controlling Jon's diabetes or whatever he has."

Abbie nodded. "Sure. The tropical fruits are delicious here. But don't buy a watermelon. They're twenty dollars!"

Carol's eyes bugged out as she pretended to faint. "What?"

"Don't worry. All the local stuff is reasonable." Abbie hesitated. "Le Marche is only a couple blocks away, but go slow, okay? Balance is still an issue for me—maybe a bit worse." She glanced away.

"I'm sorry to hear that. What do you mean by worse?"

"I have a little more foot pain and cramping which causes me to walk kind of funky." She gave a resigned smile.

Carol scrutinized her friend. "Well, grab my arm and lean on me if you need to."

"Don't worry, girlfriend, I will. Hopefully, I won't drag you down with me." Abbie laughed. "By the way, how's Roxi doing?"

Carol rolled her eyes and shrugged. "She had a meltdown when we first heard about Rob. But I'm praying she'll gradually work through the grief of losing her friend." She drew a deep breath, recalling that day's intense emotions for Abbie.

After Roxi's outburst, she and Jon waited on pins and needles at the boat. Where had she run off to? All Carol could do was pray. *Please keep Roxi safe, Lord. Hold her tight in your loving embrace and give her strength to overcome this tragedy. We all need you now.*

Hours later, Roxi stepped aboard and crept into the cabin, looking sheepish. Her bottom lip quivered. "Sorry for running off. And for what I said. I didn't really mean those things."

"Honey, you're forgiven." Carol patted the cushion beside her. "Come and sit down with us. This is an overwhelming tragedy. Feeling angry, sad, and a whole jumble of other emotions is to be expected."

Jon nodded in agreement but looked like he wanted to add something. Carol knew he must be baffled by Roxi's behavior and had no idea how to handle a teenager's emotions. Thankfully, he kept any criticism to himself.

They talked until dusk. Carol shared about the death of her first husband, Joe McKay. "Even though we were divorced, we remained close friends." For a moment, sorrow and remorse crushed her. She studied the gimballed lantern that swung over the table until she could focus on Roxi. "Your mom was only eleven when her dad passed away. Joe had never taken care of himself—alcohol, drugs, and a lousy diet. I felt so helpless and guilty, like I should have prevented his death. Time and a grief group helped me heal."

Roxi drew in a deep breath, then blew out. "That must have been heartbreaking for an eleven-year-old. Star rarely mentions her dad but keeps an old photo album buried in the back of a cupboard. Do you think she buried all those hurtful feelings too? Sometimes I do that." She made a choking sound. "I'd break into a gazillion pieces if my mom died." Her eyes darkened, and the corners turned down. "Maybe I shouldn't be so hard on her goofy behavior.

There's a lot I don't know about her. So, how did Star react to Grandpa Joe's death?"

"Your mom idolized him. She fell apart. Losing her dad was the beginning of a long downward spiral. I don't think she's ever fully recovered." Carol closed her eyes for a moment, trying to keep her emotions in check. "She became a different person after that, almost a stranger." She searched Roxi's sad eyes. She didn't know her granddaughter very well, either. But she hoped to change that.

Jon stood and stretched before grabbing a soda." He popped open a Dr Pepper and guzzled half the can. "Now, let me tell you a story. I met my first wife, Shawna, at Boeing. She worked right alongside of me, buildin' airplanes, handlin' them tools better than most men. I admired that." His face crumpled. "Cancer took her. She was only thirty-six and so brave. But I sorta fell apart after that. Didn't want nuthin to do with people, even my family, for the longest time. I moved like a robot and worked eighty hours most weeks, goin' through the motions, tryin' not to think about Shawna." He gave a wobbly smile and paused. "My savin' grace was sailin', mostly the San Juan Islands. I made peace with God there—eventually."

Carol took off her sunglasses and rubbed her eyes before giving Abbie a tight-lipped smile. "That pretty much covers what happened that night after we found out about Rob. Roxi listened and cried off and on, then told us a little about Brittany losing her mom several years ago. Life hasn't been easy for any of us." She halted outside the bustling two-story market to gather her thoughts. "Jon and I encountered Rob's two sons the next afternoon.

They'd flown in immediately upon hearing from the French authorities."

"Those poor boys must be heartsick." Abbie laid a hand across her chest.

"Actually, both are handling the loss well, showing remarkable strength. They know how much Rob suffered after their mom passed and believe their parents are now reunited." Carol grinned. "And guess what? The boys have decided to continue *Romance's* voyage around the world to complete their father's dream—a memorial to his life."

Abbie's eyes lit up. "That's wonderful!"

Carol nodded. "When we told Roxi, she seemed skeptical. 'In memory of Rob? He deserves that. Guess I could continue on also. At least to New Zealand. For Rob.'"

"God is amazing. You must be so relieved." Abbie dabbed her eyes. "And I hope Roxi will lean on Jesus to help comfort and heal her." Her smile softened. "Plus, she's got great support from you and Jon, her friends, and the whole cruising family."

"And you, God, and Jon are my support system." Carol hugged her friend. "Now, are you going to tell me what else is going on with your health?"

"Okay, but don't stress out. My doctor finally gave me a diagnosis— Parkinson's, so he put me on a couple of meds, and we're experimenting with the dosage and timing. Besides the foot issue, I'm having lots of stiffness on my right side. One day, I even needed Drew to help me dress." Abbie shrugged. "But like I said, we're getting this new phase of life all worked out."

Carol shared an encouraging smile but anxious thoughts gnawed at her insides. "I'll be praying for you." She gave her another hug.

Today I'm going sailing ... fly with a new set of wings ... Melodic words drifted in and out of Carol's consciousness.

Paul, Rob's youngest son, strummed a guitar and sang in a pure tenor about the sea and sailing. The wind tousled his long, blondish-white hair. Gray-blue eyes, so much like Rob's, reflected a deep yearning.

Friends had gathered aboard *Romance* this afternoon for a celebration of Rob's life. His eldest son, Swami V, was dressed in gauzy linen pants and tunic, his head wrapped in a striped turban. His nostalgic eulogy included childhood pranks with his brother while growing up in New Jersey's suburbs, time spent with their dad at Bell Labs where Rob had worked for over thirty years, and tales of family sailing trips along the eastern seaboard and down around the Chesapeake Bay.

A gentle breeze cooled Carol's sticky skin. She glanced toward the bow where Roxi, Brittany, and Dustin huddled atop sail bags, quietly conversing. She bowed her head. *Thank you Lord for giving my granddaughter friends along this journey, especially for times like this. I pray Roxi gathers encouragement from them but also turns to you. May she learn to trust in you and grow in faith. Guide and comfort her as she struggles through every situation.*

Through blurry eyes Carol studied the scene before her. Sailors rocked gently to the rhythm of the salt-encrusted sailboat moored in the bay. Lush green mountains rose in the distance. The sparkling sea embraced them. Soothing lyrics from one of her favorite songs wove through Carol's heart, swirling among her fellow sojourners, then up into the ever-changing cloud formations. *If I die tomorrow, I'll leave without regrets. Death can't take our love away ... My lovely lady, together, forever ...*

No more tears, no more sorrow for Rob and Jeannie. They were basking in heaven's glory. Together again. For eternity.

Chapter Nineteen: The Swimming Hole

ROXI

"All aboard *LeTruck*, folks." Red gave a dramatic sweep of his arm toward a row of unusual vehicles. "An interesting fact: Locals converted these flatbed trucks into buses by enclosing the beds with wooden structures." He and PJ crouched down to study the framework up close.

Roxi gaped at the bizarre bus by the curb. "I think I must have fallen down the rabbit hole like poor Alice."

Mama C chuckled. "Aren't those buses groovy? Their paint jobs are straight out of the sixties. Don't you love the psychedelic flowers and rainbows? Reminds me of the van I rode in to San Francisco back in '68. Not sure if we were attending a rock concert, sit-in, or—"

"Oh no, not another hippie tale," PJ moaned.

She elbowed him. "You're just jealous I was a free, peace-loving flower child while you were stuck painting Coast Guard stations and trolling Lake Michigan for boaters in trouble." She puckered her lips, kissed his cheek, and bounded up the steps of the bus before PJ could say more.

As Roxi squeezed past her archaic grandparents, she pretended like she didn't know them. They could be so embarrassing at times. Dustin and Brit followed her down one of two rows of long wooden benches. Most of the bus was occupied by sweating Tahitian men, pretty, but exhausted-looking *vahines* that held onto their loud squirming toddlers, and older women fanning themselves.

Dustin plopped between the girls and gave each a wink and lopsided grin. "This is cozy."

Brittany blushed.

Roxi rolled her eyes. "Ugh, this is like a smelly sauna in here."

"Hope you're not referring to me." Dustin pouted.

Brit giggled.

Roxi's smart retort got cut off by Mama C. "Look, Bougainville Park." Her grandma pointed out the window where an outdoor café nestled beneath a shady canopy of banyans, fuchsia bougainvillea, and plumeria. She turned to her husband. "How about a walk with our friends this evening when the weather cools down? Those garden paths are calling my name."

"Anything for you, darlin'." PJ wrapped an arm around her shoulder.

On Mama C's other side, Abbie tilted her head. "Hmm, an ice-cold drink at the café surrounded by fragrant gardens sounds heavenly. And a stroll, if I'm not too tired."

"Great. Let's tentatively plan to meet." Mama C tapped Abbie's two telescoping hiking poles. "Looks like you came prepared for our hike to the waterfall."

Abbie nodded. "Just in case. Drew made me bring both."

"Probably a good idea, although I read this trail isn't too difficult. I only hope I don't get too overheated." She pushed matted bangs off her forehead.

Roxi did the same, feeling a trifle claustrophobic squashed inside a bus surrounded by so many hot bodies. But outside the windows, waves crashed onto a rocky shoreline. A hidden cove of white sand flashed among dark boulders. If only she could be down there now, cooled by a soft breeze, the sea lapping at her feet. A rustling sound caused her to glance across the aisle. A mother cradled a sleeping infant. Beside her, an elderly woman who had black, gray-streaked hair rummaged through her straw bag. She unwrapped a small unfrosted cake and tore off a portion for the toddler seated on her lap. His dark eyes shone as he nestled back against her cushiony bosom and grinned, his mouth bulging like a chipmunk.

Roxi laughed and puffed out her cheeks. A giggle bubbled out of the youngster's mouth along with a dribble of cake.

"*Ia orana.* Hello." The grandmother smiled and spoke several more indecipherable words.

Perplexed, Roxi tried English, but the lady shook her head and squinted at her. Next Roxi tried her very limited French. "*Je m'excuse. No comprend.* Sorry, don't understand."

The woman's creamy milk chocolate face beamed. "*Voulez-vous?*" She offered samples of her cake to the three curious *popaas.*

Roxi smiled back until she took a bite. The cake had a coconutty flavor, but the dry texture made swallowing impossible. She gulped from her water bottle until the lump slid down her throat. She managed to choke out, "*Mauruuru.* Thank you."

After Dustin's coughing fit he added, "*Roa.* Very much."

Brittany nodded. "*Maitai roa.* Very good."

Really? Roxi tried not to snicker at her friend's fake politeness.

The bus veered over and stopped next to a rutted road that branched off the highway. Waving goodbye to their bus friends, the trio sang out, *"Nana."* They shouldered their packs before disembarking with the ten other yachties and gathering by a crooked, weathered plank.

"*Faarumai Falls*," Mama C read aloud. "Or however you pronounce the name." A barely discernable arrow pointed the way. Abbie studied the long road before them bordered by a tangle of greenery. "Well, off we go into the emerald jungle."

Brittany hummed and Roxi sang, *We're off to see the wizard ...*

Her singing came to an abrupt stop when she caught a glimpse of the strangest looking human she'd ever encountered. Apparently, trolls were real and living in remote parts of the world.

Brit's dad, Red, shifted, and Roxi got a better view of the short man. His large pointy ears angled through wispy black hair. "Hey, who's the goblin?" she whispered.

Brittany giggled and poked her side.

Dustin gave a conspiratorial wink. "You'll find out soon enough."

Trollman's ball bearing gaze bounced about before zeroing in on Roxi.

She squirmed. "Uh-oh."

His mouth morphed into a wide grin. One hairy arm encircled the waist of a stunning blonde half a head taller than him, and he led her over to the girls. "Hey, there. I'm Pepper, and this is my sweet mate, Sugar. And who might you three urchins be?"

Roxi's first thought was shock. These were the people who had found Rob's boat. Tongue-tied, she didn't know whether to thank the couple, interrogate them, or cry.

Brittany saved her from embarrassment by making the introductions.

Sugar spoke with a silky southern accent. "So nice ta meet ya'll. We're sailin' aboard *Escapade*. Six months ago we bid farewell to Florida and—"

"Made a right, or was it a wrong turn, from the Caribbean at Venezuela." Pepper guffawed. The swift current of cruisers heading west sucked our boat clear through the Panama Canal before we had time to say, whoa Nelly." His bulbous nose lit up like Rudolph's as his enthusiasm grew. "Nope, no easy way to get back home then except continue on around."

"So here we all are." Sugar gave them a Georgia peach smile.

Pepper patted her round bottom and gave her a lip-smacking smooch on her rosy cheek.

Roxi forced herself not to gag and breathed a sigh of relief when the group moved ahead.

Brittany's brother, Toby, led a slow march up the single lane road where walls of thick vegetation obscured what lay beyond.

Dustin kept pace beside him. "Kinda boring so far. Hope there's some rad boulder climbs at the falls."

Toby grunted and lengthened his stride.

The two girls scampered close behind the boys while adults spread out in a scraggly line. Mama C and Abbie brought up the rear. The group passed a couple of tiny rustic homes. Only two dogs barked and a few free-range chickens clucked as if acknowledging their disturbance amidst the solitude.

"Weird, no people. Think zombies ate them—or maybe cannibals?" Roxi smirked.

Brittany's eyes narrowed. "Shhh. Why do you always think up creepy stuff?" She let out a loud sigh. "I'm thankful to be off the boat. I like this peaceful place."

"You mean not exciting. And it's steamy." The tropical sun beat down causing Roxi's eyes to sting from the sweat dripping into them. She caught a glimpse of shimmery volcanic peaks through an opening in the trees. "Think we're climbing up there? Not."

"Eek!" Brittany winced. "No way, or Dustin will have to carry me."

Dust billowed in small clouds around their feet as the girls scuffled to a stop beside their fearless leaders who waited next to a poorly marked turnoff.

Toby took a long swig of water and peered at the skinny path of mire. "Think this leads to the falls?"

Dustin downed half his bottle and gave a long, loud burp. "Guess we'll find out. All part of the adventure."

Everyone in the group finally caught up and appeared to be handling the trek with the exception of Abbie. Her pale, tight expression contrasted with Mama C's cherry-red face.

Roxi exhaled a grateful breath when the group lumbered into the blissful coolness of the shaded forest and took a ten-minute break. But thirty minutes later, her sighs turned to groans from tripping over an obstacle course of gnarly roots on the zigzagging trail.

"Who planned this dumb hike? Must be a hundred degrees." Roxi itched all over and felt ready to explode.

Splotches of red, yellow, and white flowers mingled among the verdant foliage. Birds twittered in the treetops. Brittany shrugged and turned her head one direction, then another, before her gaze stopped to linger on Dustin. "I think this is kind of like an enchanted forest."

Dumbfounded, Roxi glared at her. "Seriously? You're nuts!"

Brit's cheeks flushed, and she stared at the ground. Roxi stomped away.

Dustin must have heard her outburst because he fell back in step beside Brittany. "You need to ignore Roxi. She doesn't mean to hurt people, especially you."

Well, you upset your good friend again, Rox. She bounded ahead and tried to block the pang of guilt that cramped her stomach. Following Toby through the brush, Roxi stepped into a large clearing and gaped. Wild orchids and twisty vines clung to jumbles of rocks. Her eyes were drawn to the whoosh of a waterfall cascading over a high cliff into a misty dark pool. Monstrous ferns and giant mape trees encircled the water. The mossy earth, flowering tiare shrubs, and jasmine tickled her nose and several sneezes followed.

"Woohoo! This is totally rad." Dustin dashed to the cliff's base and scurried up the boulders like a mountain goat. Toby followed on his heels, although he showed a bit more caution.

Brittany sank onto a large flat rock beside Roxi and shook her head. "I'm totally buggin'. Those two are going to kill themselves."

She felt relief that Brit was still speaking to her. "Yep, I think they've both gone ape."

"Ah-a-ah-a-ah." The sudden Tarzan call shattered the idyllic scene.

Roxi almost jump out of her skin. Her gaze veered toward Pepper as he swung over the water on a thick vine, let go, and splashed down.

"Oh. My. Gosh!" Brittany squeaked, holding a hand over her heart.

Pepper surfaced from the shadowy pool.

Roxi let out her breath. "That guy is crazy, although the pond does look inviting, and I'm melting." She started to rise. But then Trollman floated onto his back revealing a potbelly matted with a thick layer of baby-fine hair. "Oh snap, that's gross." She stuck out her tongue and pretended to throw up.

Pepper motioned to the weary hikers. "Come on in. The water's amazing." His stumpy toes wiggled, and he gave a delighted chuckle.

The girls covered their mouths, hiding smirks that threatened to burst into laughter.

A series of ear-piercing squawks contorted Pepper's jolly expression. His short arms thrashed the water.

Beside Roxi, Bobbie whooped. "That man sounds like Yackity when he gets mad."

Roxi spun around. She had met this Canadian couple today and hadn't decided yet which category they fit in. Old, but not quite dinosaurs. "Who is Yackity?"

"Our African Grey Parrot." Bobbie's husband, Tom, scratched his ample belly. "He's quite the character. Even sings and composes sea shanties."

Hmm, they definitely belong in the strange category. Roxi swiveled back around to see how Pepper was doing. The water churned. She shrieked, "Maybe there's a grindylow in the pool. That's why I hate to swim where I can't see the bottom."

Brit's eyes widened into saucers. "You think there's a scaly green water demon with razor sharp claws and teeth in there? Aren't those imaginary beasts?"

"Harry Potter's creatures are definitely real." Roxi clenched her teeth when PJ followed Red into the murky water.

The guys waded up on either side of the agitated swimmer. "What's wrong?" PJ hollered between squawks and squeals. He finally got hold of one of Pepper's flailing arms. Red grabbed the other and they stood him up in the waist-deep water.

Pepper's terror-crazed eyes peered downward. "Aargh— something's swimming around inside my shorts!" His tanned face now had a greenish hue.

Roxi glanced at Brittany. "Do you think Trollman got bitten and is turning into a grindylow?" Her friend's face turned the same greenish shade.

Red huffed. "Hold still for five seconds if you want us to help you." A smile flickered at the corners of his mouth.

No one made a sound as the bizarre scene unfolded. Pepper froze when PJ stretched the elastic band of his baggy shorts wide and gave a cautious peek inside. A long moment later he held up a foot-long, writhing black and yellow-ringed snake. "Looks like you found a new friend." He and Red high-fived as Pepper splashed wildly toward dry land.

Roxi and Brit alternated between shrieks of fright and bursts of hysterical laughter.

Pepper's crimson face glared their way as he stomped by, shaking water off like a dog.

A twinge of remorse hit Roxi. She knew how it felt to be a misfit. "I kinda feel sorry for him."

Brit's mouth bunched. "Yeah, maybe we should go apologize and see if he's okay."

"Sorry," the girls told Pepper. Roxi stared at the ground, unable to look him in the eye. When the crowd started to clap, she turned toward the water.

The two heroes clambered ashore. PJ flung the disgruntled reptile toward the pool's center.

Mama C marched up to her husband and poked his chest. "What on earth were you thinking, touching that slithery creature?" She shuddered. "That snake might have been poisonous. You could have died."

Roxi agreed. No way would she ever pick up a snake, especially here in the jungle.

PJ waited until his wife calmed down. "Well, darlin', someone had to rescue that poor guy before he had a heart attack or drowned. Anyhow, them water snakes got teensy mouths, too small to bite most folks—unless the critter woulda got hold of the webbing between my fingers." He spread them apart and grinned.

"Well, I hope you kept those sausages clamped tight." She planted a kiss on his hand. "I think you've watched way too many *Wild Kingdom* shows on TV."

He flexed his biceps. "I yam what I yam and that's all I yam."

Mama C laughed and squeezed his bulging muscles. "Okay, Popeye, but maybe you could be a little less fearless."

Roxi chuckled. "Sometimes those two are hilarious, when they're not being complete Muggleheads." She crossed her eyes for emphasis.

All the excitement died down, and everybody spread out blankets and picnic goodies to share. Everyone except Abbie whose eyes were closed and head rested in Drew's lap. Her only movement came from an occasional jerk of both legs.

Dustin and Toby scampered down off their perch near the ledge of the waterfall.

"Guess food is the signal for Dustin and Toby." Brit worried her lip between her teeth. "Hope they don't fall."

Roxi shook her head. "Don't worry. Chances are, if they do, they'll land in the water. Maybe on that snake." She cracked a smile. Brit slapped her arm. "You're bad."

144

Mama C laid out two types of French cheeses and crusty baguettes along with chunks of juicy mango, papaya, and pineapple.

The sweet mango and pungent cheese were Roxi's favorites. She glanced over as a bag unzipped.

Bobbie dug out freshly baked fruit pastries. "Sorry they're a bit untidy. Yackity managed to ransack a couple before I caught the naughty boy."

Dustin, now safely beside Brittany, snaked his arm out, nabbed one, and stuffed the whole thing in his mouth. With his mouth still half full, he tried to talk. "A little messy, but tastes totally awesome."

Pepper soon broke the languid serenity, giving an outlandish revision of his narrow escape from a landlocked sea serpent.

Sugar winked as she rubbed his plump earlobes and shrugged.

"Looks like she's used to Trollman's freaky tales." Roxi grinned at her friends, then dished up more fruit and snagged a pastry.

Brittany nodded. "*Escapade* sure is an appropriate name for their boat. Sounds like they have lots of them."

Dustin laughed. "No doubt. He's like a trouble magnet."

The afternoon heat lulled several of the older folks into an almost comatose state after lunch. The girls helped pack up the remains of their picnic. PJ and Tom seemed to be competing for who could snore loudest until PJ startled himself awake with a harsh snort. Mama C shook her head, then gazed around, a soft smile brightening her face. "This is exactly how I envisioned paradise—a waterfall's peaceful roar, the spicy-sweet and earthy scents of tropical flora and—"

"Ants." Always the pessimist, PJ brushed several of the hungry pests off the thin canvas and stowed the tarp in his pack.

Roxi closed her eyes for a moment and exhaled. "I imagined powder white sand and crystal-clear, bathtub temp water."

Brittany grinned. "I second that and soaking up a tan."

"Oh, you girls don't appreciate the marvelous smorgasbord nature has to offer." Roxi's grandma shook her head. "You can go to the beach anytime."

Roxi scrunched her face. "Yeah, well at least there you can go for a relaxing swim without a snake swimming up your shorts." That ended the conversation.

Chapter Twenty: Tahitian Melodies

ROXI

The beacon of light sank behind the island of Moorea silhouetting its craggy peaks. Evening glow transitioned from gold to orangish reds as Roxi strolled the waterfront next to her grandparents on Boulevard Pomare. An eclectic group of teenagers passed by chatting and laughing. "I wonder where they're headed. Probably to an awesome beach bonfire." Envy battled with a twinge of homesickness.

"This place is way too loud and touristy." Mama C's lips puckered in a frown. "Look at all the local cruise ships and ferries docked beside those enormous wharves."

"Well, I'm kinda enjoyin' the purty vahines hangin' out over there with the French sailors." PJ grinned.

Roxi tried to picture herself living here among the odd assortment of humans. "Papeete isn't much different from Southern California—busy streets, mix of cultures, and interesting characters. I mean, there's even Starbucks and McDonalds."

They drew near a huge parking lot. Hundreds of lights twinkled from dozens of vans set up like a gypsy camp. Aromas from grilling meats and frying veggies made her salivate. "Yum. I'm starved." She picked up the pace with PJ only half a step behind.

Mama C maneuvered her way to them through the animated crowd. "They call these food trucks *Les Roulettes*."

PJ nodded, but his knotted face showed confusion. "How're we supposed to know what they're sellin'? Everything on them signs is in other languages. And I can't understand a word they speak."

Roxi bounced from one stand to the next. She enjoyed the mystery of unfamiliar menus. "I don't know what I want to eat. There's too many choices—stir-fries, spicy curries, gooey cheese pizzas, and fried everything on-a-stick."

"And for the adventurous palate, you could try the tangy *poisson cru*." Mama C gave a mischievous grin. "That's chunks of yellowfin tuna marinated in lime juice and coconut milk."

Roxi scrunched her nose. "No thanks, I'll pass on that."

"I have an idea." Mama C's grin widened. "Why don't we pick three dinners to share?"

Roxi nodded. "Sounds like a plan."

PJ halted in front of a booth. Steak sizzled atop a grill and *pommes frites* sputtered in a large vat of oil. "Ah, french fries. Finally, something I recognize. But where's the cheeseburgers?"

"Oh no, here we go." Roxi blew out her breath.

Mama C huffed. "Seriously Jon? We've traveled almost 4,000 miles across an ocean, and you want a cheeseburger and french fries?"

Roxi snickered. She knew in the end, PJ would order his familiar humdrum foods.

She and Mama C gorged themselves on a peppery red curry dish and yummy French cheese pizza while PJ settled on fries and chicken on-a-stick.

After eating, they joined Brit, Dustin, and their families, Abbie and Drew, and a few other cruising friends. The rumble of drums accompanied by low chanting enticed the group toward the end of the lot. PJ gave a contented sigh as he licked his chocolate ice cream cone. "Come on y'all. I want front row seats for this show."

Red smiled playfully. "Righteo. Definitely need a good view of all those dancing babes."

Brittany blushed. "Dad! Give me a break." She turned to Roxi. "Those drums remind me of the Suquamish Tribe pow wows back home in Washinton that Gram and Grandpa Redfern took me to every year. Their woven baskets and beadwork are so beautiful. And I love listening to stories about my Native American ancestors."

"Hmm?" Roxi's attention had become engrossed by dancers in a small arena where colorful lights strung from poles flickered along its perimeter. The performer's palpable energy made her entire body tingle. She sunk onto a blanket beside Brit and tried to refocus her brain. "Do you know what these festivities are all about?"

"*Heiva i Tahiti* is a two-week holiday throughout French Polynesia in celebration of ... uh, let's consult our historian." Brit leaned toward Dustin. "What's this holiday for?"

He curled around Brittany and shouted over the music. "Bastille Day. Marks the fall of the Bastille in Paris during the French Revolution—July 14, 1789, to be exact."

"More info than I need to know." Roxi rolled her eyes.

Music surged as Dustin scooted between the girls. "The surrounding islands participate in these dancing and singing competitions every night."

Dancing, that's all Roxi cared about. "Shh, we'll talk later." She concentrated on an angelic troop of elementary-aged children emerging from the shadows. Clothed in colorful sarongs called *pareus*, their bodies rocked, mostly in unison, to strumming ukuleles and guitars. Flower wreaths adorned silky black hair. Dark eyes gleamed above infectious smiles. Small hands wove a simple story about swimming fish and soaring birds.

Dustin babbled on. "There are different events during the day too. Yesterday, the men ran the banana bearer's race. Those muscular dudes had to jog while carrying heavy bunches of bananas on their shoulders." He leaned closer to Roxi. "Coming up are outrigger canoe, car, horse, and bicycle races."

His breath was warm against her ear. Annoying—yet strangely pleasant. She tilted her head away.

"I'm thinking about entering the cycling competition. There's also a cool carnival that has lots of food, games, and tattooing." His voice dropped to a whisper. "You want to go with me?"

That caught her attention. Before she could reply, applause thundered from the crowd as the dance ended.

Brittany wound her lean frame, draped in a blue and lavender pareu, across Dustin. She grasped his shoulder and grinned at Roxi. "Weren't they adorable?"

Roxi nodded, still a little flustered. "Uh, yeah. Wanna learn a few of their dances with me?"

Brittany giggled. "Klutzy me?"

"Sure. Even you could do the easy ones."

Up next came the Mamas, elderly women in ankle-length muumuus, their exquisite orchid leis strung around wrinkled, cocoa brown necks. Their graceful and intricate hand and arm motions spun an ancient tale of migration across a vast sea to a new land. In between dances, harmonious choirs enchanted the audience with hymns and primitive chants, their voices swelling heavenward.

Sharp rapping made Roxi jump.

"Wahoo, the drum competition." Dustin slapped his thighs in rhythm to the clattering and hollow rumbling sounds. "The *toeres* are hit using sticks and the *ofes* with their hands."

Roxi and Brit made faces at each other, like who cared, and shrugged.

"Boyah! Now the *pahus* are beating." Dustin bounced and rocked to the rhythm. "Those are made from hollowed out coconut tree trunks. And guess what they're covered with?"

Brittany's eyebrows rose. "No clue."

"Sharkskin."

"That's so interesting." Roxi raised her eyebrows, impatient for more dancers. They had rekindled a yearning for her passion. If only Alex were here so they could practice all those fabulous new moves together. Brit was right when she admitted to being klutzy. Definitely not ballet material. Her thoughts were interrupted as drums and strings morphed to an intense tempo. Vivacious teens shot into the arena and began a rapid provocative dance, hips shifting, pelvises tilting, hopping from one foot to the other.

"Oh my." Brit blushed and gave a nervous giggle.

Their elaborate headdresses woven with bright flowers, feathers, and leaves captivated Roxi, but her eyes bugged as her gaze travelled down to half-naked breasts cupped in coconut shells. Swaying leis and shell necklaces didn't cover much. "Oh snap!" She felt a jab of envy at their extraordinary talent and slender tan legs beneath *sulus,* the vibrant material wrapped into miniskirts. She couldn't imagine ever being thin and beautiful like them. Before she could slip into a jealous sulk, the energizing pulse of the *tamure* swept her upward.

Dustin caught her hand and pulled her back down before she made a fool of herself.

"Thanks." But she wasn't sure if she was glad or mad at him.

Brittany leaned back and winked at Roxi. "Those guys aren't wearing much either. They're hot!"

Eyes wide, Roxi focused on the male dancers. They only had on *mores*, fiber skirts made from long sword-shaped leaves off the pandanus tree. Ornate tattoos covered their muscular thighs like a pair of snug cycling shorts. Sweaty brown chests glistened as they swung pandanus leaf wands in complicated patterns around their bodies.

Roxi fell deeper and deeper into their captivating story-dance until she became one with these ancient Polynesian people.

"Wow, those were some totally cool performances, huh, Rox?" Dustin fidgeted as they ambled back along the waterfront.

Up ahead Brittany, Mama C, and Abbie had their heads together in conversation.

Reflections of Papeete's lights sparkled in the bay reminding Roxi of phosphorescent seas. Her steps slowed. "Are you referring to everything or just the hot vahines?"

"Both, I guess." He gave her one of his sweet lopsided grins.

Dustin's so cute. Now where did that thought come from? Roxi turned and gazed across the Sea of the Moon toward the enchanted isle of Moorea. A quarter moon and billions of stars lit misty razorback mountains. Kyle drifted into her reverie. She imagined him walking beside her—perhaps holding her hand or his arm draped around her shoulder. She trembled a little at that delicious image.

Dustin stopped abruptly. He stared in silence across the water for a minute.

Roxi started to ask what he was looking at when he took hold of her hand. His fingers felt cold and clammy. Her stomach flip-flopped. *What on earth?*

He leaned in. "Can you believe we're really here? In paradise?" His voice grew husky. "This island is even more awesome than I read about."

A salty breeze rustled the palms. Roxi's heartbeat thumped in her ears. Her own palms felt sweaty. She wished Brittany were here—or did she?

Dustin's dark brown puppy-dog eyes drew her in. Now his warm breath fell upon her cheek. *Was he going to kiss her?*

Roxi's hand slipped out of his shaky grasp breaking the spell.

"Rox, I didn't ... mean ... to ..." Dustin stammered.

"Brit said she'd ..." Roxi lost her train of thought.

"Sorry. The music. The dancing. The magic. Guess I got caught up in all the excitement." Dustin didn't look at her.

Her voice quivered. "That's okay." She swallowed the lump in her throat and tried to concentrate. "Oh, by the way, we're supposed to meet Brit in the morning at nine to catch the bus to Maeva Beach."

Dustin hung his head, looking miserable. "Don't know if I'll go."

Roxi paused for a moment. "Brit will be *very* disappointed. She has a new French bikini. Bet it's rad."

Dustin's head jerked up, his eyes wide, his smile grateful. "Hahaha. Since you put it that way, guess I'll be forced to join you."

She cracked a smile as the tension eased between them. Dustin was a good friend. Roxi didn't want to lose that.

At the quay, Roxi waved to Brittany's shadowy form that stood a few boats away. She shouted to her, "See you tomorrow." She punched Dustin's arm a bit harder than necessary. "You too, amigo."

She bounded away before he could retaliate, relieved to have the yachts moored along the shore. No long awkward dinghy ride to endure. Roxi leaped onboard, said a quick goodnight, and escaped to the sanctuary of her cabin.

She had lots to sort out. What a night.

Chapter Twenty-One: Daughters

CAROL

"Unbelievable." Carol raised her hands, palms up. "Your daughter Hannah ran away after high school?"

Abbie's voice matched her glum expression. "Yes. Problems began her junior year when she met the "Lost Boy." That's what I called him—no direction, no goals, no faith in God." Abbie's eyes betrayed her calm exterior.

The two women sat on a wooden bench overlooking the harbor waiting for Jon and Drew. Carol tried to decipher what those pale blue eyes were saying. *How did they even get on this topic of daughters?*

Carol bit her lip and cringed at thoughts of those teen years with Shalimar. As drug use increased, her daughter's behavior plunged into a destructive moodiness. She had to swap her *understanding-friend* role for the *tough-love* parent. When money and other valuables disappeared, she had been forced to change the locks on the doors to keep her daughter and unwholesome friends out.

Carol shook her head to clear away those regretful memories. "I can only imagine what you went through."

Worry lines deepened between Abbie's brows. "At first, I blamed myself, being too tolerant yet overprotective." Her hands trembled.

"So, she ran away with Lost Boy?"

"Yep. I had no idea where they lived for almost a year." Abbie's fingers balled into fists. "She only called a couple times asking for money. I felt abandoned—by Hannah, Andy—and Drew." The last name blasted from Abbie's lips like an expletive. Bitterness puckered her mouth. "Drew retreated into his work. I had no one to share my fears and anguish."

"I'm so sorry. I understand lonely and abandoned. First Dad left after the divorce, then Mom, Joe, and my brother Jimmy died. And I lost Shalimar long before she moved away for good. *Who would be next?*

Abbie cast her eyes down as her face grew pink. "Well, I wasn't completely alone. Jesus stood beside me through everything. And he helped Drew and me muddle through that rough patch. Adversity actually strengthened our marriage." Tears rolled down her cheeks. "But I still mourn the loss of my first grandbaby."

Carol's mouth opened wide. She couldn't speak for a moment. "What do you mean?"

"Hannah left Lost Boy and came home pregnant. I reassured her that we'd help, but she chose to give the baby girl up for adoption. I still think about that precious, little granddaughter. Try to picture what she would look like now, what her favorite books and toys would be." Abbie drew in a deep breath and then blew out slowly."

Carol nodded, then patted her friend's hand. "I know what having a pregnant teenage daughter is like. Shalimar was only seventeen when she had Roxi. She refused to give her up."

Remorse welled up in Carol's heart. With her own life so complicated and busy, she hadn't volunteered to help raise Roxi. Now, she had a granddaughter struggling with emotional problems after years of instability. She prayed the cycles of depression and addiction that had plagued her daughter, ex-husband, and other close relatives could be broken and not harm another family member.

Jon and Drew strolled toward their wives, smiling, like they didn't have a care in the world. Of course, they were looking forward to another night of festivities.

Carol exhaled. Men didn't have a clue. "I'm grateful to have a second chance with Roxi, to do things right this time, and hopefully have a better perspective now. During Shalimar's difficult years, a friend from my parents' group led me back into church and into reading the Bible. A relationship with God didn't solve all my problems but sure has helped me survive them."

Abbie gazed into Carol's eyes. "Yes, with God, all things are possible. He gives us strength to endure and hope to continue living."

That balmy evening Carol sent a quick prayer of gratitude towards heaven—for how far she had come in her personal journey, for this blessed season of her life, and for many wonderful family members and friends.

Dancing bodies glistened in the arena. Drums thumped a rapid rhythm. She turned at a commotion in the crowd. Sugar yelped as Pepper leapt over the low rope border and joined performers in a parody of the *tamure*. His potbelly jiggled. His hips gyrated wildly. Stubby hands sliced an erratic pattern as he attempted to imitate the dancer's fluid movements.

Music came to an abrupt halt. A wave of chanting Tahitian men surrounded Pepper and escorted him toward a shadowy corner of the lot. Campfires cast an eerie glow. The large crowd that followed drowned out his protests.

Sugar cast a tight frown that betrayed her anxiety as she sprinted by Carol. "Oh dear, ah hope they don't hurt my darlin'. He enjoys havin' fun with people."

Abbie's face looked like a deer in headlights. "Oh no. What do you think they're planning to do to him?"

Roxi spun around in front of Abbie. "Who knows? Trollman always manages to attract the wrong kind of attention."

Carol heard Pepper's shrill squeals before she saw him. He sounded like a pig knowing it's about to be slaughtered and roasted. Pepper writhed, helpless, held between two burly Polynesian men clothed only in ti leaf skirts. His toes bounced off stones as his partners paraded across a long glowing firepit. Their eyes were glassy, as if in a trance.

Carol's heart flickered with sympathy for the odd little man. She looked over at Abbie. "Pepper finds trouble quicker than a roomful of puppies."

At the far end of the pit stood the high priest. A square chin jutted out above broad shoulders that were pulled back, emphasizing his puffed-out chest. Ignoring Pepper's pleas, he scrutinized the native men as they stepped from the searing rocks. Both dropped to their knees and bowed deeply.

Pepper fell to the ground beside the men. His glazed eyes held a mixture of fear and awe. He leaned back and gawked at the apparition towering above him. "I'm very sorry, je m'excuse, so sorry," he pleaded over and over.

The priest's unique *more* drew Carol's attention. Shells, feathers, and bones were woven onto the plaited fiber skirt. Her breath caught. *Bones?* She flashed back to the Marquesas. *Are these peaceful islanders still practicing cannibalism?* Alarmed, she studied the priest. He reminded her of a giant parrot, his long black hair braided into an ornate headdress of bright red, green, and yellow feathers.

Standing in between Carol and Abbie, Sugar moaned, then lunged forward toward her husband.

Carol placed a restraining hand around her arm. "Wait."

"Wait for what?" Roxi cried. "Poor Trollman is about to be sacrificed!"

A hush came over the crowd. The high priest raised both arms wide. His carved-rock expression transformed into a benevolent smile. Booming mirth rose from his cavernous belly. He reached down and grasped Pepper who sagged in his arms like a rag doll. The priest kissed each cheek, then set Pepper down gently. In a deep bass, the priest boomed, "*Maeva. Oramatua mauruuru roa.* Welcome. The spirits of the dead thank you very much for your performance."

Pepper's mouth opened. He wiped his sweaty brow with shaky hands and finally stammered, "*Mau ... ru ... uru. Ia orana.* Th ... th ... thank you. May you live and prosper." His smile wavered as he bowed and backed away. He walked like a duck over to his wife, protecting his singed toes. They clung to each other, laughing and crying as the audience cheered.

Late that night, Carol reclined in the cockpit. Water lapped softly against the hull. Rigging jingled. She took a deep breath of the cool air. Poor Pepper. Why was his life so full of drama? Did he enjoy all that attention, even if sometimes negative?

She sucked in her breath. *Like Shalimar.* She recalled the time her daughter cut her beautiful auburn hair and dyed it black—and began wearing only dark clothing. Her actions seemed to mirror an unfathomable darkness within that she displayed by slashed wrists and drug overdoses—desperate cries for attention. Rehab and counseling gave temporary reprieves. Eventually Shalimar had been diagnosed as manic-depressive but refused to stay on meds.

Carol grieved for her lost daughter. But what could she do?

I can love her. I can forgive her. I can pray that she forgives me.

And I can trust God. She bowed her head.

Chapter Twenty-Two: Wonderland

ROXI

Dustin steered his inflatable across Cook's Bay toward Moorea's inner reef. As the dinghy picked up speed, Roxi's grandparents clutched the handholds.

Roxi sat between Brit and Dustin, but out of his reach because he was always doing stuff to irritate her. She turned halfway around and contemplated towering volcanic cliffs and peaks that crowned jungle-clad hills and embraced the bay. Faint harmonious singing rose from a building whose white spire poked through treetops. Cotton candy clouds drifted lazily above the church, reflecting in the glassy green water where a handful of yachts lay at anchor.

Roxi exhaled as tension oozed out every pore and evaporated. "Wow, this place is like living inside a painting."

Across from her Mama C's smile broadened. "This whole area is surreal. One of God's glorious masterpieces. We need to dig out our canvas, paints, and pastels."

Roxi studied her grandma. She looked a lot better than when they'd left California nine months ago. Less wrinkles on her bronzed forehead. Deeper smile lines. Maybe a few more gray hairs in her dark auburn hair. *Those are probably my fault.*

Her eyes shifted to PJ, who sat with his arm around Mama C. A twinge of apprehension fluttered in her stomach. His muscular body appeared to be shrinking. Although his biceps still bulged, a faint outline of ribs protruded. Even his Irish complexion had a bleached-out look. Only his lively green eyes held an intensity that lit up when he met Roxi's probing stare.

PJ misinterpreted her scrunched frown. "Are ya nervous 'bout snorklin', honey?"

She wanted to ask how he'd been feeling, but instead Roxi gave a rapid shake of her head. "No way. More like excited." She playfully splashed a handful of saltwater in his direction. The water splattered across Brittany's face. "Whoops."

Before she could apologize, her friend filled the bailing scooper and poured water over Roxi's head.

Sputtering, Roxi lunged.

PJ took ahold of each girl's shoulder and pulled them apart. "Okey-doke, let's call a truce before ya'll sink Dustin's dinghy."

Roxi glared.

Brit's eyes stared at the floorboard. Her skinny body didn't fill out that flowery bikini very well, Roxi thought with a satisfied smirk. Brit had been acting weird for almost a week. Had she found out about that night with Dustin? *That near-kiss hadn't been my fault. Had it?*

Dustin cut the motor, and PJ tossed the small anchor onto a patch of sandy seabed.

"Here we are." Mama C sorted through a duffel bag of fins, masks, and snorkels until everyone had a set in their size.

Dustin somersaulted backwards into the clear aquamarine water and dove down about ten feet to the reef. Brittany moved to where Dusin had been sitting and waved down at him.

Roxi swung around with a fluid motion and dangled her webbed feet in the crystal clear water. She gazed below at the aquarium scene beneath her.

"Ahh ..." Brittany tumbled overboard into the water—all of her except one finned foot that caught beneath the outboard's protruding handle. She dog-paddled madly to keep her head above the surface.

Roxi arched and reached back, pushing the fin sideways, freeing Brit.

Brittany splashed about and finally grabbed the dinghy railing, her face lobster-red. She tittered. "Hey, thanks for rescuing the klutz." She looked down for a moment, then gazed directly into Roxi 's eyes. "By the way, I'm sorry for pouring water on you. And for being so distant lately. I can't really explain why."

"No problema, mi amiga." Roxi sighed with relief. The memory of Brit dangling from the dinghy made her giggle. Brit's hesitant chuckle turned into boisterous laughter, and Roxi joined in. Things were getting back to normal.

Brit dove under as Roxi slid into the bath-temperature sea. Saltwater enveloped her like a warm cocoon. She defogged and adjusted her mask over her eyes and nose before clamping her lips around her snorkel.

Brittany's head bobbed up, and she pulled the snorkel from her mouth. "Take a look. You won't believe the awesomeness down there."

Roxi lowered her face. Taking a breath through her nose, the mask suctioned tight against her face. *Duh. Use the snorkel in your mouth, silly. Works a lot better for breathing.*

She peered down into a mermaid's wonderland. Fish of all sizes and shapes weaved among a forest of staghorn coral. A school of at least a hundred zebra-striped fish glided past, less than five-feet beneath her.

Mama C pulled out a Ziplock bag of frozen peas and shook out a handful. Feeding frenzy! A cloud of swirling colors encompassed her grandma.

Fish nibbled at Roxi's gloved hand, seeking more treats. One swam up to her mask and scrutinized her. Laughter bubbled from her mouth as seawater rushed in. Choking, she raised her head and spit. *Yuk.*

Brittany and Dustin were already paddling off toward another coral cluster, not exactly ignoring her, but clearly not thinking about her, either. Oh well. Ahead, PJ swam in a circle. He motioned to Roxi, and then pointed down. A beach ball-sized sea anemone attached to pink table coral waved in the gentle current. Three plump orange clownfish, whose broad yellow stripes were outlined in black, drifted among its poisonous stinging tendrils.

PJ dove below for a closer look.

Roxi attempted to but kept bobbing to the surface. *Probably all that baby fat.* Kicking extra hard, she remembered to slowly deflate her lungs and glided close to Nemo. What a cutie. He darted straight towards her. To greet her or protect his home?

Roxi drifted toward the surface in a cloud of bubbles. She loved being immersed in this amazing world beneath the sea. How cool would living down here be where everything was peaceful? From the corner of her eye, she glimpsed a shadowy figure emerge from behind a gigantic brain coral. Probably Dustin trying to sneak up on her. Pretending not to notice him, she whirled around as he drew close—and almost had a heart attack.

Her eyes bulged as she stared down into two dead black eyes. Shark! The fish swished by, its tailfin stirring up the sandy bottom. Roxi kicked to the surface, yanked out her snorkel, and screamed. Frantic, she splashed to the dinghy and launched herself in.

Her grandparents were right behind.

Dustin swam up and hung on the side. "Wow. That was rad. Did you guys see that blacktip reef shark? Musta been over six feet long."

PJ scowled, arms crossed. "Yeah, and I'd say it's time ya'll got outta the water."

Roxi white-knuckled the seat. "Dustin, are you suffering from oxygen deprivation?"

He chuckled. "Black and whitetip reef sharks won't hurt you." He pulled off his mask, rinsed, then adjusted it back into place and gave a lop-sided grin. "Those dudes are mellow. Only snack on reef fish, not us tasty humans."

Roxi's eyebrows rose. "Cross your heart and hope not to be eaten? And by the way, where's Brit?"

Dustin rolled his eyes. "Come on, scaredy-cat." He dragged her into the water. "There's a totally radical area I want to show you. Brittany's there."

She gave a longing glance at her grandparents, safe aboard the inflatable, dove in, and stayed glued to Dustin's side as they wound through a coral labyrinth, all pinks and purples. Bright blue and black angelfish with yellow striped designs coasted by. Two shy, long-snouted butterflyfish fluttered into a narrow opening. Diminutive neon-blue fish zoomed everywhere, contrasting with finger-sized purple and yellow fish.

Roxi breathed easier when she spotted Brit floating on the surface. Jaws hadn't eaten her. She was engrossed in something beneath her.

Roxi swam closer. A fat purple starfish, the size of a dinner plate with dangerous-looking orange spikes, had attached itself to coral near the ocean floor. She raised her head, spit out her snorkel, and waited for Brit to look up. "What planet did that thing come from?"

Brittany giggled. "Isn't that creature cool? Professor Campbell, our marine biology specialist can probably tell us."

"That is a crown-of-thorns." Dustin frowned. "*Not* cool and very harmful to the earth's vanishing reefs."

"Really?" Brittany's brow crinkled. "How can a starfish be a *major* threat to humongous coral forests?"

"These guys multiply and gobble up coral like rabbits devour a vegetable garden." Dustin glowered at her for a moment. He took a deep breath and dove to the starfish, which he tore off the coral. Placing the creature on the sandy bottom, he hefted a rock and pulverized the freakish critter.

"Stop," Brittany sobbed. When Dustin surfaced, she thrust a wave of water at him. "You shouldn't have done that. Starfish are part of this ocean habitat too."

"Yeah, but those kind are not a good part." Dustin clenched his jaw and kicked away.

Roxi followed him and a reluctant Brit trailed behind.

Quarrels made Roxi's stomach hurt, but her tension soon dissolved. Who could stay upset when the vibrant reef rippled with tendrils of yellow and orange sea anemone, spiny sea urchins, and a collage of fish darting among lacy tube, mushroom, and delicate fan corals?

Eventually their bodies chilled and fatigued. Roxi shivered as the three amigos slowly stroked toward the dinghy. Casting a wistful glance down, she spotted a small group of green and sapphire parrotfish—the cleaning crew.

Their beak-like mouths feasted on algae that grew on the coral. *Sweet.* She needed to immerse herself in this land of enchantment one last time. Tapping Brit on the arm, they dove to the sea floor as Dustin hoisted himself aboard.

Roxi floated upwards and gave a wide grin as she held up a slim blue starfish which fit inside her hand.

Mama C took the treasure from her.

A moment later Brit popped up. A beautiful shell with intricate brown and black patterns lay in her upturned palm. "Look what—"

Dustin reached over and swiftly knocked the seashell back into the sea.

"Hey, why did you do that?" Brittany snapped and glared. She turned to dive after her prize. Dustin caught her arm like a spring-loaded trap.

He glared back. "Do you have any idea what you were holding?"

Brittany scowled. "Well, Mr. Know-It-All, that *was* a new shell for my collection."

"Wrong, Miss Smartie. That's a cone shell. And the animal living inside injects a highly poisonous dart when he's been disturbed."

"Oh my." Brittany paled and her voice shook. "I had no idea." Clinging to the dinghy's side rail, she pulled herself half out of the water and planted a kiss on Dustin's cheek. "Thanks for saving my life."

Dustin's face reddened. "No prob. Everyone needs to be aware of what you touch around here, that's all."

Mama C nodded. "That's for sure. Many dangers are camouflaged among all this beauty."

Roxi shuddered at thoughts of poisonous shells, ravenous starfish and sharks. But magic lived here also among this alien world.

PJ tugged at the anchor. "I suggest we all do a little more studyin' of South Pacific sea life before we try this again."

Dustin yanked the cord and fired up the motor. Each lost in their own thoughts, the weary explorers chugged back to the tranquil beauty of Cook's Bay shimmering in late afternoon sunshine.

Chapter Twenty-Three: Moorea Casts Its Spell

ROXI

A lush rainforest of banyans, ti, crotons, ferns, and vines obscured the Opunohu Valley from the one-lane dirt road that snaked up the mountain. "Hey, Dad, are we almost there?" Brittany's flushed face glistened.

Red's dark eyes scanned the ground like he was tracking an animal. Or maybe trying to avoid stepping on something—like a snake.

Roxi made sure to follow in his footsteps.

"Getting there." Red swiped his forehead.

Toby smirked as he walked next to his dad. He gave a quick glance back and down at his younger sister. "Wimpy."

Brittany scowled at the back of his head and stuck out her tongue.

Breathing grew more difficult as Roxi struggled to keep up with all of their giant strides. "Your smart aleck brother should be dribbling basketballs across a court, not hiking Jurassic Park." Through occasional clearings, she caught glimpses of spiny pineapple fields and the fragrant vanilla orchid vines that she loved. Community vegetable patches of taro, pumpkin, cassava, cucumbers, and kava struggled against tendrils of encroaching jungle.

"I agree, and you should be dancing on a stage somewhere. But what should I be doing?" Brittany looked lost in thought for a moment. "Maybe taking care of animals or something to do with the ocean? I love both of those. Hiking through jungles is not my thing. Looks like Dustin's mom is into this *Indiana Jones* habitat, though."

Juanita lagged, stopping to examine and collect botanical samples. Her thick braid swung over her shoulder as she bent to scribble notes and sketches in a thick journal.

Roxi snickered. "Check out her sixties-era knitted rainbow bikini under that see-thru skirt." PJ refers to her as that peace-loving flower child. He's made his views quite clear he doesn't agree with her politics. I stay clear when he gets riled up in a political debate."

"Yeah, I would too." Brittany dabbed her forehead. "I think Dustin's dad is even more spacey."

Roxi inspected Ray. His bushy salt and pepper beard made up for the shortage of scalp hair, which he covered by wearing a beat-up Panama hat. Behind his kinda cool John Lennon glasses, his squinty eyes scrutinized every scenic view, oblivious to everyone around him.

"Poor Dustin." Roxi shook her head. "He sure has strange parents." *But who am I to talk*? She didn't even have a dad, and her wacky mom who lived in soap opera land, traipsed from one audition to the next seeking the perfect role. Most of the parts never suited her or she them. Didn't really matter. The point being, Star wasn't present, even when home. Roxi sometimes fantasized about living in a normal family like Alex's.

"Hey, Brit, check out these cool flowers." Dustin spoke with an affectionate lilt.

The uncharacteristic tone of his voice caught Roxi's attention, and she realized that Brit wasn't beside her anymore. Curious, she half-turned before Mama C grabbed her hand and pulled her forward. "What're ya doing?" Roxi tugged her hand away and glanced back.

Dustin tucked a lavender orchid behind Brittany's ear.

Brit's eyes sparkled as she whispered something to him.

Roxi strained but couldn't catch a single word. Dustin must have liked what she said, though because he broke into a broad grin.

"You know Roxi, I'm growing concerned again about your grandpa." Mama C's voice intruded on Roxi's eavesdropping.

Roxi blew out her breath and turned to her grandma. A pang of worry grumbled in her gut. "Yeah, PJ doesn't seem to have much energy these days. What do you think is wrong?"

"I'm not sure, but this illness has gone on far too long. The doctor in the Marquesas was probably on the right track. Diabetes." Mama C's frown deepened. "I wish Jon would eat better."

"He's going to be okay, though, right?" Her shoulders slouched.

"Oh, hon, I didn't mean to alarm you. Your grandpa will be fine." Mama C gave a vague smile. "But I'll rest easier once he sees a doctor in New Zealand."

She didn't sound very convincing, but Roxi nodded. The road, now asphalt, grew steeper. Calf muscles tightened in protest. She turned to check out Brit and Dustin and couldn't believe what she saw. Now the two lovebirds were swinging their joined hands in unison.

Mama C reached out a steadying hand as Roxi stumbled. She peeked back to see what had caused the distraction.

"Ah hah, looks like the enchanted isle has cast another spell." She gave a knowing smile.

Roxi remained silent. She seriously doubted any guy would ever look at her the way Dustin gazed at Brit.

"Hey, Rox, beat feet. We got a ride." Dustin rushed past, pulling Brittany along.

Her grandma gave a breathless, "Thank goodness. I'm glad Jon stayed on the boat to rest today. This hill would have done him in." Sweat drenched her bangs.

Roxi stared at their ride. PJ would have called the dusty antique pickup that stopped in the road a classic. She hoped the truck could carry them to the top of the mountain. Two friendly farmers, faces and clothing streaked with dirt, motioned them over. "*Ia ora na*. Hello." Their dark faces beamed.

The group flopped into the mini-truck bed like sardines in a can. Relief showed on everyone's face as they groaned, "*Mauruuru roa*. Thank you very much."

The old truck creaked around steep switchbacks for the final mile. Red jumped off at the top and bellowed, "Whew, what a hill. Got that ride in the nick of time." He shook the driver's hand and gave him a few Pacific francs. Everyone waved grateful goodbyes.

"At least the four-mile trek back is all downhill." Roxi felt ready for a nap. She took in the breath-taking view from Belvedere Lookout. That woke up her mind and enthusiasm for an instant. Mt Rotui and Mt Tautuapae stood like sentinels, their feet bundled in a luxurious blanket of emerald and hunter green. Opunohu's azure bay glittered like a precious gem between them. "Awesome," she whispered. "Almost worth the climb."

Mama C consulted her map in the *Lonely Planet* guidebook, then pointed out landmarks. "Look, over there is Cook's Bay."

"Yeah, if so, where's our boats?" Roxi was hot and hungry. She ignored Mama C's reply. Why hadn't she stayed on *Dawn's Dove*? At least it was cool in the shadows of the bay, and she could have gone swimming after she ate all the snacks she wanted without any nagging.

A gentle sea breeze cooled sweaty bodies while they picnicked, took photos, and dozed—all except Ray. He ignored food, choosing the nourishment that creativity satisfied. Roxi munched a sandwich while she studied his techniques as he painted brilliant watercolor sketches. After a while, she grew restless and scooted next to Brit, who practically sat on Dustin's lap. Both friends gave her dreamy smiles, their thoughts clearly not on her. She felt like a third person stumbling on stage during a dance duo.

A loud ruckus in the bushes drew her attention. A clucking mother hen and her peeping flock of chicks scrambled out from the underbrush. They paraded across everyone's blankets, pecking at picnic crumbs. Once satisfied, the family vanished into the brush on the other side of the clearing.

The three friends looked wide-eyed at each other before laughter erupted.

"What was that?" Roxi choked out. Laughing with her friends again renewed her joy.

"On this journey, I'm learning to expect the unexpected." Brittany grinned.

"Words of wisdom from our wise sage." Dustin put his hands together and bowed. "Yes, this island definitely possesses a crazy, alluring magic."

Dumbfounded. Roxi thought it not at all like Dustin to blurt out such nonsense. He usually kept his emotions hidden. Except that one night, across the sea, when Dustin almost kissed her. Or had that been her imagination?

She stifled a groan. He and Brit were back in la-la land—fingers intertwined, speaking secret thoughts, their eyes glued to one another. Roxi gave up trying to figure them out. "See ya later," she murmured to the air. She walked away, unnoticed.

The following day, Roxi got to hear all the sappy details of the blossoming romance. Beneath a crescent moon set in a black velvet sky sparkling with diamonds, Brit and Dustin had tasted their first kiss. Wavelets swished around their feet as a soft breeze carried words of endearment that mingled with the rustle of palms.

Heart-shaped Moorea, isle of enchantment, had woven a spell once again. Capturing two young souls in its delicate embrace, they had clung to each other and to that moment, not knowing how much time they had together before their yachts sailed toward different shores.

Chapter Twenty-Four: Bloody Mary's

CAROL

Carol and Abbie slid off their bikes and joined their small group along the shoulder of a crude road in Bora Bora which had been built by American forces during WWII. Carol glanced at Abbie. "Sure you're up for a twenty-mile ride?"

"You bet." Abbie's smile faltered. "I get a little wobbly when I get tired, so hopefully we'll stop to rest a few times."

"Don't worry. I'll make sure we have plenty of rest stops." This time, her smile wavered. "I wish you weren't leaving for the States in two days. Our time together has been so wonderful. I always feel calmer when you're around."

"I feel the same." A sheen of tears softened Abbie's blue eyes. "But I need to get back to the grandkids. And me and ocean crossings aren't compatible with this darn Parkinson's."

"Two months is a long time to be without you, but at least we've made a supportive group of friends to share this cruising life." Carol sniffled and rubbed her nose.

Abbie's smile brightened. "And we can always talk by phone patch, or a calling card, when you arrive in New Zealand."

"Definitely." Carol readjusted her bicycle seat as their party of cruising friends prepared to pedal the island's perimeter. She hopped on her bike. "You know, author James Michener was stationed here. He modeled the mysterious island of Bali Hai in *Tales of the South Pacific* from Bora Bora."

Abbie nodded as they headed out from Faanui. "And I read that most of the filming actually took place where we were anchored in Moorea. I can't decide which island is more beautiful."

Before Carol could reply, a middle-aged couple rode up beside them. "Mind if we join you?"

"The more the merrier. I'm Carol and that's my husband, Jon, ahead of us." She smiled and studied the woman for a moment, admiring her reddish gold hair styled in a French braid. Then she raked her fingers through her own frizzy ponytail. "Wish I knew how to make your fancy braid."

"I'm Alicia. I can teach you the technique. French braiding is easy once you practice a few times." She glanced at her husband. "Paul and I arrived yesterday on *Holding Pattern*. I know that's a strange name for our ketch, but my husband is a pilot and I'm a retired flight attendant."

Jon had slowed his bike until he rode alongside the new couple. "Howdy. I remember hearin' you talk on the net durin' the crossin'. Guess you folks are used to lots of travelin'."

Paul shook his head. "Yes, but it's taken some adjustment to the sea turtle pace." He stretched his lean frame back, rolling his shoulders. "Nothing goes to windward like a 747."

Jon chuckled. "That's fer sure. Ya know, I built them planes ya flew. Retired from Boeing last year."

A few minutes later, the group stopped for a break. Roxi and Brittany cruised up to the adult pack that had sprawled beneath a huge banyan tree. "I'm pooped already." Roxi dropped her bike in the dirt.

"Ditto." Brittany set hers on its kickstand.

Carol ambled over. "Do you gals want to hike to the marae with us? The trail is only a quarter mile." She pointed to an opening through the thicket.

Brittany's smile held an apology. "No thanks."

Roxi's lip curled. "Nope. Seen one, seen them all. Not my thing."

Is that granddaughter of mine ever going to change? Carol walked away from the girls. She almost turned around when she heard Roxi say, "At least we didn't get the 'You may never pass this way again' lecture."

Brittany giggled. "Yeah, there's lots I like about these islands, but piles of old stones isn't one of them."

Abbie motioned to Carol to join the hikers, which saved her from saying something she'd regret later. *See, that's one of many reasons why Abbie needs to stay.*

Thirty minutes later, the adults emerged from the bush trail. Red called to the girls who were still propped against the banyan's giant roots. "You girls should have come with us. The stone *ahu* was massive, over one hundred and fifty feet long and nine feet tall. They used the structure as a landmark for approaching ships in the days before GPS."

His daughter, Brit, didn't respond, but continued to stare out at sea.

Roxi shrugged. "Not really in the mood for a history lesson."

As everyone got back on their bikes, Carol noticed both girls kept their distance from each other. They must have had a disagreement. Well, not surprising. Roxi was having one of her snarky attitude days. She'd probably make things worse if she intervened, so hopefully the girls would work out their issue among themselves.

Abbie's husband, Drew, asked the guys about a boat sinking last week.

Paul clucked his tongue. "Wasn't that on the reef surrounding Huahine? We spent a few days there."

Red frowned. "Those strong currents can throw off your chart position. Plus, going through the pass in late afternoon is never a good idea. It's difficult to see any coral bommies."

Jon adjusted his sunglasses. "Well, the good news is that young couple survived and hitched a ride on an older gent's boat. Everyone's gettin' the help they're needin'."

Roxi pedaled beside Abbie and Carol.

Her granddaughter glanced over, her sad eyes narrow as her mouth tightened. "If only Rob had let someone crew on his boat and help him, he'd probably still be here with us."

Abbie gave a deep sigh. "Possibly, but man can only plan his course. The Lord is the one who determines his steps."

"So true." Carol's thin smile melted into a scowl as they rounded a bend. "Oh no. What have they done to paradise?" Resorts and shops jutted over pristine water and littered the verdant valley in careless splotches. Drawing near the southern tip of Pofai Bay, her initial shock gradually mellowed when she spotted a huge hut a quarter mile ahead. Her heart rate quickened. A thatched roof adorned a cabin-sized structure constructed of logs, stones, and woven matting. "Isn't that the infamous Bloody Mary's?"

The cycling group dismounted, locked their bikes to palm trees, and ambled over to inspect two enormous tikis whose faces were carved into fierce expressions.

Roxi marched over to her grandparents and mimicked one of the monoliths. Her tongue hung out, bulging eyes crossed.

"You'll scare the enemy and locals with that there look." Jon chuckled as he snapped her photo.

"That's what I've been telling you guys forever—ugly and scary, that's me." Roxi ignored his protests as they entered the restaurant. She scuffed across the sand floor to the restroom and followed the other females in. Minutes later, she came out babbling. "Guess what PJ? The sinks in the bathroom are miniature waterfalls!"

"Ha-ha. More than that are waterfalls in the men's room." Jon winked at the guys.

Puzzled, Roxi's eyebrows scrunched together. She peeked over at Brit and mouthed, "Does he mean the urinals?" They both giggled with sudden understanding.

Carol's glare at her husband could have withered the hibiscus bush out front. But she chose to give a smile instead of a lecture and changed the subject to something more appropriate. "Let's find a table. I'm famished."

As they all studied menus, Roxi glanced across the table at Brittany. She wiggled her eyebrows and slid her gaze toward the bathrooms. Another round of muffled laughter rippled from the girls.

Thank goodness. The girls were back to their normal silliness. Carol relaxed as she took in the ambience of the room. Sixties music bounced off walls of bamboo and matting. Overhead fans spun lazily, spreading aromas of sizzling meat, onions, and garlicky pizza. Her mouth watered.

A server attired in a Hawaiian shirt and shorts soon delivered their order. Carol bowed her head. "Bless this food, Lord, and thank you for the privilege of enjoying a bit of earthly paradise among good friends."

Jon bit into his juicy cheeseburger, then dipped a fry in ketchup.

Carol pressed her lips together. *Enjoy the greasy junk food while you can, Jon, because tomorrow you're back to fruits and veggies.* That might make him grumpy but was worth it to see him regaining some muscle and vitality.

When they resumed their island circumnavigation, the men requested a stop behind Hotel Matira to hike the ten-minute trail up to where heavy seven-inch military guns and bunkers had been abandoned by the US Army and Navy after WWII.

The women chose a different footpath to the ridge where they all raved about the captivating view. A necklace of low-lying coral atolls encircled Bora Bora's magnificent blue lagoons and thriving reefs. Lush green valleys blossomed with a diversity of fragrant flowers popping in vivid reds and yellows. Behind them at the island's center towered two dramatic pinnacles capped in puffs of whipped cream. Even Roxi and Brittany seemed impressed.

"Look, there's Raiatea and Tahaa." Alicia pointed a slender finger southward. "Paul and I spent an amazing week there among remote anchorages and explored the Faaroa River by kayak. The experience was surreal, paddling through tunnels of trees and tropical jungle, chattering birds our only companions." She swiped a droplet of sweat rolling down her freckled cheek. "Did you know Polynesia's largest marae is on Raiatea?"

"Oh great. More rock talk," Roxi grumbled. She and Brit headed back down the trail.

After their hikes, the cyclists left the modern world's congestion behind as they rounded the island's eastern coastline. Tropical vegetation was broken only by an occasional primitive village, where squawking chickens skittered away from their tires. Grinning islanders waved as if they were watching a parade. "*Ia Orana*. Hello. Welcome," everyone shouted as they passed.

Every few miles they stopped, and Carol, acting as unofficial guide, would draw attention to another spectacular angle of Mounts Pahia and Otemanu. "Those basalt peaks are over 2,000 feet high. I've heard there're guided hikes, but I can't fathom climbing up there."

"No thanks." Abbie gave a little shiver. "Even if I could, I wouldn't care to traipse through all that tangly jungle and then claw my way up volcanic rocks. Not my cup of tea."

All gazes then turned toward the eastern lagoon where two sailboats anchored near a motu. Reflections of the boats shimmered in the crystal water of the low-lying coral sand islet, making the motu look like a postcard.

Red grunted. "I don't know if I'd chance taking our boat through that winding narrow channel to get inside there even though that looks like a remarkable spot. *Sea Eagle* draws seven feet." His mouth tightened. "Not much leeway for error. Teavani Pass into the main lagoon was challenging enough."

Paul nodded. "I agree. I've heard from several sources that navigating that pass can be stressful. I wouldn't want to damage our boat so far away from boatyards and marine stores."

Carol scowled at the men. "I'll tell you what's nerve-wracking—all these noisy tourists rushing around on jet skis, tour boats, mopeds, and quads." Her arm stretched toward the serene motu with three thatched huts set near a white sand beach, palm trees swaying.

"That's what Jon and I came cruising for—isolated places like that."

"Well, I didn't!" Roxi's red face looked ready to burst into flames. "Who wants to be stuck on a rock with nowhere to go and nothing to do?" She took off on her bicycle, leaving Carol speechless.

Chapter Twenty-Five: Haumata

Roxi

Wispy pines, pandanus, and coconut-laden palms sprouted near the shoreline of tiny Motu Piti Aau. Roxi splashed through the lagoon's shallows as her grandparents strolled the soft sand. Across the brushy quarter-mile strip of land, a distant roar of waves crashed upon the reef. Seagulls circled, screeching for treats.

Roxi thought Mama C seemed much calmer today after yesterday's near calamity as they had motored through the pass. The rush of an incoming tide hadn't helped. PJ had maneuvered the boat along the slim, twisty channel with the assistance of Mama C's directions. Her grandma had raced between deck and chart table recalculating their position every five minutes using the GPS to keep their sailboat from hitting any charted reefs beneath them.

Mama C used her uncanny radar and zeroed in on Roxi's thoughts. She gave a rueful grin. "I still can't believe our near mishap yesterday. Our chart indicated for us to curve right of the marker in the most critical part of the narrows."

PJ grunted. "Yep, and if we woulda done that, we'd still be sittin' atop that coral bommie. Thank goodness for clear water and that remarkable lookout at the bow." He grinned at Roxi. "Ya warned us in the nick of time."

Mama C nodded. "Our granddaughter saved the day—and our boat."

Roxi flexed her arms like Wonder Woman, then stopped mid-stride. Out of the thicket bounded a native girl, about ten or eleven years old. Her boyish body, the color of cocoa, was clad only in a pair of flowered panties. Behind the girl trailed three younger ones, similarly attired. It didn't seem to bother any of them, but she averted her eyes slightly.

"Uh, hello," Roxi said and placed a hand over her heart. "You almost gave me a heart attack jumping out of the bushes like that." The girls giggled but said nothing. She tried again. "Ia Orana."

The older girl brushed her long ebony hair away from eyes as dark as the Polynesian night and smiled slightly. "Ia Orana."

Mama C spoke in French. "*Bonjour. Parlez vous Francais? Ou habitez-vous?* Do you live here?"

"*Oui.*" The girl pointed further up the shore and motioned them to follow.

The small girls skipped ahead. In a wide clearing, a wizened old man sat in front of a stilted thatch hut patching a frayed fishing net. When he stood, he measured only a couple inches taller than Roxi, and his stomach was round as a globe. Skin the shade of old coconut husks contrasted with silvery-white hair topping his head like puffs of cotton. As he shuffled toward them, his eyes lit up and arms opened wide.

Roxi only recognized a few of the words he spoke. In a matter of minutes, a group of men, women, and children had gathered around the newcomers. A tall woman, early twenties maybe, stepped forward and spoke in English.

"*Maeva*. Welcome. My name is Mira. I'm teacher on the main island." She introduced Hitiona, the patriarch, and his large extended family. "My father invite you to rest." She pointed to a log in the shade.

Hitiona's wife, Moca carried over green coconuts that had straws protruding from rough-cut holes. Roxi took a tentative sip. The refreshing liquid had a subtle coconut flavor. She smacked her lips. "If only they had ice cubes. Don't they have refrigerators?"

PJ chuckled. "Not much electricity out this way. No refrigeration, no lights, no television."

"No way! How can people live without TV or computer games? That's worse than living on a boat."

"Mauruuru." Mama C thanked the family matriarch. She unzipped her backpack, pulling out a bag of hard candy and small toys for the youngsters crowding around her. Older kids exclaimed over colored pens, pencils, and paper. She handed a notebook-sized laminated world map to PJ.

He held the map high for everyone to see and put his finger on the west coast of North America. "This is California, where we lived." He traced their route, recounting funny and scary moments, pausing often so Mira could translate.

Haumata tapped Roxi's arm and motioned her to come away.

Mama C nodded her consent. "I know you can't get lost or in much trouble out here, but be careful."

The girls weaved along an overgrown path. Roxi slapped at mosquitos in the itchy brush until a caress of cool ocean air lifted hair off her damp neck. She peeked around Haumata. No people, only a white sand beach that cradled a scattering of top shells, bonnets, and other varieties of shells she'd been studying about. Beyond the reef stretched an endless sea painted in shades of blue.

"Sweet." Roxi melted onto a shaded patch of powdery sand next to motu girl. Above, graceful palms arched, shaped by decades of trade winds. She sighed with contentment.

Wait. She rubbed her eyes and blinked. *Am I seeing things?* Several of the shells close to the water's edge moved. She crept close, Haumata by her side. Hermit crabs in their portable homes scurried across damp sand.

Haumata placed a walnut-sized murex shell in Roxi's palm. The crab poked its head in and out. "Poor creature. I'd be freaked too if I was trapped in the hand of a giant." The scratchy feet tickled as it scrambled around her palm, and she giggled.

Her friend babbled in Tahitian. Roxi had no clue what she said, but eventually they discovered a few common words of mostly English and French. When that failed, they drew pictures in the sand or pantomimed.

Voices sounded nearby. Haumata's grandfather, Hitiona, and two young men clutching spear guns stepped from the brush and headed for the reef. Mama C and PJ followed a few feet behind the barefoot men. Roxi's grandparents waved, then tread cautiously in their reef shoes onto the exposed portion of the reef, stopping often to gaze into tidepools. The two divers clambered to the reef's drop-off, where they slipped on worn fins and masks and dove in.

Haumata pranced out barefoot along the jagged, uneven rocks and coral like they were marshmallows. She squatted beside Roxi's grandparents and studied the placid pool. Plucking out a purple sea urchin, she cracked its shell against a rock and scooped something out.

Something gross. Roxi stooped and forced herself not to gag as her friend offered her one. She shook her head no. "Uh, *aita mauruuru.*" She gulped as Haumata popped the slimy morsel into her mouth and chewed. *Well, maybe for her it was like eating potato chips or something.*

At reef's edge, Hitiona baited a rusty hook using a piece of fresh crab. With a flick of his wrist, he tossed the line out, then slowly wound in the homemade handline again and again.

Within minutes one of the divers came partially out of the water and waved a bloody snapper above his head. He gave a shout and flung the fish far onto the reef. Haumata rushed over and strung it onto a heavy cord.

In broken French and hand gestures, Mama C asked, "Why do they throw the fish way up here instead of laying their catches near them?"

Haumata's pearly teeth flashed into a fierce expression. She pointed to where her uncles were diving. "Many mao."

"There's sharks in the water?" Mama C's mouth hung open, eyes wide.

Roxi tiptoed over, stepping carefully to where another flopping fish lay and tried to pick it up. The slippery finned demon kept squirming from her grasp. She finally stomped on it.

Haumata bounded over, laughing, and grabbed the fish with one hand. "*Mauruuru.*"

"Sure, no problem." She grimaced as she rinsed the scaly stink off her hands in a nearby tidepool, then wiped them dry on her salt-encrusted shorts.

The sun was descending behind the mountainous peaks of Bora Bora, casting an orangish glow, as the group returned to the family village carrying a full line of fish, a small octopus, and bag of crabs. Roxi and her grandparents bid goodbye to their new friends.

Hitiona smiled at them and spoke in his native tongue. Mira translated for him. "My father says, 'Please, tomorrow come again'."

Days blurred together. On their seventh morning, after boat chores and schoolwork, Roxi dove into the ten-foot-deep swimming-pool-blue water and swam ashore. She helped Haumata hang laundry. Afterwards, using palm fronds, they swept around several huts. Doing chores with a friend wasn't nearly so boring as doing them alone, and what they did next made the work even more worthwhile.

Sweaty and grubby, the girls raced to the end of the motu to snorkel in a natural waterpark aptly named The Aquarium. The two girls swished through The Aquarium's canyons of coral carried by a current that rushed around the point. Roxi wore dive gloves to fend off the prickly pastel coral garden sculptures. Butterfly, zebra, unicorn, and small neon fishes drifted by her mask, completely indifferent to human intrusion as they searched for a meal. Or maybe they were having fun like her.

The virtual reality ride lasted ten minutes before the current dissipated. Then they swam to shore, ran back around the point, and waded out into the swirling waterway to float back through again. Over and over they explored the underwater fantasyland until Roxi couldn't stop shivering and her stomach rumbled.

Riding the current was sooo totally rad. She couldn't remember ever having this much fun, even with Alex. She hated to admit it, but she was glad for this special time she had been given on this secluded isle with Haumata and her friendly family.

Most days, the girls would eat lunch aboard *Dawn's Dove*. In the drowsy heat of afternoon they would curl up, side by side, in the cockpit. The sail awning provided a shady haven as they read together picture books and easy readers like Dr. Seuss.

Haumata's English vocabulary grew better every day. Roxi's French improved too. Teaching her friend fulfilled a need she didn't even know she had and gave her a new purpose. Something had altered inside her, although she couldn't pinpoint what was different.

Unfortunately, not much had changed on the outside. Roxi still waited with impatience for her chipmunk cheeks to hollow out and freckles to blend into a flawless tan. Her goofy hair screamed, "hopeless." Although it had grown a few inches and now shined with golden highlights, her locks remained a tangled mess. If only she had Brittany's straight hair.

"Poor Brit," Roxi thought. Could she still be moping for her now steady boyfriend Dustin? He and his parents, aboard *Harmony,* had left a week ago and headed north to the Cook Islands. And Brit's yacht, *Sea Eagle*, had sailed almost the opposite direction towards Tonga. As usual, Roxi had been testy with her friend when they talked on the VHF radio. But honestly, what was the big deal? The two lovebirds would only be apart for a few weeks until they reunited in New Zealand. *Maybe I should have encouraged Brit's dreams instead of making fun of them? Sometimes dreams* were *all you had. All that kept you going.*

Haumata nudged her. "What you think?"

"Huh? Oh, wishing Brit could be here too. She would love this place"

Haumata's eyebrows rose. "Who she? A friend?"

"Hopefully she still is." Roxi pointed toward the profusion of fluttering palms on shore. "What do you use all those coconuts for?" She hungered to learn everything about these Polynesian islanders and their land. Their lives were so different. So uncomplicated. The opposite of hers. Everyone took care of each other, which must give them a sense of belonging and security. She tried to imagine growing up here among so many brothers and sisters as she French-braided Haumata's thick hair.

Her friend replied in sing-song English. "Green coconuts we drink. White meat good to eat. Brown nuts shred meat, make coconut cream. That my job. Old nuts dry for copra.

Roxi finished the long braid. Far from perfect, but she had improved. "Anything else?"

Haumata's hands wove pictures for each use. "Make cup and bowl from shell. Use palm frond for matting, baskets, and more."

"Sounds like you use everything from the tree for many purposes. Nothing is wasted." She grinned. "You shouldn't ever have to worry about running out among these hundreds of trees and new ones sprouting everywhere."

Two weeks had passed since they dropped anchor in Bora Bora's eastern lagoon. The leisurely pace on motu time had affected *Dawn's Dove*'s entire crew. Even master planner Mama C could be found taking afternoon siestas or swinging in the foredeck hammock while reading. When PJ wasn't catnapping, he would tinker on the boat, fish with the local men, or practice new wood carving techniques with Hitiona.

Out near the point, Haumata, her young sisters, and Roxi put final touches on their huge sandcastle. She rose to take a quick dip and rinse off the itchy sand caked on her sun screened legs and arms. Thigh-deep, out of the current, Roxi closed her eyes and plunged beneath the surface.

Breath burst from her lungs in a cloud of bubbles. Something had clamped vise-like around her right ankle.

Shark! Is this going to be the final day of my brief insignificant life?

Chapter Twenty-Six: Kyle

ROXI

Panic-stricken, Roxi gave a fierce kick to dislodge the maneater biting into her lower leg. Desperate for air, she thrashed her way upward. As her head broke the surface, she screamed, but only a choked gurgle emerged.

As quickly as Jaws had attacked, the beast released its grip. Stinging saltwater blinded her. She could only imagine the bloody mangled remnant that used to be her foot. Odd though, because she felt no pain. She launched herself toward the blurry shore—and smacked into Kyle.

Kyle? They hadn't seen each other since Hiva Oa. Clinging to his rock-hard arms, she sputtered, "There's a ... what are you ...?" After a moment realization dawned on her. She raised her foot from the water. Still there. No gory stump. Terror dissolved into relief before igniting into fiery outrage at his prank. She pummeled his chest using both fists.

"You jerk! Thought I was a goner." With one hand she swiped her dripping hair off her face. "And what are you doing here, anyway?"

Kyle's mouth twisted, trying to hide amusement. "Whoa, Little One."

Searching his eyes, Roxi's fury reflected back at her as she continued her tongue-lashing.

Kyle's eyes frowned. "Honest, Roxi, I'm so sorry. I only wanted to have a little fun and surprise you. I never meant to frighten you." He brushed a few remaining strands of hair off her cheek, tucked them behind her ear, and cleared his throat. "By the way, it's great to see you."

Her anger melted like butter on a stack of hotcakes. She slumped against him, the adrenaline rush gone. He held her close against his chest and she listened to his strong heartbeat. It felt good, in a weird kind of way, to be in his arms. After a minute, she disengaged herself and backstroked away.

"We've got lots of catching up to do." He flashed a smile. "Want to go to Stingray City this afternoon?"

Excitement swirled like currents in the pass. "Awesome. I'll check with my grandparents." Suddenly she remembered Haumata and pointed over Kyle's shoulder. "Can I bring a friend?"

He turned and looked toward the island girl on the beach. She gave a friendly wave, and he did the same. He glanced back to Roxi and nodded. "I'll pick you both up at 1400. At your boat?"

She grinned. "We'll be waiting."

Kyle's dinghy bounced around Bora Bora's Matira Point, then planed across the water as the inflatable gathered speed. Flashes of color zipped beneath Roxi and Haumata.

"Looks amazing down there," Roxi shouted above the motor's whine.

Kyle leaned toward her. "Fabulous snorkeling. Let's come back tomorrow."

Minutes later, they slowed over a sandy shelf on the reef. Hordes of tourists from three boats splashed and hollered like a bunch of hunter seals. Kyle shook his head and anchored several yards away. "I'll be shocked if there's any sea life around for miles with all that racket."

Roxi nodded as she slipped on her mask and inserted the snorkel. The three eased into the aquamarine water. She and Haumata balanced on tiptoes to keep contact on the bottom. She laid her face in the water and peered down. Several dark shapes glided their way, and she pulled her legs up, treading water. Raising her head, she spit the snorkel out. "Hey, don't rays sting or bite?"

Kyle shook his head. "Only if you startle or make them mad."

"Great. How do you know if you do that?"

"Guess when they sting or bite you." He snickered.

Haumata giggled, then dove under and swam away.

Roxi gathered her nerve and lowered her head again, floating on the surface. *Whoa.* A dozen diamond-shaped eagle rays swirled along the bottom in the most graceful ballet. They had the cutest faces with perpetual smiles and trailed long skinny tails. She held very still and took shallow breaths as one that had about a three-foot wingspan passed between Kyle's outstretched legs. Beneath her, Haumata glided by holding onto one!

Roxi lowered her legs in slow motion until her toes snuggled into the sand. A few seconds later, the tickle of a soft wing brushed her calves. She willed herself not to jerk her legs up to her chin and inhaled a few calming breaths. A baby ray circled several times, probably searching for food like the tourists fed them. The eagle ray rolled on its side and rubbed its smooth belly against her shins before departing. She looked up as the last ray coasted away.

"That was sooo rad! Like one of those scenes in a National Geographic special."

Kyle yanked off his mask. His blue eyes sparkled like sunbeams dancing on the lagoon. "I told you this area is amazing. I've never seen this many rays at once, and they weren't a bit shy."

"Did you catch the little sweetie that rubbed my legs? Its tummy felt like satin."

Beside her, Haumata squealed with laughter and then somersaulted backwards under the water.

Roxi couldn't stop grinning. "Just another typical day in paradise."

Today was their last day at the motu, and Hitiona's family were preparing a farewell celebration for them. Roxi sat cross-legged beside Haumata and helped the women wrap taro root, breadfruit, and fresh fish along with other ocean delicacies in large banana leaves. She blew out a lungful of air. She had tried every excuse to convince her grandparents to stay longer. All had failed—even the nightmare she had a couple of nights ago where she and her grandparents were sailing through a wild storm. The boat pitched forward and backward, side to side, throwing them around the cabin like rag dolls in a dryer. She had awakened drenched in sweat and tears. In the morning, when Roxi warned Mama C, her grandma had figured the dream was another one of her ploys to stay. True, she'd do almost anything for another week with her friend. But she really did have that vision, and that was worrisome.

Roxi focused on the island men who tended a three-foot deep pit lined with coral rocks. Coconut husks smoldered.

Once the stones were hot enough, women carried over the wrapped food and placed it on top of them. Steam arose. More layers of banana leaves were then placed over the pit.

"This our oven," Haumata explained. "Called *umu*."

Roxi stared at her friend to see if she was joking. "Really? You cook your food in the ground?" Visions of bugs, worms, and other revolting crawly things squirmed through her brain. Guess they'd get baked too. Yuk!

Haumata nodded. "Yes, for ... um ... special day, like today." Her eyes twinkled with merriment, but a melancholy smile betrayed her sadness.

Moca shuffled over to the girls. "Take two, three hours cook. You go play." She patted each of their bottoms, shooing them away.

Both girls stood motionless for a moment, not sure where to go as the men meandered away to nap in the shade of rustling palms. Women busied themselves, picking up, sweeping, and preparing more dishes for the early evening feast.

Mama C crossed her arms and shook her head. "Boy, no matter where you are in the world, women are always working—cooking, cleaning, taking care of kids. Which reminds me, Jon." She gave him a playful scowl. "You and I have work of our own to prepare for tonight's festivities— potatoes to peel and veggies to chop."

His sea-green eyes peered with longing at the men stretched out beneath the trees. "Hmm. Yeah, I guess we should head back to the boat. But maybe a short siesta first?"

She tugged on his arm. "Nice try."

Roxi and her friend ambled along the motu's shoreline. Their last day together. Unspoken sorrow hung between them, knowing their paths would not likely cross again. "Will you write to me?"

Haumata's radiant smile spread to her eyes. "Oh yes. Need work more on English."

Roxi's own smile dimpled her cheeks. "I'll try to write you every week and send books whenever I'm able." She crossed her heart.

Seated on hand-woven pandanus mats in late afternoon, Roxi scrutinized the unusual cuisine that filled large shells and steamy banana leaves that were partially unwrapped. Haumata grabbed one and scooped something mushy onto her clam shell plate using her fingers. There were no forks or spoons.

Roxi leaned toward Kyle. "What do you think that is?"

He shrugged. "Maybe breadfruit?"

Feeling bold, she followed her girlfriend's lead, plucking out bits of sticky mush, crab, lobster, and even octopus.

PJ filled his shell only with identifiable foods such as Mama C's potato salad, vegetable stir-fry, finger-size bananas, and chunks of cooked grouper.

Mama C plopped a teensy portion of taro root on his plate. "Try this. Tastes like sweet potato."

His mouth bunched, but Roxi knew that he knew better than to complain. Instead, he pushed the weird potato to the side of his plate.

The soft babbling of Hitiona's extensive family accompanied boisterous laughter, smacking lips, and an occasional belch.

After the meal, Mama C gazed around at each of the motu family members. "Thank you all. Everything was delicious." She presented gifts of cloth, needles, and thread to each woman amid much oohing, aahing, and hugs.

Then PJ and Kyle passed out fishing line and hooks to the men, who all shook his hand.

Roxi finished handing out coloring books and boxes of crayons to the little ones before squatting down in front of Haumata. With a flourish, she set her favorite purple backpack in her friend's lap.

"Oh, this so pretty." Haumata's eyes widened when she unzipped the large pocket stuffed with books. From a side pocket she pulled out and unrolled a watercolor Roxi had recently painted. It showed their serene motu set in the shimmery glow of early morning.

Haumata's dark eyes filled. "Oh Roxi, *mauru roa*, much thank you." Her voice quivered. "I always remember you." She took off her shell necklace and slipped the gift over Roxi's head.

She reached out and gave Haumata an impulsive hug. "Me too."

Soon everyone was embracing or shaking hands. Tears of farewell glistened on cheeks.

As the sailors shuffled back along the shoreline of the lagoon, Mama C sniffled. "Saying goodbye seems to be the hardest part of this journey." They each agreed and took turns sharing special memories of their time among the motu people.

Kyle cleared his throat as they approached the dinghies. "Jon, Carol, if I have your permission, I'd like to take Roxi for a final spin around the lagoon."

Roxi's stomach flip-flopped.

PJ glanced at his wife.

Mama C nodded. "Okay, but be careful, both of you. It will be dark soon."

Kyle pushed his dinghy into the shallows. "No worries. We won't be gone long."

After wading into knee-high water, Roxi hopped aboard. Eyes still watery, she waved as Kyle headed the dinghy across the deepening blue lagoon.

He cut the motor halfway out, and they drifted. Roxi had the uncanny sense they were suspended somewhere between heaven and earth as the glowing orange sun descended through a Prussian-blue sky, casting a glimmering trail in the still water. The orb slowly melted into Bora Bora's silhouetted peaks.

Enraptured by the surreal beauty, the island seemed to beckon to their young hearts, whispering, *Come to me, come to me and stay for a while, or forever.* Roxi knew she'd never forget every detail of this moment.

As they headed back through the twilight, Kyle kept glancing at her like he wanted to say something. He finally reached over and took her hand.

"I could die this very minute and be perfectly content," Roxi said in a hushed voice.

At *Dawn's Dove*, Kyle raised a protective hand to her back as she climbed on board. "This was such a lovely day, Rox. I'm going to be awfully lonely on that crossing to New Zealand, but I'll look forward to catching up with you there." He gazed deep into her eyes. The warmth from his expression made her heart skip a beat.

The pair jumped when PJ coughed. They turned toward him.

"We'll be based outta the Bay of Islands, Kyle, and keepin' a close lookout for ya." He stood, stretched, and then started down the companionway steps. "Have a safe trip, and stay alert." He gently closed the doors and slid the hatch shut.

Roxi memorized each feature of Kyle's face in the shadowy light, including the golden stubble on his chiseled chin and cheeks. *What would kissing that full bottom lip feel like*? She gave her sweetest smile, but it turned to a frown. Worry scrunched her brow. She leaned over the rail. "I will see you again, won't I?"

Kyle stood in the dinghy grasping the railing with one hand while he lightly caressed her cheek using the other. "Of course, Rox. There're still lots of countries to explore, and touring will be much more fun together."

For a split second, she thought he might kiss her. At least she hoped he would. But he pushed off and sped away, leaving a phosphorescent wake on the indigo lagoon, now lit only by the reflection of awakening stars and distant resort lights.

Butterflies fluttered in Roxi's stomach as she watched until the last sparkles of the trail that led to Kyle faded. Now she understood why Brit had been so dejected when Dustin left. Her friend had asked, "Is there something wrong with missing my boyfriend?"

"Well, you're not my boyfriend—yet, but our paths will cross again," Roxi whispered. "And I hope it's soon."

Chapter Twenty-Seven: Going In Circles

ROXI

"Blue-footed boobies?" Roxi shifted the radio transmitter to her other hand and scratched her ear. She braced herself with her feet as the boat rose over another swell on the vast ocean. "Are you making that up, Dustin?"

"I swear that's what they're called. They have bright blue feet and aren't very smart, but hilarious to watch. Flocks of adults and fuzzy baby boobies swarmed Aitutaki while we were there." He paused as if he were waiting for Roxi's giggling to subside. But of course he couldn't hear her laughter if she weren't pressing the transmit button. "My favorite part of the Cook Islands was spelunking in a couple of rad caves."

Roxi waited until static interference died down, then clicked the transmit button on the ham radio. "I wish we could've explored those islands with you, but then I wouldn't have met Haumata and her family." Talking about her friend, now hundreds of miles behind, made her yearn for those delightful days together.

"When do you plan on arriving in New Zealand?"

"PJ said at least seven more days at sea."

Dustin's voice held a hint of concern. "Well, hope the weather holds for you. An earlier report of a severe low headed towards the east coast of North Island came over our friend's weather fax."

Kyle popped into her mind—snorkeling with the rays and their last evening on Bora Bora made her long to be with him. And now he was out there, somewhere, sailing alone on *Songwriter*. That troubling thought made her stomach hurt. Rob had also been solo and look what happened to him—he'd fallen overboard. Hopefully, Kyle had gotten ahead of the latest series of storms. He was intelligent and strong. Well, except when he got sick.

Dustin interrupted her thoughts. "We weighed anchor a week ago, so we should get to New Zealand a couple days ahead of you."

"Sounds good." She glanced up to see PJ signaling her. "Well, better go. Our batteries are getting low."

"Yeah, Dad gave me a look too." He paused. "I can hardly wait for us all to be together again, Rox."

"Yep. I look forward to having lots of new adventures. Hope Brit's here for the next radio sched. I'm anxious to see you both. Be safe." She switched to her official radio voice. "This is KE6CIM with KD7CAT, and we're clear."

"How's the gang on *Harmony* doing?" Mama C asked as she finished washing the final dish and sat down.

Roxi turned off the radio and hung up the transmitter. "Everyone's fine, and Dustin said they're about two days ahead of us." She stood and stretched. "Guess *Robyn* was having alternator trouble in Aitutaki."

PJ frowned as he walked to the chart table. "That's not good. If Tom had to order one, could take a week or more for the part to be flown in."

"Island time—it's great when you're not in a hurry." Mama C shook her head.

"They're okay. Paul loaned them his spare one." Roxi stepped into the head to brush her teeth.

Mama C poked her head through the bathroom doorway. Several emotions played across her face. "That's what I love about cruisers, always helping each other. Once we reach civilization, there will be plenty of everything available, and we'll have six months to stock up. And play tourist while waiting out cyclone season." Her smile drooped. "Roxi, honey, I hope you decide to stay and continue on with us."

PJ cleared his throat. "Now, Carol, the child needs to make her own decision, whatever will make her happy, not you or her mama."

Roxi scrubbed her face and wondered. *What* will *make me happy*? She climbed onto her bunk and dug through messy shelves until she found Mom's letter they'd picked up at the Bora Bora Yacht Club. She reread the crumpled letter for the hundredth time written in Star's large loopy cursive.

Dear Baby Girl, I miss you so much. I've been thinking it's not good for a mama and her daughter to be apart for so long. When you get to New Zealand, maybe you can fly home like we talked about. I'm working steady now on the set of All Our Lives, except when these darn allergies flare up, which are getting worse, along with stomach issues. Call me when you get there, and we'll figure out what to do. Don't you ever forget how much your mama loves and needs you!!! Your Shining Star.

Roxi stuffed the letter under her pillow. "Guess you forgot I'm not a baby, but will be fourteen in a couple weeks. And why do you really want me to come home? Are you between boyfriends?" Yes, she missed Star, her bunny, and her dance buddy, Alex, although both of them were making new friends. Also, something seemed to be evolving between her and Kyle, and that made her shiver with anticipation.

Far into the night, she tossed and turned. Her mind rocked back and forth like the boat in rough seas. She no longer felt so much like a burden to her grandparents. They actually seemed to enjoy sharing their time and experiences and were kinda cool for ancient relics.

The six a.m. watch came way too soon. Wind had built to a steady thirty-five knots, gusting higher. Roxi scrunched into one corner of the cockpit behind the dodger and stared at PJ, her eyes heavy. He slumped opposite her in foul weather gear, his chin bobbing on his chest. He'd been up and down all night adjusting sails. His snoring rose to a crescendo and then subsided, almost in perfect time to the ten-foot swells crashing onto their starboard beam.

At eight o'clock the next morning, Mama C called them below for a simple breakfast of cereal and fruit. Roxi sipped hot tea but picked at her food. Her stomach felt queasy, so she stretched out on the settee cushions behind the dining table.

Every ten minutes, her grandma checked for ships as she cleaned the galley. "Jon, I—" The boat lurched, and she clung to the post beside the sink. "I hope this weather doesn't last for the rest of the crossing. The rolling makes doing even the simplest chores exhausting." She glanced at Roxi and then at him. "You both look like the morning after a wild party."

PJ ran his fingers through his messy hair and yawned. "Well, the good news is, if we maintain this speed, we all could git to the Bay of Islands ahead of schedule. Maybe a whole day if you gals can take the beatin'."

Roxi squeezed a pillow against her stomach. "Let's get this crossing over with."

The boat tilted, and Carol fell into her husband's lap.

"Well, good mornin' darlin'." He wrapped his arms around her and swayed back and forth.

Mama C laid her head on his shoulder and exhaled. "I can handle the discomfort if it's only a few days, but can *Dawn's Dove* hold up to all this pounding?"

He rubbed her back. "We built her strong. She can withstand much worse than this."

Conditions did not improve over the next two days. Ship traffic increased as they drew closer to land. Most daylight hours, Roxi hung out in the cockpit. Her gray mood reflected the overcast sky and churning sea. Indecision about returning home or continuing on with her grandparents swam around her muddled brain and gave her a headache. One part of her chanted, *Hurry, hurry, hurry* while the other said, *Slow, slow, slow.* Either way, she had a serious choice to make—stay on this voyage or fly home to Mom. This was an impossible dilemma, and someone was going to get hurt.

A wave slammed the boat at the perfect angle and covered her in an icy sheath. "Ugh, I'm done and going below." She scooted with care down the steps, shivering, as the boat swayed like a metronome.

That evening, Mama C served leftover navy bean soup and cornbread to warm them up.

PJ kept checking the wind vane, their course on the compass and GPS, and then would plot their position on the chart. "Darn, these rough seas and the current keep shiftin' the boat off track."

As they ate, Mama C ruminated. "We've crossed the thirty-two-degree line in the southern hemisphere. Shouldn't temps be rising, not growing colder?" She wrapped her hands around her mug of tea. "For heaven's sake, it's November. Summer season is almost here."

Roxi shuddered. "If this is what their warm season is like, then I hate to imagine winter." After dinner, she snuggled deep into her sleeping bag, secure behind the lee cloth attached to hooks at each end of the main salon settee. The boat's movement had become way too rough to sleep in her forward cabin.

She yawned for what felt like the hundredth time, but couldn't fall asleep. Even having pillows stuffed all around her didn't help with the constant rolling that kept her muscles tense and achy as if she'd been dancing all day. And the jittery tingle in her stomach, like before a test, didn't help.

Mama C volunteered to take the evening's first watch until midnight.

PJ had nodded off twice during supper, and they had to catch his soup mug from sliding across the table. Now he listened to Russell Radio, chin cupped in his palm.

Des, who ran the radio station based in the Bay of Islands, had broadcast an unfavorable forecast for tomorrow.

Mama C pointed to the aft cabin. "Better get some rest, hon."

PJ nodded, did a quick check-in before turning off the radio, then gave a peck on her cheek before crawling into bed. He fell asleep before his head hit the pillow.

Mama C shrugged her heavy jacket on over a sweatshirt and pulled on fleece gloves. "Feels like I'm preparing to play in the snow."

In reply, a thunderous snore erupted from the aft cabin.

"No one ever listens to me." A gust of damp frigid air blew in as she stomped outside.

Roxi stared through the clear hatch cover above her head. The sky was as dark as the Sierra Nevada cave she'd almost gotten lost in. Heavy clouds blanketed the comforting glow of moon and stars. Her grandma's footsteps thumped above on the wood grating that lined the cockpit floor. Mama C was probably scanning each horizon for lights from container ships and other boats. Like every watch, you had to look forward, behind, and to both sides for at least one minute in each direction.

The yacht tilted upward, then crashed down with a teeth-jarring thud. Companionway doors creaked. Mama C had to be huddled against them for protection. The boat quaked, and Roxi did too, her nerves as taut as piano wire. *We're so alone out here, at nature's mercy. Are we all crazy to be doing this, risking our lives? And for what?"*

Water rushed past the hull sounding like a thundering river dashing against boulders. Wind howled through the rigging. Roxi pressed a pillow over her ears to muffle the chaotic noise and thought about finding her headphones so she could listen to an audio book. But that would mean leaving her snug cocoon. She curled tighter. For the moment, she felt warm and safe. That's all that mattered.

Roxi's eyes flew open. Something was wrong. She lay still in the darkness. Her heart pounded.

There. She strained to make sense of the sounds—sails snapped, lines flogged, and then a rapid pounding of footsteps above. As Roxi rose to her hands and knees, the boat heeled violently to starboard, almost throwing her over the lee cloth and onto the table. She clung to the bookshelf rail until the rolling subsided, then half crawled to the companionway.

In the aft cabin, Mama C slept soundly. PJ must be on watch now. Roxi pulled herself up three steps grasping the handholds on either side of the double doors. As she got one door partially opened, the boat listed hard to port. The door flew out of her hand and crashed against the bulkhead. Horrified, she watched PJ fly across the cockpit. His hand dripped blood as he reached for the tiller.

Roxi cried out. "Mama C, come quick! Grandpa's hurt, and I think something's wrong with the boat." She pulled herself onto the flooring and crept toward him. Her teeth chattered.

Her grandma's head appeared in the doorway, eyes drooping with fatigue. She sounded annoyed. "What on earth is going on out here?"

PJ appeared dazed. "I got no idea. We were sailin' along hunky dory. Then without warnin', the sails backwinded."

The sailboat settled for a few seconds, giving Roxi a chance to scoot closer to him. Then the frenzied motion started again.

Mama C braced herself in the doorway. Her gaze shifted about, searching for an explanation. "Did the wind change direction?" She rubbed her forehead. "Maybe there's a squall approaching."

PJ shook his head. "That was my first thought, so I readjusted the sails and double-checked the wind arrow on the masthead." He winced as he wiped his injured hand on his shirt. "Within moments we were backwinded again. Makes no sense."

"Jon, is your hand all right?" Mama C shone the flashlight on him.

Roxi peered at his hand in the ring of light where a jagged gash across his palm oozed blood. Her stomach flip-flopped. The erratic boat movement wasn't helping her nausea either. She gagged and willed herself not to lose her dinner.

PJ reached out and used his good hand to unhook both lines that attached the self-steering Monitor wind vane to the tiller. He pulled it towards him. The tiller flew over too quickly. He pushed the handle away. When the boat didn't respond and change direction, his head jerked up, and startled eyes locked on his wife. "It's not working!"

Roxi yelped. "Are you saying we can't steer the boat?" Terror clawed its way from her brain to her stomach. She studied the compass. Normally the numbers held steady within a few degrees but now swung crazily. She screamed, "Oh snap. We're going in circles!"

PJ grabbed the flashlight and picked up the boat hook secured against the bulwark. Lying on his belly, he bent over the stern and poked around with the pole in the churning water.

He spun around and faced them. His voice cracked like he was about to cry.

"There's nothin' down there. The rudder's gone"

Roxi slumped to her knees and wrapped her arms around the binnacle. She whimpered as she prayed to a God she wasn't even sure existed.

Chapter Twenty-Eight: Obstacles

CAROL

Carol scrambled into the cockpit, numb with shock and a touch of hysteria. "How could we have lost our rudder? We just put a new one on in Mexico."

Jon rubbed his face, smearing blood onto his cheek. He shouted above the howling wind, "I have no idea. Right now we need to get the boat hove to. Then we can figure out what happened and what to do."

"Okay, but let me wrap your hand." Carol pulled a bandana from her pocket. "This will have to do until we get things under control."

Jon assumed his role as captain, giving orders as he adjusted the main and secured the other sails. The boat came about until facing into the wind. With the boat hove to, the violent rolling ceased. Now they could move about a bit easier.

Her anxiety subsided slightly, and Carol prayed, *Lord, please help us*. She and Roxi gathered and coiled all the jumbled lines sprawled across the deck.

Jon surveyed the topsides a final time before Carol directed them all below. Her hand shook as she flipped a control panel switch that lit the strobe atop the mast, a warning to approaching ships. On the VHF radio, she put out an alert for anyone in their vicinity. There was no need for a mayday call. They weren't sinking and Carol had confidence in Jon to find a solution to this latest setback.

Roxi slumped onto the nearest seat cushion. "Are we going to die?" Her lip quivered.

Jon's head jerked up, and he gave a half-hearted smile, but his mouth puckered as Carol poured peroxide over the large gash in his hand. "We'll be fine, sweetie pie, but we're gonna need your assistance. Can you look up Taupa Radio's frequency and give 'em a call on the ham radio?"

Roxi gave a hesitant nod. "I guess, but what do I say? That's New Zealand's biggest marine station. I don't want to sound stupid."

"You need to explain the situation and give our position. But be sure to tell 'em there's not an emergency—yet."

Half an hour later, the boat remained somewhat stable in its hove to position as they sat around the dinette table in dry clothing, sipping hot chocolate like any normal evening. Jon's eyes held shadows of doubt.

Carol felt like she'd aged twenty years.

Roxi hugged her knees in a tight embrace as they formulated a plan. "Wish I'd never left home. Not that I had a choice." A solitary tear slid down her face.

Carol scooted beside her. "Oh, honey, everything will be okay, I promise." She massaged Roxi's taut neck muscles. "You know, your grandpa can fix or build anything. Why do you think I brought him along?"

A teensy smile escaped Roxi's terrified expression, then became a huge yawn.

"Think we'd better all git a little shut-eye." Jon stretched arms over his head and swayed, looking like he was about to topple. "Come dawn, we're gonna be mighty busy figurin' a way to steer this boat."

The misty light of early morning cast a dim glow through the portholes. Jon and Carol sipped steamy cups of Earl Grey while they conversed in hushed voices.

He smiled as Roxi stirred. "Mornin' Sleeping Beauty. Gonna make us a new rudder today?"

"What? Thought you'd have one built by now. What have you been doing?" She burrowed deeper into her sleeping bag. "Be sure to wake me *if* we make it to New Zealand."

Carol tapped the top of Roxi's head protruding from her warm nest. "Rise and shine. Quick breakfast today." She handed her a granola bar and carton of juice. "We've been kicking around a few ideas to get the boat moving, so there's lots to do." She turned the kettle back on. "Tea or hot chocolate?"

"Tea with lemon and extra honey." Roxi stretched like a cat before she sat up. "Feel like I've been hit by a tidal wave."

"We're all sore from last night's rock and rolling." She handed Roxi her favorite mug that had dancing ballerinas painted all over it.

Jon dragged heavy rope down the center aisle from the forward chain locker. He carefully figure-eighted the line onto the cockpit floor so it wouldn't get tangled. Roxi finished her meal and slipped on her jacket to help let out the four hundred feet of five-eighth inch line over the stern. She gave a puzzled look. "What's this supposed to do?"

Carol held up both hands with all fingers crossed. "We're hoping that the dragging line will be heavy enough to assist in letting the boat sail on track."

Jon pulled up more sail and adjusted each until the boat's bow inched away from the wind. All three froze, waiting to see if the simple procedure would work. And it did—for about five minutes. Gradually they drifted off course and swells slapped the beam, spray dampening tired bodies and downhearted spirits.

Roxi and Carol clung to the siderail as the boat began another round of wild bucking.

Jon spread his legs wide for balance and worked the traveller lines in the cockpit to shift the mainsail until they were hove to again. He secured lines in their cam cleats, then turned around, massaging his forehead. "Doggone. What a waste of time. Now we gotta drag all that soggy anchor line back on board."

Dejected, Carol pinned her lips together and handed them each a pair of thick gloves. She and Roxi took turns cranking the winch and winding the heavy rope in as Jon stood at the stern, straining and pulling at the same time.

Jon grunted. "This is about as easy as yankin' a wigglin', four hundred pound snake outta quicksand." Finally, all the line lay on board. Carol and Roxi coiled it between the coaming and bulwarks. Jon then secured the rope to the stanchions along the railing, making several half-hitches.

Too exhausted to complain, Carol pulled off her gloves and rubbed her hands. They throbbed from handling the rough line. She looked at her watch. "Uh-oh, ten past eight. we need to check in on Russell Radio and give Des a report. Then, we can get started on our second option." She shoved frigid hands into her jacket's fleece-lined pockets.

Roxi led the way below, turned on the radio, and adjusted the frequency.

Jon poked his head in. "Carol, where's our spare wood? I'm gonna need a couple of thin pieces of plywood, about twelve inches by twenty."

"I think there's several small pieces beneath the dinette cushions and a few more under our mattress."

Roxi shook her head. "How can you remember where everything is in this jumble of lockers and hidden compartments?"

"One of my many talents."

"And one of many reasons I married you." Jon grinned.

After completing the radio check-in, Roxi handed the mic to Carol who updated Des on their failed attempt. His mellow tone and reassuring support soothed everyone's frayed nerves. Then he gave a two day forecast for their area.

Jon halted his search for wood and tools. He frowned when Des relayed more unwelcomed news about an approaching low pressure system that would pass over them sometime in the next twenty-four hours as the disturbance made its way toward New Zealand.

"Might get a bit bumpy for you folks, but no serious worries." Des cleared his throat. "However, those yachties closing in to land should make a dash. Winds along the east coast are predicted to reach fifty knots, gusting to sixty within two days. That's even a tad brisk for us Kiwis. Give me a noontime check-in to update any progress."

Roxi paced the cabin. "Oh no, where do you think Kyle and Dustin and Brit are? They're all going to be tossed about and battered into driftwood."

Carol signed off and stared at her granddaughter. "Honey, you're as white as our mainsail. I'm sure our friends are already in Kiwiland. Thinking the worst isn't going to help anyone, but praying will." She ignored Roxi's eye roll. "When you're ready, come help us outside."

On the cabin top, Jon lowered the twenty-foot aluminum spinnaker pole off the mast track and laid it alongside the bulwarks. He stepped past Carol and opened the heavy aft locker lid that was packed to the brim with gear. Roxi stepped over and held the lid up while he rummaged around. After he tossed out a mildewy duffel, he unzipped the bag and pulled out a greenish halyard. "This line oughta do the trick."

Roxi pinched her nose. "Whew, smells like something died in there."

Jon chuckled. "Or maybe I need a bath." He chuckled.

Carol knelt by him and held two boards sandwiched on either side of the pole as he lashed everything together. As he tied the last knot, she inclined her head toward him. "And where exactly are we going to attach this monstrous contraption?"

"Good question. Been thinkin' and got things figured out. We can take hardware from the mast track, secure that to the self-steering wind vane frame, and then clamp this pole onto to the sturdy frame."

Carol thought through his plan and nodded.

Roxi's face was one big question mark. "I didn't understand a single word of what you said, but hope this plan works."

By mid-morning, the hardware was ready for the pole. Even with a leaden sky and ocean, Carol still felt hopeful. She trusted her husband's ingenuity. All three of them were needed to wrestle the pole over the bouncing stern pulpit, then hold it while Jon locked the post onto the frame.

He lowered the paddle end into the water, then moved forward to readjust the sails. The boat inched away from the wind.

"We're moving forward," Roxi shouted. Everyone cheered.

Due to mounting wind and seas, the paddle bounced out of the water at irregular intervals, losing its effectiveness to steer. The boat tried to round back into the wind each time, but under close supervision and constant adjustments, Jon kept them somewhat on course.

Carol eyed the GPS. "Hey, we're rollin' now, almost four knots, headed southwest—that's even the right direction. Watch out New Zealand, here we come."

Chapter Twenty-Nine: The Slick

ROXI

The next morning, a shrill screech jarred Roxi awake. She poked her head out of the companionway and seized the handholds as a monstrous wave crashed against the beam. The makeshift pole helping to steer *Dawn's Dove* twisted, then popped off the wind vane.

PJ jumped up from the cockpit, lurched for the safety line, and secured it to the stern rail. The line snapped taut. "Carol, grab the end of this other line, wrap it around the winch, and start crankin'. We gotta save the pole."

The boat began the now familiar circle dance, even more chaotic in the confused seas. Roxi's emotions shifted from disbelief to fear as the pole sank beneath the surface, along with her hope. "Now, what are we going to do?"

Mama C only groaned as she struggled to crank the line in. "Jon, this is impossible with the boat rolling. Plus this thing is heavy with water."

He fought to help her wrestle the jerking line in. Between jagged breaths, he stammered, "Roxi ... bring the traveller ... to center when the ... boat faces into the wind."

She tried to remember how PJ did this as she studied the wind arrow on top of the mast. When the arrow pointed straight ahead, she thought, *now!* Roxi yanked up on the traveller's port line with her left hand and controlled its slide through her shaky fingers while pulling the mainsail to center using her right. Then she locked both lines down.

The boat shuddered for a moment, as if deciding whether to pirouette one last time, then settled into the wind. Roxi drew a deep breath. She'd done a good job.

"That was perfect, sweetie. Now the real fun begins—pulling that darn stick aboard." PJ hunched over the winch, and with Mama C's assistance, they cranked the line in.

Inch by agonizing inch.

Roxi shouted. "I see the pole. The line's around the middle, and the darn thing is bouncing all over the place."

Two loud thuds sounded.

Carol's head shot up. "What was that?"

"The pole smacked the boat."

"Not good. That will damage the fiberglass." PJ put all his weight into cranking the winch. The line didn't budge. Sweat covered his beet-red face and a low moan escaped as he let go of the handle.

Mama C winced. "Hon, are you okay?" She grabbed his elbow and guided him onto a cushion. "You rest, and tell me what I can do to help."

PJ's chest heaved. "Just ... give me ... a minute." He sucked in a few erratic breaths. "Feelin' a little puny."

Roxi's gaze connected with Mama C's anxious eyes. "What's wrong with him? PJ never complains." *What would they do if something happened to him*? She scooted next to her grandpa, not sure how she could help.

Mama C leaned around him and mouthed, "He's going to be okay." She stared toward the back of the boat, then glanced around. "Roxi, hand me the end of that spare rope behind you." She tied a bowline, making a large loop.

"Now, can you pull about six feet of the line across the cockpit?" Mama C wound a portion around the starboard winch and ran the loop end outside the stanchions and back to the stern.

PJ scratched his head. "Whatcha thinkin' Carol?"

"If we can slide this loop over the pole's paddle, maybe we can swing that end up. Might make it easier to haul onboard."

PJ still sweated, but his breathing had returned to a more even rhythm. He cupped his chin in his hand and gave a slight nod. "Guess that idea is worth a shot."

"Yeah, I think that'll work." Roxi nodded several times. "Tilting should drain the water and make the pole lighter."

"Good deduction." Mama C gave her a heartening smile.

The compliment made Roxi feel like her opinion mattered, and she gave a thumb's up.

After several frustrating attempts, her grandma managed to lasso the paddle. Mama C scooted off the stern bench and joined Roxi at the starboard winch. The two worked in time with the boat's pitching and managed to crank the pole's paddle end up a few inches. As water drained, the pole got lighter, and by then, PJ could assist by winding in the port line.

All three of them struggled to tug the cumbersome post back onboard. Mama C bowed over, forehead touching her knees. "Praise the Lord. Thank you, God, for giving us strength for this task."

Relief surrounded Roxi like a fluffy blanket. She had no idea what came next, but she felt confident PJ already had a plan. Her watch beeped. "Wow. Is it only noon? I'm ready for a nap." As she tottered toward the companionway, something made her glance back.

PJ stood, framed by whirling ball-bearing clouds and mountainous gray foamy seas. He leaned into the wind, a somber expression on his face. "We need to think about deploying the sea anchor soon."

Stony-faced, her grandma nodded. "I agree. This wind must be up to forty knots. Conditions are worsening." She staggered toward the door. "I'll fix us a quick bite to eat first. I feel like I've run a marathon. We're going to need to keep our energy level up for whatever lies ahead."

PJ's voice shook. "Okie dokie. A short break works. But there's still a hunk of work that needs doin' before the weather deteriorates."

Mama C's face blanched, and her words grew shaky. "We're not in any real danger, are we?"

Was the cold wind making her shiver? Or were her grandparents also scared? Roxi didn't want to hear anymore and clambered below to check in on Russell Radio. A few minutes later she called outside. "PJ, Paul wants you on the radio."

While Mama C ping-ponged around the galley making lunch, PJ and Paul discussed plans for building an emergency rudder which would attach to the Monitor wind vane.

Hope that stays on better than the pole did. Roxi snuggled into a bunch of pillows in a corner of the dinette. *Mmm, feels so good. Wish I could stay curled up in this spot, secure and cozy, until we reach New Zealand. If we get there.* Background sounds faded as her eyelids drooped.

Eww. What on earth? Something scampered along Roxi's arm. She awoke, disoriented, and thought that a mouse was nibbling on her. She yanked her arm away as her mouth opened to scream.

"Lunch is ready." Mama C knelt on the settee, gently rubbing Roxi's forearm. "Are you holding up okay? This certainly wasn't on our itinerary."

Roxi's muddled brain bounced to her recurring bad dream of a raging storm. Maybe these past twelve hours were all part of it. She started to rise. The boat rolled and her head banged into the bookshelf. "Ouch! Nothing like a knock on the head to let me know this nightmare is real."

"Unfortunately, this situation is, but only temporary. You need an ice pack for that bump?"

"Nah. I'm starved." She grabbed her tuna sandwich with one hand and rubbed her forehead with the other.

While everyone ate, PJ studied their book on sea anchor setups. "By the way, Carol, where is our parachute anchor?"

She pointed to the fore cabin. "Behind the forward bulkhead, on the left, I think." She massaged her temples using small circular strokes. "Roxi and I are hoping to wake up soon and realize this is all a terrible dream."

"Hah. Then we're all havin' the same one. No such luck." He climbed off the V-berth and hauled the large nylon bag up the steps.

On deck, they all moved like robots. Too little sleep and the morning's workouts battling the rope and pole had taken a toll. The brewing gale slammed against Roxi. She teetered, then planted her feet farther apart. After stuffing her stocking cap over burning ears, she cinched the furry hood of her jacket.

Sinister clouds loomed in the northeast. Walking upright was almost impossible. Sometimes Roxi had to crawl on all fours as she followed PJ's instructions. There wasn't time for whining or being afraid. Her grandparents were depending on her to do her part. Like Harry Potter said, "You never know what you're capable of until you try." She wouldn't give up or let them down.

By mid-afternoon, the parachute sea anchor had been deployed off the windward side of the bow. They froze like ice sculptures as the contraption sank into the churning current. When the four hundred-foot line stretched tight, the eight-foot chute should open like a real parachute beneath the ocean's surface and create drag.

Mama C scrutinized the spot where the sea anchor line met the water. "Why isn't this working? Do you think the parachute opened?"

PJ adjusted the harness lines until their vessel lay forty-five degrees to the wind. Within seconds, the incessant rolling decreased.

"Look!" Roxi pointed, not believing what she saw. The frothy seas had smoothed directly in front of them. "Wow. This calm is magic."

PJ slapped his thighs and whooped. "Well I'll be. That's called a slick. I read how the chute will slow a boat's drift and create an undisturbed area, but seein' the parachute actually work is somethun' else."

"Great job, honey." Mama C's broad smile wavered and fatigue glazed her eyes.

"Yeah, PJ. Now I don't have to waddle around the deck like a penguin." The past two days had given Roxi a new respect for her grandpa. He always knew what step to take next and never showed defeat—even when sick, frustrated, or worn out.

PJ kept a wide grin as he circled the deck, double-checking each piece of hose he'd slipped over the harness lines to prevent chafe on the fiberglass hull.

Roxi followed Mama C into the snug cabin, appreciating its protection. She poked her head back out.

PJ had begun to triple-reef the mainsail into a small triangle.

"Hurry up. The cabin is warm and dry inside."

The roaring wind carried Roxi's words away, and PJ didn't respond.

"Come on in. Grandpa will be down as soon as he secures and triple-checks everything." Mama C hesitated and her next words quavered. "That storm will be hitting us soon."

Goosebumps popped up on Roxi's arms. "We're gonna be okay, right?"

"You bet we will. Our boat is sturdy, and now, we're set up to ride out anything that rolls our way." Mama C engulfed her in a hug.

This was exactly what Roxi needed, although she'd never admit it. Strength flowed from the warm embrace, and a calm settled over her.

A fitful sleep plagued them all that night as the barometer continued to drop. Every two hours PJ zipped into foul weather gear and ventured out to inspect everything. Roxi awakened each time the door creaked, letting in a gust of bitter wind and spray. She followed the sound of his footsteps and held her breath if the silence lasted too long. Her tense muscles wouldn't relax until the hatch slid back, and he clomped back down the steps. Then her breathing would slow, and she'd pray again for daylight.

All things felt better in the light of day. PJ promised to build them a new rudder come morning to steer them to New Zealand. And he always kept his promises.

Chapter Thirty: Hope Blossoms

ROXI

In the dismal light of early morning, Roxi and her grandparents lingered a few precious minutes after a lukewarm breakfast of oatmeal and stale muffins. *Dawn's Dove* lurched over eighteen-foot swells. Force eight winds tore at the handkerchief-sized triple-reefed main sail.

After Des ended his weather forecast for New Zealand's North Island, Mama C turned off the radio and wagged her head. "I don't want to think about what would have become of us if we'd lost the rudder near shore."

No one spoke. They probably envisioned the same scenario as Roxi. Their boat breaking apart on a rocky strand. Water-logged bodies smashed into fish food.

PJ interrupted her imaginative demise. "Reckon we all better get movin'." He stood and gave a loud exhale. "Carol, can you help gather up my tools?"

"Sure. What do you need?"

"Everything." Then he pointed to the built-in teak bookcases. "And Roxi, can you clear the books off the shelves?"

"Okay, but why?" Her mouth opened as he unscrewed the first plywood panel. *Has he finally lost his mind?*

Mama C stroked the glossy wood. "I sure hate for you to tear up my beautiful bookcases. But guess this will be worth the sacrifice if they can be useful for helping us build this rudder so we can get to New Zealand."

Intent upon his work, PJ didn't answer. He laid the two rectangular pieces of wood on the table, now transformed into a workbench, and studied them. "Yep, a bit of trimin' and shapin' should do the trick."

As the sawdust flew, Roxi's hope budded. *Unbelievable.* Building an underwater steering mechanism from bookshelf planks and random nuts and bolts? That would make a funny story when she saw her friends again. Not *if,* but *when.* She kept trying her hardest to stay optimistic, but her smile faded as she recalled the morning report for the eastern coast. Fifty to sixty knot winds were creating monstrous waves which battered the shoreline. Several yachts had suffered severe damage, but no lives had been lost.

Thank goodness they had heard on the radio that *Sea Eagle* and *Harmony* had arrived safely in Whangarei. *But where was Kyle? Could he be struggling for his life this very minute?* With no ham radio, he couldn't check in or put out a distress call. And so far no one had spotted *Songwriter* among New Zealand's many small islands.

By late afternoon, PJ had assembled a temporary rudder by fastening the wood panels around the self-steering wind vane paddle using at least twenty sheet metal screws and through bolts.

"That looks really strong. This has gotta work." Roxi gave a tentative smile.

Mama C's lips pressed together. "You're not building the space shuttle. Let's get this device hooked up."

PJ ignored her and dragged out the belt sander. "Needs a little final shaping."

She looked mortified and pointed toward the door. "No way are you doing that in here!"

Roxi gave a nervous giggle. She felt a little concerned for him as he threw an extension cord into the cockpit and hefted the rudder onto his shoulder. Minutes later, the whine of the sander penetrated the cabin. She glanced out and chuckled. PJ straddled the paddle like a rodeo bronc rider as their sailboat reared and dipped. Sawdust powdered his face around a snorkeling mask used for eye protection.

"Oh, snap. You look like Rocky Raccoon." She grabbed her camera and captured a picture of him spitting out woodchips as he gripped the shifting beast beneath him.

Sometime during the night, the back edge of the storm skittered past on a southwesterly course. PJ rose before daybreak. "Come on, sleepyheads. Time to get to work."

He focused on attaching his rudder to the wind vane frame and then rigged the lines.

Roxi attempted to assist, but choppy seas kept jouncing them about. "Ugh. This isn't easy." Her foot slipped, and she landed on one knee. She screeched and muttered a couple of curse words.

The hatch slid back and Mama C poked her head out. "Hey, you two. Come below and have a quick bite."

Whew. For a moment Roxi thought her grandma might have heard her. Mama C always seemed to know what she was thinking, saying, and doing, even when they weren't in the same place. She and her grandpa headed down into the warm cabin.

"I'm purty sure we got everything hooked up." PJ's hand trembled as he bit into his oatmeal raisin muffin. Dark rings rimmed his cloudy sea-green eyes.

Roxi rubbed her sore knee as she studied him. She hoped the lighting was what made him look so spooky.

Mama C must have had similar thoughts. "Jon, you must be exhausted. I hope you can take a break soon and get some rest." His only reply was a huge yawn.

After breakfast, the three trudged up on deck while morning's golden rays beamed down. The sunshine renewed Roxi's strength and spirits as they hauled in the sea anchor line. She squealed. "Yuk. What on earth is slimed all over this rope?"

Mama C bent close, squinted, and poked the mystery substance. "Hmm ... feels sticky like jelly."

Roxi glanced over the side of the boat. "Oh my gosh. There's hundreds of aliens down there." A flotilla of miniature sapphire-blue creatures sporting transparent puffy sails skimmed by along the sun-dappled ocean.

PJ's eyebrows drew together. "The storm must have carried 'em here. Probably a type of jellyfish."

Mama C shook her head and grinned. "Not true jellyfish. They're called *By-the-Wind-Sailors*. And thankfully not poisonous, but I'd suggest washing your hands when we're done."

Roxi immediately wiped her hands on her shorts. "There's sure never a dull moment out here."

By 9:00 o'clock, they were underway once again. PJ had to experiment with various sail and motoring combinations to balance the steering. Each of them took turns manually guiding the boat by using the self-steering wind vane's upper paddle as a tiller. This meant standing for two hours, but at least conditions were now comfortable and everything seemed to be working. Finally.

A terrific bang woke Roxi around midnight. *Did the engine blow up? Or a whale ram them?* For a minute, too terrified to move, she listened for water rushing through an imaginary hole. But all was quiet. Too quiet. Gathering courage, she leaped up and grabbed her life jacket before bounding up the steps. "Now what happened?"

PJ knelt in the cockpit, a grim expression tightening his face. "Far as I can figure, a line come loose, and some musta slipped overboard. Just our luck the durn thing wrapped around the engine prop."

Mama C continued to work the paddle, glancing between the compass and her husband. "Ah, that explains why the motor quit. That horrific noise nearly stopped my heart too. So now what?"

"I'm glad to hear we're not going to be fish food. And we can still sail, right?" When PJ nodded, Roxi unzipped her life jacket and flung it below.

"Definitely, but without the engine, we'll be a might slower, down to about three knots." He looked at Mama C. "Any idea how many miles we got left?"

She frowned. "About seventy, but that will put us in the bay at night. There's no way we can navigate that maze of islands in the dark, even using GPS."

He scratched his head. "Guess tomorrow, we'll have to heave to at dusk and wait for daylight."

Mama C groaned. "Not another night out here. I'm completely exhausted. All I can think about is dropping anchor in a quiet harbor and sleeping for a month."

PJ stared into space and scratched his head at the new dilemma. "Well, our only other choice is gettin' in the water and cuttin' that line off. Then we could motor and pick back up to five knots."

"That would get us in by tomorrow afternoon." Mama C's brow creased. "But that sounds dangerous. Let's see what conditions are like in the morning."

By dawn, Mother Nature had pulled another trick out of her bottomless bag. The wind had circled around to the west and increased to thirty knots, which made holding their desired course impossible. PJ wrestled into his wetsuit. "Those doggone swells are makin' us jump around like a rabbit crossin' a desert highway at noon in July."

"That's what I'm trying to tell you. Don't go in. The conditions are too risky," Mama C's voice held an edge of panic.

PJ's mouth set with a stubborn determination as he headed up the steps.

Roxi had one ear tuned to their conversation, the other to Russell Radio. She also tried to find a way through that thick skull of his. Maybe scare tactics would work. "What if the boat slams down on your head and knocks you out and you drown?" she shouted at his back.

Before he could reply, she heard Des calling, "*Dawn's Dove*, are you there?" Roxi answered the radio and gave a quick update on the frightening situation. She listened for a minute and then called outside. "PJ, Des wants to talk to you about a possible solution."

As Des explained how they could unwind the line without going in the water, PJ's shoulders relaxed down to their normal position.

The anxious expression on Mama C's face dissolved. "Tell Des I'm going to give him a big kiss when we meet him. He's saved the day."

Roxi sighed with relief.

PJ rummaged through his tool bag, then motioned her over. "You're gonna hold my pipe wrench like this and turn the upper portion of the propeller shaft in reverse. I'll be crankin' in that troublesome halyard on a winch. Can ya do that?"

"I got this." Roxi laid on the floor, rolled on her side, and crammed into the narrow space in front of the aft bunk. Then she had to contort her arm into the 4x6-inch locker behind the engine compartment. For once, she counted being small a blessing.

"You guys did it. The line is free!" From the cockpit, her grandma's voice resonated with renewed hope. Roxi climbed on deck and sat down beside her as Mama C coiled the line, then secured the cause of their problem to a cleat.

PJ strode from stern to bow, double-checking every line to prevent any further mishaps.

"Everything's secure." He leaned against the boom gallows and gave the go-ahead to Mama C.

She pushed the start button. The engine fired on the first try. "Oh, what a beautiful sound. We're on our way—again." She glanced at Roxi. "Mind taking first watch?"

"Not a problem. Can you hand my book up when you go below?"

Mama C nodded.

PJ trimmed the sails and joined his wife at the chart table. From the companionway, Roxi observed as they plotted the boat's position and calculated the approximate time of landfall at their current speed.

Twenty minutes later, her grandparents returned to the cockpit. PJ scowled. "That doggone wind is keepin' us from steerin' a proper course. No way we're gonna make the Bay of Islands now."

Roxi inhaled sharply and grimaced. "Really? Why not?"

Mama C's lips thinned as she snarled. "We're only fifteen miles south of the Bay, but because of this lousy weather ..." Her voice cracked. "Might as well be a hundred."

Baffled, but not defeated, Roxi jumped to her feet. "This is not fair. After everything we've been through and how hard we've worked, we're not going to make it?" Tears gathered in the corners of her eyes, but her chin came up. "PJ, there's got to be a way."

He rubbed his grizzled chin. A cloud passed in front of the sun and the certainty that had gleamed in his eyes only thirty minutes ago dimmed. "It will take a miracle."

Salvation came on the noon radio schedule when Paul announced, "Several cruisers in Opua organized a meeting with the local boaters and have devised a plan to help you guys. And a boatyard owner has volunteered to use his trawler to tow you the remaining twenty or so miles. We're heading out in the next half hour."

PJ hung up the transmitter, his eyes wide with disbelief. His voice cracked. "Sounds like we got that miracle after all."

He must have been hiding most of his tension, because his whole body slumped.

Roxi had to admit she admired this courageous man who she now considered to be her real grandpa. In a spontaneous and uncharacteristic move, she leaned over and hugged him.

Mama C walked over and wrapped her arms around them both. They stayed like that for a long moment.

By 2:00 p.m., elation over the impending rescue had once again been replaced by discouragement and numbing exhaustion as the barometer plummeted. Another storm system headed their way. Roxi tucked her body into a cockpit corner and scanned a portion of the horizon. "What if our rescuers can't get to us?"

No one answered.

Suddenly, a vision rose on the crest of a gigantic swell. An angelic creature plowed through the rough seas as if they were ripples in a pond. The trawler made wide circles around them, drawing closer with each pass. She read the name on the stern written in tall block letters. "*WARRIOR*. Should be called *SAVIOR*," she exclaimed as the boat's back end surged high out of the water. The three-foot prop's shrieking roar seemed to be shouting at the waves, "Out of my way! I'm more powerful than you."

Paul and two other men leaned against the rail, waving.

Roxi raised her arm in greeting, then rubbed her eyes. "Is that Pepper in the back? What on earth would he be doing out here?"

Mama C waved back to the crew. "Can't tell for sure if that's him." She hurried below to listen for instructions on the VHF.

Roxi took her grandma's place at the stern and craned her neck so she could hear and relay messages to PJ who stood near the bow.

Heavy seas made it difficult for *WARRIOR* to move in close enough, not wanting to cause a collision. They drove donuts around *Dawn's Dove* and attempted to throw the towline across several times. PJ eventually snagged the heavy rope. He secured the line around the Sampson post that stood behind the bowsprit, and then around a large cleat. He signaled, using a thumbs up with one hand.

Captain Jim eased his trawler forward, taking up slack in the rope. The voyage commenced, but aiming toward the protected waters of the Bay of Islands brought them beating into the wind and crashing waves. PJ lay prone over the bowsprit and lashed towels around the towline to prevent damage as the rough rope chafed against their yacht's shiny gelcoat.

Roxi and her grandma huddled behind the shield of the dodger. They both gasped as a tower of green water dashed over the bow. "Where's Grandpa?" A scream lodged in Roxi's throat.

PJ reappeared, water streaming off his body. His arms and legs were locked around the bowsprit like a toddler on his new rocking horse. What a comical sight, but neither she nor her grandma were laughing.

Mama C poked her head outside the dodger. She yelled into the shrieking wind, "Get back here—now!" Her words blew back into her face, and she shook her head. "I swear, that man is going to give me a nervous breakdown one of these days."

Me too, Roxi thought.

Her grandma's vibes must have reached him, because PJ raised his head and stared right at her. He crawled to the side rail and slunk along the deck until he slumped into the welcoming arms of his wife. He looked as pale as a new moon and trembled uncontrollably.

After a long hug, Mama C barked out orders. "Get yourself below and out of those wet clothes. You must be freezing. I'll heat up soup for all of us."

The enormous pressure of the past two days must have overcome them. They both staggered down the steps, looking ready to keel over. Come to think of it, Roxi thought, she wasn't feeling so hot herself. Released from their intense struggles to survive, she soon followed her grandparents into slumberland.

Chapter Thirty-One: The Rescuers

CAROL

The squeak of fiberglass rubbing against fiberglass awakened Carol.

Jon pulled the companionway hatch fully open.

A shaft of golden light blinded Carol for a moment, and she squinted.

"Wake up, sleepyhead. You're missin' the view."

She yawned and stretched before joining Jon on deck. Sliding her hand into his, Carol drew in a puff of crisp, pine-scented air. She glanced up and gawked. "Land! We made it." No longer did the panorama only offer an endless ocean. The trawler towed their sailboat past tall, rugged cliffs and iridescent green valleys. Forested hillsides provided a backdrop for boulder-strewn sandy shorelines. Shadows deepened as the sun melted into towering pines, momentarily igniting them into golds and reds. "What a gorgeous country."

Jon's grin broadened. He pointed ahead. "Hot diggity, will ya look at that?"

Roxi poked her head out the companionway, rubbing her eyes. "Hey, isn't that Hole in the Rock? Saw a picture in one of your magazines. We're definitely in the Bay of Islands now." She pulled her hair into a messy bun before taking a seat in the cockpit. "Bet PJ could sail *Dawn's Dove* right through that opening."

Jon raised his eyebrows. "Is that a challenge?"

Carol flinched. "I'm sure he could if the boat had a new rudder, but don't be putting any more crazy ideas in his head. I've had enough excitement for one decade." She closed her eyes and took a few deep breaths. Grateful. That's how she felt. She gave a prayer of thanks for God's protection and their rescuers.

"Amen," Roxi whispered. She raised her head and looked around. "This place looks like something out of Tolkien. I wonder if they have hobbits here?"

Carol chuckled. "I think they're all hunkered down on South Island."

Jon scratched his head. "I don't know what in tarnation a hoe bit is, but there are wallabies and kiwis."

Roxi's eyebrows shot up. "I thought kiwis were a fruit."

Carol chortled. "True, but the national bird goes by the same name. I have no idea why."

The two boats wound through the calmer waters between several islands. Carol turned her focus on the hillsides. "I'm so excited to hike here. I've read they have the most wonderful, well-maintained trails in the world."

"Yeah, even I'm looking forward to tramping a bit." Roxi giggled when Carol's jaw dropped. "What? Don't look so shocked."

"I guess we're all ready for a little exercise on solid ground." Her heart beat with renewed hope. Maybe her granddaughter planned to stay with them after all.

Roxi rubbed her hands together and shivered. "I'm freezing. Gonna go below and warm up."

Jon wrapped his arm around Carol. Huddled close, they stared into the New Zealand twilight. Their hair and clothing might be disheveled, but Jon's face glowed, and her head buzzed. She was so excited. "I can't believe we survived the rudder fiasco and are almost to Opua."

He turned and embraced her. Passion shone in his hazel eyes. "I have to admit, there were times I got so worried that somethun' would happen to you or Roxi and—"

She interrupted him with a kiss. "You're the bravest, smartest man I know. In spite of tremendous obstacles, you got us here."

His eyes sparkled. "And you, my dear, are quite a first mate, stayin' calm in the face of disaster, and workin' nonstop without complaint."

A warm smile spread across her face. "Guess we make a pretty good team, hmm?" She nudged him using her elbow.

"Yep, and how 'bout that granddaughter of ours? She's got spunk." He tickled Carol's ribs. "Takes after her grandma, I reckon."

"Our Roxi is definitely one of a kind." Her smile drooped. "I hope she decides to continue the voyage with us. I can't imagine going on without her."

"Now, honey, that's her decision." Jon rubbed her back in slow circles. "Have faith. She'll make the right choice."

Carol helped Jon secure *Dawn's Dove* to a mooring across the bay from the historical town of Russell. Only a few lights twinkled amidst midnight's darkness. *WARRIOR* tied alongside, and their makeshift crew clambered aboard.

Paul led a weathered, but still handsome man over. Before making introductions, he slapped Jon on the back and gave Carol's shoulder a squeeze. "Sure good to see everyone again. I believe one of our last days together, we spent riding bikes around Bora Bora. That seems like ages ago. Glad we've been able to keep in touch on the radio. By the way, this is your rescuer, James Ashby."

"Evenin' mates. Welcome to Opua. You folks must be worn out. And please, call me Jim."

The captain's thick accent delighted Carol, but Jon's brow furrowed, clearly perplexed at Jim's pronunciation. He reached out, and the two men shook hands. "Don't know how to thank you, James, uh, Jim."

Carol did. She stood on tiptoes and planted a kiss on Jim's chin.

The seasoned sailor blushed. Ashby's tousled hair was a mixture of blondish-brown interwoven with gray, and his piercing green eyes seemed to be searching for the next challenge. His hands waved about until he stuck one in a pocket, and with the other, he patted Carol's head like he would a large dog.

Steven lumbered over to rescue the captain and pulled Carol into his massive arms for a bear hug. "Thank God you're all okay."

His greasy overalls looked as if he'd emerged from an engine room. Carol forced herself not to back away and vaguely recalled he repaired engines, refrigerators—anything electrical or mechanical. A handy guy to have out here. She took a small step away and smiled with sincere gratitude. "It's wonderful to see you again. We seem to meet in the oddest places. Our first encounter was when I kissed the ground in the Marquesas. By the way, how's your wife, Susie, doing?"

A lanky stranger with a jovial face interrupted them. His deep voice held a slight lilt. "G'day mates. I'm Warwick, one of the captain's mules at his boatyard." His accent was even more difficult to understand than Jim's.

Roxi giggled. "That's an odd name," she blurted.

He chuckled, but not before Carol gave Roxi a meaningful look, aghast at her brazen manners.

After Carol shook her head, her eyes widened. Roxi had been right. Pepper clenched the back rail, looking deathly ill.

"Excuse me for a moment." She brushed past Steven and the young Kiwi. Yes, she thought to herself, there were actually three types of Kiwis in New Zealand. She'd explain that to her granddaughter later, when things settled down.

Roxi followed in her wake. "Oh, snap. It's Trollman."

"Shh, be nice. His name is Pepper." This sure wasn't the loud, obnoxious man she remembered. She moseyed up beside him and tapped his arm. "Hey, are you all right?"

His eyes slowly swam into focus. He opened his mouth, but only a low moan came out.

Carol surveyed his greenish pallor, took his hand, and guided him to the cockpit. "Sit, lean your head back against this cushion, and close your eyes for a few minutes." She looked over to Roxi. "Can you get Pepper a ginger ale, please?"

Roxi handed Pepper the can, and he took a few sips of the beverage, burped, then gave a sheepish grin. "Whew, that feels better. I didn't realize the seas would be so rough out there when I volunteered to be part of the rescue team." A twinkle of mischief crossed his face. "Well, to be honest, the boaters chose me since I happened to be the only one at the meeting who had a medical background."

Carol tried to keep her skepticism from showing. This prattle was more like the old Pepper. Always joking around. He probably meant his many experiences as a patient, seeing that he always managed to find himself in jams.

"Really? And what exactly is your specialty?" She mashed her lips together.

His chest puffed out as he sat up. "Been a paramedic for twenty-five years."

Roxi's jaw flew open. "Are you serious? That's totally rad."

The acknowledgment floored Carol. Who would ever imagine such a goofball being a real-life hero? An imperceptible voice crept into her head, reminding her not to be fooled by the outward appearance of something or someone. Like a geode, its beauty lay hidden within.

"Well, don't take this the wrong way, but I'm thankful none of us needed your services." Carol hesitated before reaching out to shake his hand. He surprised her when he grabbed her shoulders and pulled her towards him into a quick hug.

Roxi stared at him, her eyes shining admiration. "Thank you, Pepper. Coming out in that storm to help us was really, really brave."

"You're very welcome," he said a bit gruffly, then patted her back.

Tears glinted in his eyes.

Carol's own filled for no good reason, except for the realization that she had a new friend. And the pure joy of being alive—in this place—at this moment.

Chapter Thirty-Two: Decisions

ROXI

Roxi stretched as she gradually awoke from a deep sleep. Her mouth watered at the aroma of bacon sizzling in the galley. She hoped pancakes swimming in a puddle of warm maple syrup and scrambled eggs with melted cheese were on the menu.

She sat down and drummed her fingers on the table while her grandma flipped pancakes. "Looks good. I'm starved." Roxi's stomach growled in anticipation.

Mama C glanced up. "Good morning, sunshine." She removed the bacon and grease from the pan, then stirred the eggs. "Ready to put your feet on solid ground?"

"Only you know how much." Roxi loaded her pancakes with butter and syrup and took a large bite. "Yum." Mama C scraped scrambled eggs onto Roxi's plate, and Roxi added a spoonful of salsa to them. "So, my first priority is a hot shower at the cruiser's clubhouse."

"I second the motion. I can't believe our last *real* showers were over six months ago in Mexico. Solar bag showers just aren't the same." Mama C shook her head and called PJ down for breakfast.

PJ's eyes bulged, then brightened at the feast that lay before him. "You really outdid yourself, sweetheart." He embraced her before diving in.

With full bellies, they motored their dinghy toward the village of Opua where buildings peeked through bushes and pines. PJ tied the dinghy to a well-worn floating dock. A long ramp and short path led up the hill to the one-story, white clapboard clubhouse trimmed in blue.

Roxi giggled when her grandma went through her kiss-the-earth ritual. But she had to admit, she felt like doing the same. It had been that kind of crossing.

Before she knew what was happening, they were gobbled up by a crowd of jabbering well-wishers all asking questions. Roxi felt herself squeezed and patted by friends and complete strangers. Like a celebrity, she smiled until her face hurt. Inching away from the chaos, she swallowed her disappointment. Where were Brit and Dustin? Her eyes scanned the premises and finally spotted them emerging from a camper van that had seen better days.

Roxi yelled at the top of her voice, "Brittany! Dustin!" and sprinted towards them. She and Brit embraced, jumping in circles like they'd been apart for years, not weeks. Someone tapped her shoulder.

Dustin gazed at her with his big brown puppy eyes. "Hey, Rox, did you forget about me? I'm glad to see you safe and crazy as ever."

Roxi punched his shoulder, and he grabbed her hand. He grinned and pressed a stick of gum into her palm. She'd missed that crooked smile. "You'd be bonkers too if you'd gone through the past few days alongside us." She crossed her eyes and tilted her head before popping the peppermint gum into her mouth.

"Sorry we couldn't get here sooner, but we're both in the process of hauling our boats out down in Whangarei. Lots of projects to do now. We were too busy having fun in Aitutaki to work on anything." He gave a wistful sigh. "I wish you could have joined us there. That place was totally rad."

"Or sailed to Tonga with *Sea Eagle*. Then maybe we would have been closer to help when you guys lost your rudder." Brittany stared at her friend, her eyes huge, as if Roxi were some sort of apparition. "Did you totally freak out? I would have had a meltdown for sure." Her lower lip quivered. "I didn't think I was ever going to see you again."

"Yeah, ditto." Roxi squashed those terrifying memories into a box to replay later, or maybe never. Right now, joy filled her heart at being reunited with her two friends. Her two *best* friends. Her breath caught when the thought struck her how much she'd missed them—how important they had become in her new life. "I'm so thankful that we're all together again." Brittany sniffled and Dustin blinked like he had something in his eyes.

"Group hug," Roxi exclaimed, surprising herself. She disengaged after a few seconds and answered a couple more questions before holding her hands up. "Whoa, enough talking. I'm exhausted and beyond gross and smelly. Show me the showers, and then, don't disturb me for at least an hour."

Steamy clouds blanketed Roxi. She moaned with pleasure at the simple act of rinsing her hair for the third time. This yacht club might not be fancy, but its narrow shower stalls were a haven for crusty sailors needing a wash down after local races or a long voyage.

Still basking in the squeaky-clean warmth of that sweet bath, Roxi and her grandparents met up with Brit, Dustin, and Brit's dad. The three amigos slid into Red's van behind the adults for the short dash up the highway to Pahia. He pointed out the post office and marine store before turning onto the main road.

"Wow, I can actually understand the signs here." Roxi twisted back and forth trying to see and read everything.

Brittany smiled. "I know. Life is so much easier in a country where everyone speaks your language."

Dustin elbowed her. "You forgot about the Maori."

"Who's that?"

"The Polynesians who settled here first in the late 1200s. They—"

Mama C screeched after they curved right off of a roundabout and entered the left lane on the new road. "Get over! What on earth are you thinking?"

Roxi almost swallowed her gum at the outburst.

Her grandma sat up front between the driver and PJ. She must have realized her mistake and turned to Red. "Whoops. Sorry for giving all of you heart attacks. I forgot they drive on the wrong, I mean the left, side of the road here."

He patted her shoulder with his bear paw and chuckled. "No worries. We've all done that more than once since we arrived. Takes some getting used to."

The group, with Dustin out ahead, strolled Pahia's downtown consisting of about four square blocks that bordered a boardwalk and beach. Roxi peered into several touristy shops. Brittany stopped in front of one. Skimpy bikinis and short sundresses adorned mannequins along with vibrant pareus wrapped in a variety of styles. "We definitely need to go shopping."

"Yeah, a couple new pairs of shorts and T-shirts ought to take care of that." She laughed at her friend's shocked look. "Close your mouth or you'll catch a fly. I was kidding." But not really. She didn't like shopping and all that fancy stuff like Brit wore.

Brittany gave her an uncertain smile. "Don't you love this place? Everything looks so normal."

A pensive sigh escaped Roxi. "Kind of reminds me of home." She glanced away and murmured, "Which I do miss, but California seems so far away and long ago." They picked up the pace to catch up with the adults on a cobblestone walkway that wove past burbling fountains in the center of two courtyards.

Kek kek kek. Kek kek kek.

Roxi looked to her right, then left. "What's that sound?"

Mama C slid her sunglasses off and squinted at a nearby tree. "Oh, those are kingfishers in that Norfolk pine. Aren't they lovely?"

"Kind of irritating, but I can't blame them. We're probably disturbing their rest or whatever they're doing." She pointed to a couple of funny-looking trees. "Those trees remind me of umbrellas."

"They're fern trees, one of my favorites. The forests here are filled with them."

The sun broke through the gray cloud cover reminding Roxi of June gloom in southern California which usually burned off by early afternoon. Sunlight sparkled on the choppy bay where a small group of sailboats raced between orange buoys.

PJ stopped to watch them. "That wind must be blowin' at least thirty-five knots."

Red chuckled. "A mild sailing day for the hearty Kiwis."

"Kiwis?" Roxi chirped, picturing the New Zealand bird. "Don't you mean soaring, not sailing?"

A hearty laugh erupted from Brit's dad. "New Zealanders are also called Kiwis."

Roxi was still shaking her head when the group entered a tiny produce shop and a cheery clerk greeted them. "*Kia ora*. Hello. Let me know if I can assist you."

Mama C and PJ raved about each fruit and vegetable as if they were precious gems. Roxi's face reddened as she pulled Brit and Dustin into a corner of the store, as far from her grandparents as possible. "They're acting like complete geeks." She slunk even lower when her grandma lifted a huge, shiny apple to her nose and inhaled deeply.

"Can you imagine its crisp, juicy flavor?" She offered one to PJ.

"Is this a real apple? It looks fake." PJ held the fruit to his face and scrutinized it.

A bell jingled above the door. Alicia and Paul, off *Holding Pattern*, came in and strode over. "The apples are even better if you take a bite," she kidded with a friendly smirk.

Roxi turned to Brittany. "All this food is making me hungry again."

Alicia glanced over at the teenagers, and then back at Mama C. "You guys should join us when we're all done shopping. We're headed down the block to the Ferryman's, the local's favorite pub with the tastiest fish and chips south of the equator."

"And maybe sample a New Zealand brewski or two?" Dustin's eyes held a hopeful gleam beneath arched eyebrows.

"Ha! In a few more years, boyo." Red rubbed his knuckles across the top of Dustin's bristly crewcut.

"Hey, don't be abusing my guy." Brittany gave a mock pout and pushed her dad's hand away. She reached up and ran her fingers against the front of his scalp to get the longer hair to stand back up.

After a final mouthful of lunch, Roxi licked salt and vinegar off each greasy finger. "Delicious, but now I'm stuffed." Her stomach churned, and she tried to stifle a fishy burp. "Excuse me, need to use the restroom." She hurried through the door, locked it, and leaned over the sink, moaning. The food soured in her stomach as she thought about the phone call she had to make soon—to her mom.

Her thoughts jumped back and forth along with the beat of her heart.

She needed to make a decision.

But when she did, how would she tell those she loved?

Chapter Thirty-Three: Prayers & Promises

CAROL

Jon pushed away from the table and stood. "Those fish and chips filled me up, but an ice cream cone couldn't hurt." He fidgeted with a button on his shirt when Carol gave him the evil eye. "Ah, come on, sweetheart, we deserve to celebrate."

She gave a tight-lipped smile, trying not to get upset in front of their friends. "Maybe, but don't forget, you're supposed to be on a strict diet until we hear otherwise."

Alicia looked at Jon and frowned. "Are you still not feeling well?"

He shrugged and scooted away to join the men by the door.

"I don't understand his illness. His symptoms seem to come and go." Worry tightened Carol's neck, and she massaged the muscles as the two women and Roxi strolled the waterfront pathway.

The husbands lingered behind after everyone stopped at an ice cream shop. As usual, they were talking boats, storms, and technical jargon.

Roxi shuffled alongside the two women since her friends seemed to have vanished. She licked the drippy coconut ice cream off her sugar cone as Alicia gave Carol the name and phone number of a doctor's group down in Whangerai. "It's frightening being so far from the US and our familiar clinics and doctors. We've been treating Paul's headaches for years since his accident, but their frequency seems to be increasing." She shook her head. "Luckily, Norma, Opua's wonderful postmistress, gave us a referral and he's scheduled for tests next week. It didn't take long to get an appointment."

Carol jotted down the information and then waved to catch Jon's attention.

He swaggered over. "Missin' me, sweetie pie?"

Ignoring his flirtation, she used her no-nonsense voice, wagging her index finger for emphasis. "We need to make a phone call right now. Alicia gave me the number of a reputable group of doctors, and we're not going to put off getting you checked out another second. Your illness could be serious, and you need to get whatever this is taken care of."

She purchased a phone card and located a phone booth. Jon squirmed as if he had sand in his shorts. "You know, Carol, I've been feeling much better lately. Do you think this is really necessary?"

She knew his aversion for doctors, but she wouldn't let him weasel out of this.

He leaned against the open door of the booth tapping his foot.

She set up his appointment for early the next week, hung up the phone, and stepped out.

"Well, that's set." Hands on hips, Carol turned and raised her eyebrows to her granddaughter. "Next in line for the phone?"

Roxi shook her head and backed away. "Not ready." She turned, spotted her friends, and fled down the steps to the beach where Brittany and Dustin sat cuddled close together.

"You're going to have to talk to your mom soon," Carol called after her, then sighed, because she knew she also needed to speak with Roxi's mother. Never an easy task, but she kept hoping someday, somehow, through grace, both she and her daughter could forgive past mistakes and move forward into a healthier relationship. Was that even possible with someone who had a mental illness? *God, I really need your guidance. Please tell me what to say and do.*

After a couple of days getting settled in, Carol and Jon hiked a wooded path up to a grassy hilltop to express their gratitude to Des, the man who had given so much encouragement and advice throughout their ordeal at sea. Their Russell Radio guru answered the doorknocker, appearing as an unassuming white-haired man. His inquisitive dark gray eyes gazed at them behind black-rimmed spectacles.

"We called earlier. I'm Jon, and this is my wife, Carol." He crushed Des's hand in a vigorous handshake. "We all don't know how to thank you."

She stepped forward and gave Des a zestful hug. "What an honor to finally meet you in person after all those conversations on the radio."

His eyes twinkled merrily. "Only doing what I love, helping folks. Please, come in." He led them to his cramped office where two ham radios, a VHF radio, weather fax receiver, printer, and computer consumed most of the space.

Jon gaped at all the equipment, but Carol's attention was drawn to a huge picture window. She gazed out, growing excited at the prospect of exploring Russell across the bay and what lay beyond. Several islands appeared to float between heaven and earth, their green heads reaching into a bright blue sky as puffy white clouds paraded by. "What a view."

Des came and stood beside her. "Yes, I'm rather fond of it, especially watching storms approach."

"Oh, I almost forgot." Carol unzipped her backpack and handed him a homemade card that included a poem she'd composed.

He pulled out a photo tucked inside. "Your yacht, *Dawn's Dove*, I presume?"

"Yes, taken in the lagoon at Bora Bora." She grabbed a final item at the bottom of her pack. "Banana bread, baked this morning. It's not much, but we wanted to show our appreciation for all your assistance."

Des blushed. "Well, thank you, but not necessary. The radio gives me purpose and enjoyment since I retired."

Jon put his arm around Carol. "We better head to the boat, hon. Let Des get back to monitoring calls."

She smiled. "It's been a pleasure to meet you."

Des nodded. "For me also. Cheers mates. Hope you take time to enjoy our beautiful country."

As the two tramped back down the path, Carol reflected on all they'd gone through to get here. "We definitely need to take advantage of our six month stay in New Zealand—get to know the people, culture, history, and of course, tour its diverse landscapes."

A glum expression replaced Jon's contented look. His eyes swept the bay before landing on her. "Don't know 'bout doin' any of that. First off, we gotta figure out the rudder situation, or we won't be continuin' this trip." He got that stubborn look on his face that made Carol cringe. "We'll probably have to build our own, and there're several other boat projects that need doin'."

A black cloud of bitterness eclipsed her earlier joy. "It isn't fair. We've worked so hard to get to this country." She turned away as her vision blurred. Neither talked until they reached the yacht club.

"We can continue this conversation tomorrow." Carol's eyes didn't quite meet Jon's. "I'm going to sit here awhile and ponder."

Jon made an unintelligible sound and headed inside the clubhouse. She glanced about for a secluded spot where she wouldn't be disturbed. Beneath a tree sat a vaguely familiar figure who faced away from her. Carol's heart leapt. The blondish hair had a shorter cut, but could it be? "Abbie?" she cried. "Are you real or am I dreaming?" She half ran, half stumbled over.

The woman turned, then stood and held out her arms. She raced into them and smothered her friend in a fierce hug. Abbie wobbled. "Whoa, girlfriend. You all right?" She rubbed Carol's back until she calmed.

"I can't believe I found you. I had been wishing you were here to talk with." Carol choked up.

"I know. Isn't God amazing how he promises to always provide what we need? And he does!" She plopped onto the wooden bench and Carol joined her.

"I thought you wouldn't be here for another week."

"I really missed Drew and was able to move my flight up." Abbie smiled, but her eyebrows drew together. "We've got so much to catch up on, but first, tell me what's going on. Is it, Roxi?"

Carol gave a small shake of her head. "No. Would you believe we're getting along better?" She rubbed her temple. "Although I am worried whether she's going to continue on the trip with us."

"Oh, I hope so."

"Me too." For a moment she studied the water where the afternoon breeze had begun to ripple its glassy surface. "No, what's upsetting me right now is Jon and I had a major disagreement."

"I'm so sorry." Abbie's eyes glistened. "I hope you two can work things out."

Carol cleared her throat, trying not to break down again. "I don't know how." She told her what Jon had said. Her mouth drooped. "We've come halfway around the world and had planned to travel across both these magnificent islands. There're awesome hikes through spectacular forests, river rafting, islands to explore, and so much more. Sitting in a boatyard is not on my itinerary."

Abbie closed her eyes and bowed her head for a couple of minutes, then peered at Carol with a stern expression. "I understand your disappointment, but let's look at the bigger picture." Her soft tone conveyed compassion. "First of all, the three of you and your boat got to New Zealand unharmed, minus a rudder." She gave a rueful grin. "Second, that can be replaced or rebuilt, and should only take about six weeks, not six months. And third, you have a loving husband and beautiful granddaughter you are sharing an amazing adventure with."

Carol reflected on what Abbie had said and felt a twinge of shame for not being more grateful. Before she could respond, her friend continued.

"Our lives are full of opportunities, but there are no guarantees how things will turn out. We need to face all of the hills and valleys with an enthusiastic faith in God." She grinned. "Oh yeah, and fourth—you have a wonderful friend who loves you dearly."

A low, half-moan, half-chuckle escaped from Carol. "How did you get to be so wise? You always remind me of what's most important."

"I've learned lots through my many mistakes and failures. Believe me, I'm far from perfect."

Growing serious again, Carol asked, "Mind taking a short walk?"

"Sure, as long as we can go slow and the pathway is on level ground. My balance isn't great today, and I don't have my walking stick."

The two women ambled along the dirt road leading towards the marine store and Ashby's boatyard in comfortable silence. Carol stopped. Her jumbled mess of emotions made formulating the right words difficult. "I've had, that is, I've got one more challenge to tackle. And I'm kind of dreading it."

That was yesterday. Now the time had come—to make the call to her daughter. "Why is this so difficult?" Carol whispered as she stood in the phone booth and punched in the number.

The phone rang several times before being picked up. "Hello," a provocative voice answered. "This is Star."

"Hello, honey, this is your mom." Her voice shook a little. "I wanted to let you know we arrived safely in New Zealand. How are you doing?" She regretted the question as soon as the words were out of her mouth. Her daughter, a hypochondriac, always had a lengthy list of varying ailments. But Shalimar surprised her.

"Fantastic. I'm starring in the most captivating role on daytime drama. And the best part is the leading man, Owen, is also my real-life boyfriend." She squealed. "Can you believe it? A nobody like me living with one of the hottest actors in Hollywood?" She got quiet. "Whoops. Wasn't supposed to share that. I know you don't approve of living together before marriage."

Carol took a deep breath. This might be a good time to admit her own failures. "God is the one who doesn't approve. But I did the same thing when I was about your age, and that didn't turn out well."

"What are you saying?" Shalimar growled. "That my romance with Owen is doomed?"

Carol grew frustrated, then remembered Abbie's advice. *Speak from the heart and forgive.*

"Not at all. Every relationship has its challenges. Sometimes, they don't turn out the way we'd hoped for." *Like the one I envisioned with you when you were born.* Carol took a deep breath and prayed for wisdom and the courage to continue. "I'm sorry I've failed you in so many ways. We've hurt each other, but we can't undo the past." Her mouth went dry, and she tried to swallow. "But do you think it's possible for us to make a fresh start?" Her hands felt cold and clammy as she waited for a response.

Shalimar's acidic words burned. "Are you for real? You can't just apologize and expect forgiveness for everything you've done to me. You killed my dad when you divorced him, kicked me out of my home instead of protecting me, and stole my daughter. Shall I continue?"

The harsh words cut deep into Carol's heart. She couldn't breathe for a moment. "I'm sorry you believe those things. Your accusations only contain a small amount of truth. I admit I've made mistakes, but I've always loved you, and I always will."

Shalimar hung up.

Filled with remorse, Carol covered her eyes with both hands and sobbed quietly. Yes, she'd made many poor choices she now regretted. But at the time, they had seemed right, and she'd never meant to hurt anyone, especially her daughter. Everything Shalimar had accused her of had been taken out of context.

A gentle presence embraced Carol as she felt peace like a gentle river flow through her shattered heart. She would never stop loving Shalimar or hoping for a renewed relationship. In the meantime, she planned to nurture Roxi and their growing bond—if their granddaughter stayed. And she needed to be more patient and supportive of Jon.

But for now, all Carol could do is pray and trust God's promises.

Chapter Thirty-Four: The Journey

ROXI

Roxi squirmed beneath Mama C's scrutiny as she tapped the toe of her shoe against the phone booth.

"You really need to call your mom and let her know your decision—to stay or go." The last word wobbled. Her grandma hesitated. "I feel bad enough she accused me of kidnapping. I don't want her thinking I won't even allow you to talk to her."

"Yeah, Star has probably already had a couple of panic attacks and wonders what has happened to me." Roxi's heart thumped along with the high-pitched ringing in her ears. She felt like she might be having one of those attacks.

"Are you okay, hon? Your face is white as a ghost."

Roxi nodded and focused on breathing until her heartrate slowed. She wanted to put this call off indefinitely because she knew it would trigger a theatrical response from her mom. "Guess it's now or never," she wheezed.

"Also, you might not want to mention the rudder incident." Her grandma leaned against the booth and shook her head. "You know how nervous Shalimar gets over the smallest things. I'm sure that would send her over the edge."

"That's a kind way to describe Star's freakouts." Roxi waited for Mama C to ask the question that had made her pinched lips turn down. She hated to stress her grandma out, but right now, she needed to focus on what to say to her mom. She edged inside the booth and banged the door shut.

Mama C shuffled over to a black wrought iron bench, hovered on the seat's edge, and bowed her head.

Roxi bit her lip. *I need you too, Lord.* A jumble of anxiety and hope flip-flopped in her stomach. She punched in the number. The phone rang and rang, reverberating in her ear. She knew her mom better than anyone and wasn't afraid of Star's tantrums. However, threats to harm herself or someone else frightened Roxi. Wouldn't be the first time. She wished her mom wouldn't be home and she could leave a message. Then the ringing stopped.

After a long moment of silence, the familiar deep, flirtatious voice answered. "Hello, Star speaking."

A painful longing surged with conflicted memories. Building a sandcastle together and decorating using smooth sea glass and shells until the sculpture had dissolved with the incoming tide. Often hiding beneath her bed with a flashlight and book because she'd heard scratching noises at the window while Star went out. Her tenth birthday—when there hadn't been cake or presents, but they'd had a private party while the stereo blasted and they sang and danced around the apartment for hours.

In a high voice she hadn't used since she was small, Roxi said, "Hi, Mommy." She fought the urge to burst into tears.

"Oh, snuggle bunny, it's sooo wonderful to finally talk to you. I've been telling my new honey, Owen, all about you and have been worried sick. It's been sooo long." Star gave a little sniffle. "If anything ever happened to my baby girl, I would curl up and die."

Roxi rolled her eyes. She could hear the pout and excuses as Star rattled on and on about herself without a break. Roxi ground her teeth as she tried to work up the courage to burst her mom's euphoric mood with her bombshell decision. Star's words suddenly seized her.

"So this isn't a good time." A stinging heat spread across Roxi's face as if she'd been slapped.

"Anyhow, sugar lamb, I've been thinking I might have been an itsy bit impulsive in that last letter to you."

You mean the one that says it's not good for a mother and daughter to be apart for so long? The one that says how much you need and miss me? The one that almost made me choose you?

Star gave a nervous chuckle. "There's so much happening right now with my career and getting settled at Owen's in Santa Monica. Of course, he had to practically beg me before I agreed to move in." She chortled. "But honestly, that made such perfect sense, being closer to the studios and the whole Hollywood scene, which I absolutely adore."

Roxi wanted to scream, "Stop! I get what you're telling me. But why don't you adore me?" The words lodged in her throat.

"And I don't have to bust my behind each month scrambling to pay the rent and bills. My Owen takes care of everything," Star purred. Her breathing came in little puffs.

Roxi's mouth twitched. "So, what about me? Your daughter," she bellowed. "And what did you do with Thumper and all my stuff?"

"Ahem. Don't be mad," Star faltered. "Everything is working out. Your pal, Alex, took the rabbit, and um, most of your things are in the trunk of my car." She gave a dramatic sigh. "Don't you understand? This is the break I've waited for my whole life! Give me a few more months until the money's rolling in, then I'll send my private jet and bring you home."

Tears spilled over, and Roxi rubbed at them with clenched fists. "I don't believe you," she said in a low growl. She took a few ragged breaths and tried to calm herself. Then she remembered. This is good news, right? What she wanted—to stay with her grandparents. Star had made her decision easy. A smile played on her lips. "Whatever. Whatever you say. It's okay."

"Are you absolutely positive?" Star's light tone betrayed her relief. "Ooh, I do miss my snuggle bunny."

Roxi wrinkled her nose at the stupid baby name and wound a clump of hair around her finger, yanking until fresh tears threatened. Her mom could be so aggravating. It was time to end this call. "Well, gotta go, Star. I've used up the time on our phone card," she lied. "We'll talk soon." Another lie. "Love you." Was that a lie too?

Mama C's downcast eyes glanced up as Roxi approached. A distressed meow, like a kitten whose tail had caught in a door, escaped.

Roxi swallowed the lump in her throat, then the corners of her mouth curled up. "I'm afraid you're stuck with me awhile longer. That is, if you and PJ still want me."

Her grandma's slumped shoulders straightened, and she jumped up. "Of course. I mean, hmmm. Papa and I will have to think hard about that." Her wide grin said otherwise. "So, how did Shalimar take the news?"

"Let's take the path along the shore, and I'll tell you all about our conversation." Roxi concentrated on the stony slope until they reached the bay trail. *Where to begin?*

She blurted, "Star didn't flip out because that's what she'd already decided. And she didn't even ask what I wanted."

"What? Oh." Mama C's brows formed a V. "How do you feel about that?"

"How do I feel about staying here or about being rejected by my mom?" Roxi's lower lip quivered.

"First, tell me what *your* decision was." Her grandma's calm brown eyes steadied Roxi.

They ambled along the worn path until Roxi stopped, picked up a rock, and heaved it far over the water with all her pent up resentment. She let out a long breath. "I chose you guys. I'm tired of being the parent to a childish mom who constantly changes her mind and throws temper tantrums if she doesn't get her way."

Mama C shook her head. "I understand. It's difficult to live with someone who has you walking on eggshells. Someone you can't always depend on."

Roxi twisted and pulled on the bottom of her shirt. "That's what I like about you. I can count on you to listen and at least try to understand me, even if we don't always agree. You've believed in me and taught me to believe in myself. And helped me along my faith journey too." She gave a lopsided grin. "Also, you don't have crazy spells like Star."

Mama C placed a hand on Roxi's shoulder and pulled her into a hug. "Thank you, sweetheart. I'm so grateful we can share our feelings and have this time together." She pulled away to gaze at her. "I hope you know I love you very much, and I'm certain your mom does too."

"Yeah? Well, she has a funny way of showing her love." Roxi frowned. "She chose what she wanted, not what I needed."

Her grandma held up her hand and shook her head. "She's not perfect. None of us are. Try to be patient with her and keep praying. God is working in all our lives but on his time schedule. Trust him."

They reached the end of the trail near the clubhouse. Roxi scanned the cloudless sky and sucked in a lungful of cool ocean air. "I'll try," she promised and crossed her heart.

"Hey, wait up." Brittany brushed aside thin branches that sprung back as she followed Roxi along the fern-lined coastal trail towards Pahia the following day. "What's your hurry?"

Roxi glanced back and slowed at the rustic bridge that spanned a bubbling creek. "I'm trying to work off a few pounds after all those days at sea." She puffed out her cheeks and let the air escape little by little. "I want to be in shape whenever I run into Kyle again."

"Oh, sorry I'm so slow. But truly Roxi, you look great. You've lost weight since Mexico and I think you've grown a couple inches."

Roxi beamed. "Thanks, but I still have a ways to go." Thirty minutes later, the girls crested the rise and rested beneath a tall tree in a pasture so green it didn't look real. A small flock of sheep grazed in the distance.

"What a beautiful scene." Brittany lifted her head. "And I love these New Zealand Christmas trees. Look, there's already a few of those cute bottlebrush flowers blooming."

"Give them a couple more weeks and the whole Pohutukawa tree will be decorated in fuzzy red flowers."

Brit's eyebrows rose with a question.

Roxi chuckled. "The only reason I know anything about those trees is because Mama C has pointed out at least ten of them since we arrived."

"I guess we're fortunate to have grandmas that take the time to teach us all kinds of weird stuff—like Grandma Redfern taught me basketweaving." She grinned. "Because you know that's a skill everyone needs."

Roxi laughed, then grew serious. "Do you want to hear the good or bad news first?"

"Definitely good."

"Well, in case you're a teensy bit interested, I'm not flying home."

Brit squealed, bounced onto her knees, and wrapped Roxi in a hug. "Thank you, thank you, thank you." Pulling back, her lips puckered, and she squinted. "So what can the bad news be if you're staying?"

Roxi's mouth tightened. She snapped, "My mom doesn't want me. She's too busy with her job and new boyfriend." Her eyes narrowed and she hugged herself. "What kind of mother doesn't put her daughter first?"

"Oh, Roxi, I'm so sorry. I'm sure she loves you, but from what you've told me she has serious issues." Brittany's fingers ran through her silky blonde hair. She looked as though she wanted to say more but struggled with how to say the words.

"I don't understand. Why can't I have a normal mom?"

"And why did mine have to die?" A tear slid down Brit's cheek.

Roxi grimaced. "Why does life have to be so hard?"

Her friend took a deep breath and exhaled slowly. "Gram always told me that in every squall there's a gift."

"What does that even mean?"

"I have no idea."

Both girls giggled as they stood. Roxi brushed off her jeans and looked at Brit. "Thanks for the talk. Guess we're both trapped in this strange way of life for a while longer."

"I kinda like cruising now, most of the time. I'm sure glad we found each other. It helps to have someone else who's been through painful stuff and gets you."

"Totally. And I'm sort of getting used to all these loony adventures." Roxi grinned. "Also doesn't hurt that we both have rad boyfriends."

They laughed and high-fived.

Back in Opua, the girls ran into Dustin near the marine store. Roxi left her googly-eyed friends after the three made plans to meet tomorrow. She traipsed along the gravel road deep in thought. Sadness lingered, and she could feel a thin layer of childhood peel away, painful like a sunburn. But with the change came a lightness, like freedom as a baby bird leaves its nest and soars into the unknown. She didn't know whether to laugh or cry so did a little of both.

A soft voice spoke inside of her. *Life isn't all sadness. There is also joy in this world. And my joy is in you too, a wide, deep river that will never run dry.*

"Thank you, God, for always being with me," Roxi whispered. Then she blinked in disbelief. A vision from her daydreams sat on the cruiser's dock, leaning against a piling as dinghies bobbed in the water around him.

"Kyle," she hollered.

He lifted his head, then stood and waved to her.

Roxi skittered down the grassy slope toward the boy whom she now felt certain was part of her destiny. They had both survived so much. There must be a reason why their lives kept intersecting. "Oh my gosh. I've been so worried about you since the storm. Where have you been? Are you anchored here in the bay? What are your plans?" She panted as the words tumbled together, and her heart beat wildly.

Kyle's laughing smile widened and his blue-green eyes sparkled like sunlight on the ocean. "Well, to answer your last question first, I'm going to continue to follow the sun— wherever it may lead me. As we sailors like to say, 'Life is a journey, not a destination'." He took her hand and squeezed. "Care to come along, Roxi?"

Nautical Glossary

- **binnacle**: Built-in housing post for a ship's compass.
- **boom**: The horizontal pole where the foot of the mainsail attaches.
- **boom gallows**: A raised arch on which the boom rests when not sailing.
- **bosun's chair**: A canvas seat secured in a bridle of ropes, used for going aloft.
- **bow**: The front end of the boat.
- **bowsprit**: A spar extending forward from the bow to which the forestays are fastened.
- **bulkhead**: A load-bearing wall within a boat's hull.
- **bulwarks**: An extension of the boat's sides above the level of the deck.
- **cleat**: A device used for fastening a line on a boat or gangway.
- **coaming**: The raised edge of the cockpit.
- **cockpit**: A seating area towards the stern that houses the rudder controls.
- **companionway**: A hooded entrance hatch with a ladder leading below.
- **dodger**: A hood forward of the cockpit that protects the crew from wind and spray.

- **fender:** A flexible bumper used to keep boats from banging into docks or each other.
- **forestay:** Long cables that connect from mast to bow for support.
- **galley:** The ship's kitchen.
- **halyard:** A line used to raise any sail.
- **hatch:** The cover to an opening.
- **head:** The ship's bathroom.
- **helm:** The boat's steering mechanism such as a tiller or wheel.
- **hove or heave t**o: Stop a sailboat by backing some of the sails to allow the vessel to drift.
- **knot:** A unit of speed equal to one nautical mile per hour/approximately 1.151mph.
- **latitude:** The distance north or south from the equator.
- **longitude:** The distance east or west of Greenwich Meridian.
- **parachute (sea) anchor:** A stabilizer deployed in the water for heaving to in stormy weather.
- **polliwog:** A novice sailor.
- **port:** The left side of a vessel when facing forward.
- **rudder:** A steering device hinged to the vessel's stern and connected to the helm.
- **shroud:** A cable used to support the mast from either side.
- **shell-back:** A veteran sailor.
- **sloop:** A single-masted sailing rig.
- **spinnaker pole:** A pole used to help control a headsail.
- **stanchion:** An upright post forming a support.
- **starboard:** The right side of a vessel when facing forward.
- **stern:** The rear portion of a boat.
- **winch:** A mechanical device for pulling on a rope.

- **windlass**: A winch mechanism designed to move heavy loads such as an anchor.

About the Author

Cheryl Fitzgerald grew up in California with the Pacific Ocean as her playground, but never imagined that one day she and her husband would sail across that vast sea and several other oceans. Today, she seeks adventures among nature's wonders with grandkids, and while land-cruising in their RV, hiking, cycling, and kayaking. You can follow her journeys at www.cheryldfitzgerald.com.